Rockers of Steel

R🎸CKERS
OF STEEL

RIVER JAMES

USA TODAY BESTSELLING AUTHOR
M J FIELDS

MJ FIELDS

Copyright © 2016 by MJ Fields
1st Edition Published: January 31, 2016
Published by MJ Fields
Cover Design by: Kari March Designs
Cover Model: Branden Haley
Photo credit: Scott Hoover
Edits by: C&D Editing
2nd Edits by: Kellie Montgomery
Interior Formatting by: Jersey Girl & Co.

First Edition: January 2016
ISBN-13: 978-1523719235 | ISBN-10: 1523719230

10 9 8 7 6 5 4 3 2 1

TABLE OF CONTENTS

FOREWORD

Dear Reader,

A big thank you for checking out River James.

If you are new to my work, let me take the opportunity to give you a brief overview of all things STEEL.

Steel men, whether it be *Men of Steel*, *Ties of Steel*, or the *Rockers of Steel*, are not for everyone and, more importantly, not for every woman. They are highly sexual, highly inappropriate, and sometimes ... high. They are not always mature, are hard to handle, and most of them would prefer to be the handler. They are man-whores who love all women...until they make the decision to love one woman.

They are undoubtedly Alpha males, each on his own path to finding out what that actually means. When they figure it out, there is no turning it off or turning back. They are genuinely good hearted and have a deep loyalty to those they consider family by blood or by choice. They are all that and then some...until River.

Warning To The Reader #1:
River seriously has issues, like *big-ass* issues. I feel the need to warn you all...

He's an addict.

He's immature.

He has the sex drive of a madman.

He is a victim and an abuser.

He has no regard for rules or laws.

He has no filter, no off switch, and no desire for either.

His loyalties are...sporadic, his mood swings epic.

River James is…a very unlikely hero.
I have asked myself more than once what I was thinking taking this on because, fiction or not, it's an emotional read and a mind-fuck to boot.

Warning To The Reader #2: I am not responsible for damage done to your electronic reading device due to the fact that during one, if not all, scenes, you hide it to make sure no one sees you reading it, throw it because you are ready to kill River, or damage it caused by tears from emotion or laughter.

Warning To The Reader #3: There are, without a doubt, triggers for some in this book. Sexual and physical abuse is touched on in this book. It was done as tastefully as possible, but I needed to put it out there.

Promise To The Reader: As raw and gritty as the situations, words, and scenes are in this book, there is heart and emotion in abundance.

Thank you so much for opening your mind and hearts to an unlikely hero because everyone deserves a chance to heal and be loved. — MJ

P.S. Make sure to check out the link in the back for information on how to claim a free "Rocker, Surprise."

INTRODUCTION

When he fell in love, he fell hard. When he lost her, he lost his will.

Drugs, sex, and rock and roll — in that order — became his life.

River James, the drummer for Steel Total Destruction, loved the brotherhood he formed with his unlikely best friend, the band mates from Steel Total Destruction, and the family he found in his label, Forever Four.

Then one tragic accident takes it all away in the blink of an eye. Twisted metal, shattered bones, crushed dreams, and torn wreckage causes deep, dark secrets to be revealed. One collision causes him to lose all hope, with no one but himself to blame.

Now facing harsh realities, which have never been one of River's strengths, he turns to the sure things in life: drugs and women who oh so willingly give themselves to a tall, dark, and tattooed rocker like him.

Will he find himself in the wreckage of twisted metal and crushed dreams? Or will he lose his way in the smoke and debris?

****

The first person in her family to graduate from high school and college, Keanna Sutton is flying high on her accomplishments and hard work. She has the career and man of her dreams … or so she thought until she finds out he is cheating on her. Ending the relationship, she begins rebuilding her shattered self-esteem.

Then a chance run-in with a tall, dark, and handsome, silver-tongued drummer tests her strength and ability to hold her own tongue while trying to ignore the implausible attraction to a man she knows will be no good for her.

Now a second run in at O'Donnell's pub while under the influence of drink, music, friends, and a fight makes Keanna throw caution to the wind, and she finds herself getting rocked the only way a badass like River can: hard and nasty.

Will the hottest night of her life end there? Or will she lose herself in a man who gives no promises except the lady always comes first?

PROLOGUE

Six years ago...

The first time I saw Jesse, she was wearing a jean skirt with a frayed hem, and she had on knock-off Ugg boots and a Buckeye hoodie, the same shit every girl in this hell hole of a town wore. She was totally townie, but hot as hell.

Her long, strawberry-blonde hair hung to her waist in ringlets, but not the kind of ringlets that came from a salon; that was all her. She had big green eyes and pale skin. She also had a round ass and the biggest tits I had ever laid eyes on when it came to a frame that size. She had curves for days—hell, weeks and months ... could have been years...

I was at Roundy's place. He was a friend of Steps, my cousin, who was three years older than me. I was sixteen years old and hanging out in a trailer in the middle of bum-fuck nowhere, getting fucking high for the first time in my life.

She looked at her friend and then around the smoke-filled room. She appeared to be nervous and immediately asked for the bathroom. I probably should have warned her that she should take her chances out in the woods with the poison ivy instead of going in to that shit hole, but I was high, and the words didn't form quickly enough.

When she came out, the bowl was being passed around, and she reached for it. Roundy looked at her, nodded, and she hit it hard several times. After a killer coughing fit, she sat down between her friend Tom-Tom and me, looked at me, and nodded with no smile on her face, not even in her eyes.

At the time, it made me laugh. I mean, what the fuck did a girl who looked like that have to be so pissed off about?

"Aw, you've got jokes," she said, rolling her eyes.

"I've got jokes for days, red." I winked.

"Not interested in days," she muttered, taking the bowl. "Just moments." Then she hit it.

I smirked. "If I can make you laugh, Joker, you've gotta give me something."

Tom-Tom leaned forward. "If you can make her laugh, I'll give you a blow job."

"It's on, then," I said to Tom-Tom, a girl I already knew, but winked at the girl who now looked annoyed.

It didn't take long. Being high probably helped.

When she smiled, I leaned forward then nodded expectantly to Tom-Tom, and Jesse looked annoyed.

"What?" I asked her, still laughing.

"Her or me," she said, standing up and crossing her arms while glaring down at me.

I looked over at Tom-Tom, and she shrugged.

I stood. "You."

That night, we had a moment. It was the first of so many things: blow job, finger banging, and getting high. She was skilled. I was not. I kind of blew it fast, but she only shrugged then started again.

The next day, we got high and fucked, and the condom broke. It didn't matter to me; I wasn't worried one bit. I was just happy as fuck when she lay back down and cuddled up against me with a smile—an almost smile—on her face. We fell asleep, looking at each other.

We woke up to Tom-Tom yelling that the Whites were there for her.

She jumped up, threw on her jean skirt and hoodie, and then took off out the back.

When I finally got up and dressed, I looked out the door to see a large man carrying her, kicking and screaming, toward a van. I started out because shit didn't look right to me, but Tom-Tom held her hand in front of me.

"They're her foster family. She ran away."

A tall kid got out of the van, pulled his beanie down, and then held the door open for her. I couldn't get a good look at him. Then I really didn't want to when she dove into his arms and cried.

"That's her boyfriend."

"Her, what?" I asked Tom-Tom in shock.

"The guy she was running from."

"Well, why the fuck—"

"That's how she is, River. It makes no sense." She shakes her head.

It made no sense to me, either. She had been running from him, and now she was running to him. I was a little pissed off, jealous maybe. I didn't need to feel that shit, so I went inside and got a little more fucked up.

Two days later, she showed up again. I woke up to her hand down my shorts and her telling me to make her laugh. She was jerking me off, and I was telling her jokes. Fucked up as hell, but then, when she smiled, rolled a condom on me, and mounted me, fucked up met don't give a fuck.

This went on for a week before I went back home. To hell.

A couple of months went by before I got a call from a girl crying. I knew immediately it was Jesse.

"I'm pregnant."

13

"Okay." I didn't feel numb or nervous as I waited to hear her voice, which always told me in the past what she was feeling.

"I need money," she declared, sniffing loudly into the phone.

"For …?" I sit up in bed and look over the side where I dropped my pants last night before climbing in, high as hell.

"He wants me to keep it. He says we can have a family. He says it like he believes it." She was pissed.

I knew she was talking about the boyfriend she had admitted to having yet told me he was too straight-laced for her. He didn't understand her like I did. I was her light, her white knight.

"Is it his, or is it mine?" I asked softly, knowing at any given moment, my mother or that fucking asshole stepfather could walk in my room without notice or care for my privacy.

"If it was yours, what would you say?"

From what I had seen from her, she couldn't handle being a parent any more than I fucking could.

"I would say, if you wanna keep it, cool. If not—"

"I can't have a kid, River! I'm not ready. I'm fucked up so much, and when I'm not, I want to be." She started sobbing. "Please help me! Please."

"Calm down, Jesse. You know I will." I swung my legs over the side of my bed and grabbed my jeans. "Text me the time and place. Everything will be fine."

I met her and Tom-Tom halfway between her place and mine. She talked Tom-Tom into staying the night, and we slept in the back of the SUV, twisted up in each other. She was a mess. Her pain became mine.

I told her to terminate—begged her to—and it made her happy.

The next morning, she took off. We had a plan.

Two days later, that plan was dead in the water…and so was she.

ACCIDENT

"Grab me that Thermos?" I ask the girl we call Yaya, pointing to the floor of my new ride. I haven't needed a vehicle in years. I'm too fucked up to drive most of the time, anyway, so why bother?

Finn, my best friend of over six years, is fucking shit up, not that it should surprise me. He has done it before. Now, because he doesn't want to be around Yaya, I have to leave the party celebrating the end of our first headline tour to get her back to Taelyn and Xavier's Steels'. X is the owner of our band's management and production label, and his mom, or Momma Joe as we all call her, is watching their kid and Sonya's — Yaya — four-year-old boy Noah.

We come to a stoplight, and I pour a cup into the Thermos cap and offer it to her. Her hand comes up and hits the cup.

"Fuck!" I yell as the hot liquid soaks through my shirt and hits my skin.

"Oh, River, I am so, so sorry," she tells me.

"No big deal," I lie. It fucking hurts! "Take the cup?"

I hand it to her then pull my shirt over my head, dab up as much of the spill on me as I can, and then reach in the back to grab a sweatshirt and pull it on over my head.

"See? All better." I wink and look up as the light turns green.

When we get to the next light and stop, I look over. "It's no big—" I stop when I see her looking at me strangely, waiting for her to say whatever it is she has going on in her mind.

"Was that tattoo a Joker?" she asks.

"Yeah." I smile and nod, then look back at the light.

"How old is it?"

"Fucked up question, Yaya. Most people ask, 'did it hurt?' 'What does it mean?' 'Why the fuck would you do that?' " I chuckle.

"*Did* it hurt?"

"It didn't tickle." I smirk as the light turns green.

"What does it mean?" she starts in on the same damn questions I fed her as I pull forward.

"It's someone I knew a long time ago," I answer truthfully. "She never smiled, so I gave a nickname that made no fucking sense, because she didn't make any sense."

She is quiet and then asks, "Did you love her?"

I laugh out loud. "Sixteen-year-old boys who get a blow job for the first time think they love whoever's mouth is involved, Yaya."

"You were sixteen?"

"Yep. First blow job one night and fucking her the next." I should stop, but why? It feels good to talk about her, and it's not like anyone would have a fucking clue who it's about, anyway. She is dead, so is the baby, and no one is any the wiser. I have to live with that all by myself. Well, me and weed, pills, or whatever I need to use take my mind off it.

I stop at another stoplight and look over, and she is looking at me like she is in shock.

"You okay?" I almost laugh, but she is in a state, Finn just having sent her away and all.

She shakes her head back and forth for a few seconds then asks, "Does Finn know about you and Jesse?"

As a car beeps its horn behind me, I look away from her and hit the gas. My breath is immediately lost as I accelerate. The wind has just been knocked out of me.

Her hands come up and grab the dashboard. "Please slow down. You are making me nervous."

The light turns from yellow to red, and I hit the brakes hard while throwing my hand out in front of her to stop her from hitting the dash.

"River," she voices quietly.

I still can't talk, can't say shit.

"He would understand if he—"

"Like hell he would!" And with that admission, years of undiluted, suppressed anger and emotion boil over. "He's sending you away because you know about her. Can you fucking imagine—"

"He's sending me away because—" she begins, but I cut her off.

I don't care. I don't fucking care.

"I hated him," I seethe. "For six fucking months, I hated him and didn't even know who the fuck he was."

The way she looks at me … The fucking look on her face is one of confusion, of pain, then of understanding.

Bright lights hit my peripheral, and then her look changes to horror.

"River, look out!" she screams.

The sound of the collision is deafening; the unbelievable pain from the steel crushing me is agonizing. Glass rains in on me while metal tears at my flesh. The smell of burning rubber and smoking brakes causes immediate nausea. The copper taste of my own blood intensifies the sickness in my stomach.

I look at her face while I close in on her, terrified I will crush her. She scrunches her eyes shut. Then I feel her hand grasp mine tightly. She screams something, but I can't hear a damn thing.

"You're gonna be okay," I repeat over and over, wanting to believe it, needing it to be true.

I can't lose her…

I can't lose Jesse…

Blackness consumes me.

*****

"Get the fuck out of here! I'm fucking done! Did you hear the fucking surgeon, man? I'm fucked, totally fucked. I can't feel my goddamned hand! Just get the fuck out!" I scream at Billy and Memphis to leave me alone. However, they don't, so I grab the bedpan with my right hand and chuck it at them. "Piss off, fuckers! I fucking quit!"

They leave.

I lie in bed, hitting the button in hopes the automatic drip on the morphine isn't shut off. I want more. I want to sleep. I want it all to go away.

Then I hear them.

"Man, don't go in there," Memphis warns. "He's wrecked."

Finn comes back with, "Didn't plan on it."

Fuck him. Fuck him!

"I fucking hear you, Beckett! Stop being a bitch and face me like a man!" I scream in hopes of egging him on. I want him to feel the hate I suppressed for years. I want him to hurt like I do.

"Changed my mind," he states before walking through the door.

I lift my arm to him. "You fucking did this! You are the reason this happened! 'Take care of the girl.' Isn't that what I do for you? Isn't that what I have always fucking done for you?!"

"If you're referring to Jesse, you didn't take care of shit. She OD'd. She was pregnant with my kid and she died," he yells, his fists balled at his sides.

"You sure it was your kid? My dick was in her, too, Beckett. My kid could have been growing inside her. Whoever's it was fucked her up. She was — "

"You're all sorts of willing to share that you were fucking my girlfriend now. Why the fuck did you wait six fucking years?"

Contempt covers his face, the same contempt I buried deep inside of me for him. Contempt once overshadowed by recognition and pain is now unearthed and raw again.

"You wouldn't let her get rid of it. I begged her to. She wasn't ready for a kid any more than you or I were. She deserved to live her life, but you had to fucking preach to her. Do the right thing? The right thing for who, you or Jesse?!"

"Six years, River. Six fucking years of lies, you son of a bitch. Six years, I trusted you like a brother, and for six years, you felt this way toward me?"

"No, motherfucker, I loved you. I felt the same burn inside as you did after losing her. I didn't know who you were mourning over a pile of coke. I just knew you lost something. When I figured it out, there wasn't shit I could do about it. But you stand there, judging me—"

"I intend on doing just that. I wish you the best, but you and I, we are nothing."

His words fuck my feelings ... hard. Not a good mix: narcotics, emotions, and pain.

"Fuck you and fuck the bitch you're putting it in!" I scream.

He takes a step toward me, wanting to strike, and I want him to. Something comes over him, though, and as quick as he was to step, he turns and walks out the door.

"Find a replacement or I'm done," I hear him say.

"You shitting me? Find a replacement? Motherfucker has a year of therapy and surgeries ahead of him; don't walk now. He needs you—not me, not Billy. He needs you to tell him you understand, that you—"

"No. Find a replacement or I'm out." Finn's voice drifts off, and so do I.

Feels like Propofol.

I'm five when I wake up because they are fighting. Mom and Dad always do. This time, he doesn't fight back, and she is screaming for him to leave.

I stand at the top of the stairs, looking down as the last of the party guests leave. When the last one is out the door, he walks past her. I can't see him under the stairs. I just see her. She stumbles a bit in her heels, the ones she bought this morning when she dragged me to the shoe store again.

They were high, and she smiled at herself as she turned in the mirror. "Do you think he'll like them, River? Do you think Daddy will think I look pretty in these?"

I smiled and nodded. "You're beautiful, Mommy."

As she kicks off the red heels and throws them against the wall, he reappears with his suitcase – no, there are two. He isn't going on a business trip this time. I know it, and so does she.

Her fists hit his shoulders as she sobs. "Why am I not enough? Why?!"

He brushes her hands away easily. "Get yourself together, Gloria. You're a mess. No man wants a messy woman."

"Whores!" she cries. "They're all whores, Robert."

He walks past her, shaking his head.

"Please don't go. We can work this out."

His pace doesn't slow.

"What about River? Do you want his life to fall apart?" comes out with obvious desperation.

"He'll be fine. He is half James," he replies as his hand hits the door knob.

"Don't go. Please don't go."

"Don't worry, Gloria; I will still feed your ... shoe addiction."

Before he closes the door behind him, she hurls one of the red heels and just misses him.

"Pathetic," I hear him murmur.

With that, she crumbles to the floor in a pool of silky black material, sobbing.

I wait until I can no longer see the lights of his car as he pulls out of the driveway before running down the stairs to her.

"Mommy," I whisper as I throw myself into her arms.

"I'm so sorry, River. I am so sorry I couldn't make him stay," she says against my cheek.

I wake in the morning to music playing through the surround sound. When I walk downstairs, I see two boxes by the door full of shoes, her beautiful high-heeled shoes. I walk toward the source of the music – Dad's home gym – where she is on her TreadClimber.

She looks at me as I enter the room and smiles. "Good morning, handsome," she greets without breaking her stride.

"Morning, Mommy. Who is this?" I point up so she knows I am asking about the music.

"Nirvana," she answers, wiping the sweat from her brow.

"His name is Nirvana?" I ask.

"No, his name is Kurt Cobain."

"Is he your friend?"

"No, he's a rock star – well, was."

"Did he quit?"

"No, he died three years ago yesterday – April 5th, 1994."

"That's sad, Mommy."

She smiles. "Sometimes, things happen that we can't change." She increases her speed. "Sometimes, change is bad, and sometimes, change is good." I recognize the sadness through her smile.

"Your shoes are in boxes."

"I don't need them anymore. The shoes don't make the girl, River. The girl makes the shoes. Mommy is going to change herself, get herself back. Mommy is going to be beautiful again."

"You don't need to change. You are beautiful."

"Thank you, baby, but the mirror doesn't lie, and I don't like what it's telling me. Why don't you go and see what Ms. Nancy has for you for breakfast?"

"Aren't you gonna eat with me?" I ask because she always does.

"No, baby, not today."

I wait a few moments until I realize that, this time she means it.

*****

I wake to see Taelyn Steel sitting beside my hospital room bed, typing on her iPad. Usually, seeing her makes me happy. Today, I want to send her away.

"You don't need to be here." My throat hurts when I say it.

She looks at me with sadness in her eyes, so I close mine. I don't want to see it.

"The specialist will be here soon."

I clear my throat. "That doesn't mean you need to be." I hope I don't have to be a complete dick to make her leave.

"You're not gonna be alone, so stop trying to push me. Your mother will be here in a few — "

"My, what?" My eyes pop open, fixing a glare on her.

"She's your moth — "

"You shouldn't have called her," I growl, hitting the call button.

"You need people, River. You are gonna get through this and —"

People. Fuck people. People mean pain, the kind that hurts inside. I hate it almost as much as I hate my mother.

"I need fucking drugs!" I shout as the nurse walks in.

I turn to the nurse. "What can you give me? On a scale of one to ten, my pain is at a twenty," I answer the question I know is coming. They ask every time.

I hear a message alert and look at Taelyn. Her eyes leave the screen and shift to me.

I shake my head, knowing damn well Gloria has arrived.

The nurse removes the blood pressure cuff she strapped on when she came in, directing my attention back to her.

"Hit me with whatever you have, and hit me hard."

"I'll see what I can do," she promises. She's new. I haven't seen her yet in the past three days I have been here, which means she hasn't been exposed to my outbursts.

When I look her up and down, she blushes.

Then I look to see Taelyn standing by the door and leaning toward the nurse.

"I want a sponge bath with special attention paid to my cock."

The nurse's eyes widen, but she doesn't look pissed.

"See what you can do." I tell her.

"Um, maybe later?"

"Make it happen." I lean back and close my eyes. "I really need it."

"I'll be back," she says in a naughty kind of way.

"I'll make sure you get yours, too," I promise.

When the nurse leaves, I clear my voice, getting Taelyn's attention. "Get rid of her," I demand, talking about my mother.

"Let's just see—"

"Taelyn, I have mad respect for you, but I am telling you that I am in no shape to deal with her." I close my eyes and hit the call button again.

"You have done so well, River—"

"Taelyn—"

The nurse comes in again and interrupts. She doesn't say anything, just shoots something in the IV. "This should help."

I feel the sting of the narcotic as it enters my vein. Then the burn blazes through me until nothing else matters.

My eyes grow heavy, and I smile. She smiles back and winks.

"Better?" Taelyn asks.

"Yeah," I respond then ask the nurse, "How long will this stay in my system? The other shit wears off too damn fast."

"It should last four hours, Mr. James."

"Good." *I won't have to deal with Gloria.* "Thanks."

I hear her heels click across the tiles on the hospital floor. I smell her musky perfume, and I hear her full of shit voice.

"My boy."

I keep my eyes closed, hoping she gets bored, thinking I am asleep, but then I flinch when she touches my face. I despise her.

I know she's wearing fur because I feel it against my cheek as she draws her hand back.

"Thank you, Mrs. Steel, for calling me. I'm sorry it took so long to get back to you. I was out of the country, and reception is horrible in Guadalupe. Thank God Herbert has his help run into town and check our calls when we are otherwise disposed."

Herbert, husband number five, is on year seven. He has lasted longer than the rest of them. Coincidence? I think not. Fucker is rich as hell.

Husband two, Juan, was the fucking neighbor's pool boy until dear old Mom realized his business didn't make bank like Father always did. He was actually the easiest to live with. Husband three, Skipper, was a fucking fat bastard who came from money and slept all day. When he wasn't asleep, he was yelling for me to get him a drink or food or the remote. Lazy fuck. The fucking slob would have stuck around, too, if dear old Mom hadn't found Henry, who was a fucking scumbag police officer, living off a healthy-ass trust fund. I'm certain she sucked him off to get out of a ticket, because I once heard her tell Skipper she got a ticket and needed two grand for fees and fines. Then she came home with the lips of a Kardashian.

None of her men let her go without. She was treated like the queen she thought she was while she looked the other way when shit was not right.

Henry, her fourth husband, was the worst. He was a monster—worse than a monster because monsters aren't real.

"You're here now, and that's all that matters."

"If it wasn't for my boy, I would have found it very hard to leave my husband, but River is worth it," Gloria bullshits.

"He has a long road to recovery, but I am sure he'll pull out of it just fine."

"How long exactly?"

God, I hate that woman. I don't give a fuck if she pushed me out of her vag. I hope that shit hurt. I hope it still does.

"The nurse said possibly four months," Taelyn answers, "which is much better than the year they originally told us."

"Oh." Her response hangs in the air.

No way is Gloria going to leave if I don't say something. Therefore, I clear my throat and open my eyes.

"Oh, honey," Gloria cries, bending down for a kiss, but I move my head, and she gets my cheek. Her eyes shift from me to Taelyn and back. "Tell me what I can do for you."

"Nothing," I answer, looking at Taelyn who seems perplexed. "I'll be fine."

"Of course you will." Gloria again reaches out to touch my cheek, and I flinch.

She glances at Taelyn. "My son is too old for—"

"I'm going to sleep. I'll call you if I need anything," I say as I let the drugs take hold.

"I should get a hotel," she says in her show voice.

"No, I'll call if I need anything," I grumble.

I fall asleep, listening to her spew bullshit to Taelyn about how she wished I would let her stay, but boys will be boys. I allow it because I just want her to go the fuck away. Besides, it wouldn't matter if I told her that shit. The one time I told her what I knew she could already see, she didn't listen. I told her I wanted to go and live with my father, and she wouldn't even call him.

Never again.

Feels like morphine.

I'm fifteen years old with full access to the world. It is literally at my fingertips.

The Internet, every adolescent boy's filthy dream and dirty, little secret. A boy who comes from a "privileged" lifestyle has that shit tenfold. Cell phone with unlimited data, a laptop with the same, mix that up with the smarts to erase my browser history and disable cookies to boot, and you have a kid whose hormones are on steroids.

"What the fuck do you think you're doing?" Henry, Mom's fourth husband grumbles as he walks in my room.

I jump and adjust myself through my sweatpants. Then I quickly minimize the screen so he can't see what it is I am actually doing.

"Goddamned kid doesn't even have hair on his balls yet and he's jerking off." He stumbles over to me. Obviously, the smoke has worn off, and he turned to the bottle.

"Fuck you," I mumble under my breath as I stand as tall as my five-foot-six ass can.

"What did you just say to me?" He grabs me by the back of my neck and pushes me down across my desk. "Someone oughta teach you a lesson."

"Fuck you," I hiss as I try to stand up, but he's too fucking big, too damn strong.

"Stay down and take what is coming to you."

I continue to struggle while he pushes harder, his body leaning over mine. I hear the clank of his belt buckle, and then he grips the back of my neck hard, mashing my face into the keyboard on my desk.

My pants get yanked down, and then the leather belt hits my back when I try to escape. Then it hits my ass.

I cry out in pain as his malicious laugh grows deeper.

I yell for my mother, scream for her.

One hand covers my mouth, and then …

"No! No! Please no!" My scream is in vain.

I plead to God for my end.

O'Donnell's Pub

Three months ago...

I walk into the gym for the first time at the twenty-four hour fitness center. I made a promise to myself that I would join once I lost twenty pounds, and this morning, I hit the twenty-pound mark!

It's intimidating as hell, but I am strong, beautiful, and in control of my own destiny. I am well-educated, stronger than any man I have ever come in contact with, and loyal to a fault.

I decided I was no longer destined to be the one left behind by the men who departed from my bed, only to wind up in the bed of someone thirty pounds smaller and ten skin shades lighter.

I look at myself in a mirror as I walk by one. I have never hated my curves. I used to love them. They made me feel ... sexy. But after Miguel's last "fuck up," I see them as a curse.

When I walk up to the registration counter, a brunette with way too much energy gives me the once-over then turns on a smile that isn't all that genuine. I give it right back.

"What can I help you with?" she asks.

I want to say, "What the fuck do you think you can help me with?" But I don't. I'm smiling, you see, and even though it's not beaming from the inside, I am ever so hopeful it will sink in.

"I'd like to sign up for a membership."

"We have a special going on. You can get a one-week trial membership." She nods and winks. "Helps new clients figure out if this is the right match for them."

"Sounds good," I say, reaching for the application she pushes across the counter. Then it hits me: this bitch thinks I'm playing.

"But not good enough." I push it back. "I want to join, become a member, so I'm not interested in this." I wave my hand at the application.

After getting everything set up, I hit the track. During two rotations around the circuit, I watch her judging me. After forty-five minutes on the treadmill, legs burning, sweat pouring off, unsure if I will be able to walk tomorrow, I am judging her.

*****

One month ago...

I shower after my workout then walk out, glancing at the wall of mirrors I used to avoid. Ten more pounds gone and my curves are tight and not lost. I am again confident with myself. I know it's ninety-nine percent because he is gone, and I don't have to see him eyeballing size two women when he is out with me.

When my phone rings, I grab it out of my bag and look at the caller ID. Natasha, otherwise known as the brunette with way too much energy who works the desk part-time at the gym, has now become one of my very best friends.

"Hey, girl," I answer.

"Keanna, I'm behind at the office. Will you pick up—"

"Jordan from school? Of course. Meet you at the office?"

Natasha's ex is doing a stint in the state pen for armed robbery. She had no idea he had a gambling addiction or was capable of something like that. She doesn't trust his family with her child after they took him to visit his father in prison and failed to tell her. She found out when he woke from a nightmare about the cage Daddy was in. Luckily, she has her family and me. I gladly help out whenever I can.

"You are the absolute best. I hope you know I—"

"I know," I cut her off, knowing she could go on for fifteen minutes about how appreciative she is. "See you soon."

My girl has issues.

Don't we all, though?

*****

Jordan and I walk into Jersey Shore University Medical where Natasha and I ran into each other after I joined the gym. She is a physical therapist, and I am a registered nurse. My attitude about her changed when I got to know her, and I am so glad I did.

"Can I push the button?" Five-year-old Jordan jumps up and down, his green eyes shining and his mop of brown hair bouncing under his hat.

"Sure can. Four—"

"Fourth floor," he finishes the sentence for me.

The entire way up to the fourth floor, Jordan giggles as he holds his belly. Then, when it stops and does the little descent elevators do, his big, green eyes widen, and he looks nervous, but only until it stops.

I take his hand and give it a squeeze. "Ready?"

He nods, smiles, and steps toward the door that's opening.

I look down at him as we walk hand in hand toward the physical therapy center Natasha works in.

"When I was younger, I used to get so scared of elevators," he says, as if admitting a deep, dark secret.

"Wow, I would have never known," I play along as I push the door open and snatch the hat off his head as we walk in.

"That's 'cause I'm a big boy now." He smiles and looks around for an empty place for us to sit.

Normally, there are two, maybe three, people in the office this close to closing time. Today, the office is abnormally busy for a Thursday at five-thirty. There is one entire row of people in the back, against the wall. Two men are playing on their phones, both undeniably good-looking. One has dark hair, the other a dark blond color. Two women are next to them. One is a blonde and a redhead sits next to the dark-haired guy.

Jordan leads me to the row of chairs facing them. We sit, and Jordan grabs his little Superman backpack out of my hand and opens it. He reaches in and grabs his tablet.

"You wanna play?" he asks.

"Sure, little man." I drop my brown Coach purse down next to me. "You're gonna have to teach me, though."

His face lights up. "You wanna watch first?"

"Sure thing."

As he starts talking about his game—Angry Birds—I see a black pair of boots walk past us.

I glance up to see the owner of said sexy biker boots sit in the only empty seat across from us.

"See, Keanna? Like this." Jordan draws his little finger backward on the screen and releases. The bird goes flying.

"You good?" I hear one of the men ask.

"No. I don't wanna be here. No sense in it. Waste of fucking time," a gruff voice answers, and immediately, I feel its seediness in my core.

"We're here for you, man," another man's voice chimes in.

"You're here because you thought I wouldn't show," biker boots replies with some bite.

I force my eyes to stay trained on Jordan and his game.

"River," a woman scolds quietly.

"I swear to whatever the hell is up in the sky playing master puppeteer of my life, I don't wanna hear it. It's a waste of time. It's not healing and—"

"My mom will fix you," Jordan announces, looking up. "She's the best. Isn't that right, Keanna?"

Shit, I mumble in my head. "She sure is, Jordan."

"See? You're gonna be fine," Jordan assures before looking back down, continuing his game.

"Let the healing begin then, little man. Send her right on over here and—"

"River," the same woman's voice scolds again.

"Hey, Momma, your boy says you can heal me. You wanna give it a go here, or you think I can sneak you off—"

"Enough," one of the men snarls.

I look up briefly, and my eyes meet his, hard and angry.

"What say you, Momma?"

I point to myself. "Me?"

"Little man says you can fix me, so how about you—"

"Please excuse him," the red-haired woman interrupts.

"*Excuse me?*" he huffs.

I force myself to speak. "Do I look like his momma?" He starts to answer, but I hold my hand up, stopping him. "You are in the wrong office for an eye exam. I will give you a hint, though. This young man here is not my son. Hell, we aren't even the same color."

The dark-haired man smirks. "Don't stop now; keep it coming. His ass needs to be put in check."

"Lust knows no color," the man they call River says, looking at me as if he may be amused, but hell if I know what's going on with his crazy ass. "If you have some special healing power, by all means, come on over and let the healing begin. Lay your healing hands—"

The redhead elbows him, stopping him from finishing his sentence.

"Crazy." I shake my head then look at Jordan, who is engrossed in his game. "Didn't your mother teach you not to talk to strange people?"

"Strangers," Jordan corrects me.

"Well, I'm here to tell you, add strange people to your do-not-speak registry," I whisper to Jordan.

I hear a gruff chuckle and look up into the very amused eyes of the man I now know as River. I shake my head, then look away.

"River, sorry to keep you waiting," I hear Natasha say, and Jordan jumps up.

"Mommy." He runs to hug her.

"Hey, bud." She returns his hug and kisses the top of his head. "Can you and Keanna give me half an hour?" She looks up at me, and I nod.

"Come here, little man. Let's play." I hold his tablet up.

When I hear River chuckle, I look up as he walks by, adjusting himself. He stops and whispers, "Big man wants to play."

My jaw comes unhinged. However, I quickly snap it shut, not wanting the inquisitive five-year-old walking toward me to ask the hundred questions I am sure he would if he thought I was even a little off balance. Kids sense it, and they do it all the time.

"Give my boy your digits. Let's make it happen." He winks, then is gone before I can give him one of my infamous quick-witted comebacks.

"Ready to play?" Jordan asks as he bounces in the seat next to me.

"Yes, of course, let's play."

I am admittedly frazzled, and he looks at me. I don't give him the chance to start the questioning. I point to his game.

"Show me two more rounds. Then I am gonna destroy you."

"It's on, Keeana." He giggles.

"Like Donkey Kong," I remark, snickering.

"Like who?"

*****

I take Jordan to the café across the street for cocoa while Natasha sees her patient.

The over six-foot-tall, hazel eyes, pillow-lipped, silver-tongued sex god makes me uncomfortable in ways that floor me. He's crude, has no filter, but the way he looked at me made something inside me shift, and I am not at all okay with it.

He's the kind of man I am sure could have any woman he wanted disrobed in a matter of seconds. The look in his eyes held nothing but confidence, which I can only assume meant he could deliver.

My phone rings. It's Natasha.

"We're across the street," I tell her.

"On my way. Oh, and by the way, the drummer —
"

"Who?"

"River." She laughs. "He says, '*I'm just a drummer.*'"

"You like him?" I ask, because if she says yes, maybe I won't think about him.

"Who wouldn't, but he fucked your name with his mouth right in front of me. He's into you, girl."

"No. Not happening." I shake my head furiously back and forth, though she can't see it.

"He asked for your digits."

"You didn't," I gasp.

"Heck no. But I should have. See you in a minute."

*****

Today

It's three-thirty in the afternoon on a Friday, and I am walking out of the hospital, feeling like a new woman, and looking forward to my weekend off. As usual, I am heading to the gym. But first, I drive home, drop off the car, grab my gym bag out of the backseat, and wait for a cab. I'm not driving tonight. I'm going to be busy drinking.

After changing into my workout gear, I hit the elliptical to loosen up my fatigued muscles. Thirty minutes later, I do the circuit. Then I shower at the gym because I promised Natasha I would meet her and a couple of her office friends for happy hour at O'Donnell's pub.

My phone sounds off as I am trying to make sense of my makeup. Looking down, I see a message from Natasha.

Where are you? We're on round two.

I message back, *Be there in five.*

Which is bull. I won't be, because I am ten minutes away if traffic is good, and I haven't even finished with my eyes.

*****

I can hear the music from the street as the taxi lets me off in front of O'Donnell's. A live band is playing, and I immediately freeze, hoping like hell it isn't the band of Miguel, my ex-boyfriend's cousin.

"There you are." I look left and see Natasha walking up to me. "You're here!" She dives forward and hugs me, laughing. "I'm a little tipsy."

"I'm here." I fake a laugh as I try to stay present in our conversation while also trying to listen to the music. "Who's playing?"

"Not sure. They started as I walked out to go grab some gum from the store next door." She giggles and repeats, "Store next door. I'm a poet, and I didn't know it."

"You sure are," I agree because, hell, she's having fun, and Natasha doesn't do fun often. "You staying with me tonight?"

"Mom has Jordan," she says, opening her wintergreen gum. "I haven't been out in months. If I don't find someone to take me home, I am certainly going home with you."

"My girl needs to get laid." I smirk, pointing at her. "Hoochie dress, stripper boots, hair on point—I don't think you'll be going home with me."

"From your mouth to God's ears." She giggles, then covers her mouth. "Oh, that's bad."

"Embrace bad," I tell her as I open the door to the pub. "You deserve it once in a while."

"So do you," she replies from behind me, loud enough for me to hear over the music. "Follow me; we have a table."

She walks around me, her dark hair hanging down her back in loose curls that cover part of her open back, deep red dress that falls just above her knees, nearly touching the black leather boots with the four-inch heels. My girl is looking hot tonight. Her attire conveys confidence, and I am ecstatic for her.

I look up as I follow her through the crowd of Jersey Shore-like men. I am certain they are all spray-tanned and waxed ... everywhere. They are without a doubt fine-looking—*mmm-mmm-mmm*—but I can guarantee they spend more time in front of a mirror than any man should.

O'Donnell's is nice with dark green painted walls, light oak flooring, and a matching light oak bar that spans nearly the entire length of the place. Built in coolers are centered behind the bar and seem to hold every beer imaginable. Plus, there are drafts in all assortments.

A twenty-ish, blond-haired man, who is hot as hell, is behind the bar with a woman standing nearby who has lighter skin than I, but she is of African-American descent. She is tall, thin, stunning, and clearly with the blond man. The way he looks at her is a little unnerving, like he wants to eat her up or just has. It's hot as hell. And she looks at him like she's the canary to his cat.

"Have a seat," Natasha offers, drawing my attention away from the couple I would probably ditch my no threesome rule for if they simply asked.

I sit down, still staring at my surroundings.

"Keanna, this is Tiffany and Erin. Tiff and Erin, this is Keanna."

I smile, looking over at them. "Nice to meet you."

I hear one laugh. "Hot, isn't he?" I glance at the girl. "I'm Tiffany."

I shake her outstretched hand and smile. "Hell yes, he's hot."

"My friend Bekah is married to one of his friends. His name is Abe, and the woman with him is his fiancée, Nikolette."

"Lucky bitch," I remark, shaking my head.

"Yeah, lucky indeed. I'm Erin," the other girl adds as she takes a shot from the tray in the center of the table, then hands one to me. "We are way ahead of you. Drink up, Keanna. It's gonna be one hell of a night."

As soon as I do the shot, another is handed to me by Tiff. As soon as it's gone, Natasha hands me yet another.

"You trying to make me—"

"Loosen up. It's girls' night!" she interrupts with a drunken grin.

"Cheers to that." Erin raises her beer, and I tap her glass with my shot.

Tiffany then disappears to grab another round, and I watch her walk up to the bar. She's five foot nothing, pushing her way through the crowd with the attitude of a six-foot-three man. She is wearing a short, camo skirt over black leggings; an Army green jacket over a black T-shirt; work boots; and her hair is loosely tied back with waves spilling out from the hair tie. I already know I'm going to like her.

"The band's good," Erin exclaims, drawing my attention back to the table. "Apparently, the owner—aka, blond hottie bartender—is gonna do live shows here once in a while to find talent for a friend of his. These guys"—she points to the small stage—"are local, just starting out and opening for the next band, Inappropriate Thoughts. I love listening to live music."

Son of a bitch, I think to myself, looking around and hoping I don't see Miguel, who periodically travels with the band as their on again, off again manager. His cousin, Anthony Masterson—or "The Master" as he is dubbed—is the frontman of Inappropriate Thoughts.

I am happy when I don't see him until I spot Anthony walking onstage, donning his almost obscenely skin tight, black leather pants and his black tank top with a new band logo — one I haven't seen — with his black hair down and out of the everyday bun it's usually in.

"Holy hell," Natasha mutters, ogling him.

I understand why. He's beautiful, and the fact that he is hung like a fucking mule is unmistakable in his pants. Who am I kidding? It's unmistakable on Sunday afternoons at the Masterson family dinners when he is wearing loose jeans.

Tiffany returns with four glasses full of a dark tap beer and sets them in front of us. "Hottie bartender says this is the best tap beer. I kind of believed him. How fucked up is that? Just because he looks like a god, I take his word as gospel."

They all laugh until Anthony's voice comes over the microphone.

"You ready to let me play with you for a while?"

"I'm ready to let you play with me all night," Natasha's voice booms over a crowd that quieted as soon as his voice stimulated their ears.

When his eyes narrow as he scans the crowd, she covers her mouth, appearing mortified.

"You just fucked with the wrong guy." I can't help giggling.

"You have no idea what you just got yourself into," he says, his eyes meeting hers.

She points to me as her face flushes furiously. Anthony glances at me, gives me a smirk, but looks back at her and shakes his head, pointing directly at her. "I'm gonna own you for one night."

Deeds, singer and guitarist, laughs and starts playing "Take me deep."

"You better run, little red dressing hood. He's a freak," I warn, feeling almost sorry for her.

"*Pft*, no man can own me," she declares with a nervous tremor in her voice, still looking at the stage.

"He sure could try owning me for the night," Erin chimes in.

I hear Sticks begin to beat on the drum and look over, but it's not Sticks.

"Oh, my God, is that—"

"River James," Natasha interrupts. "He's healing well. The band's drummer is playing with Steel Total Destruction until he is cleared to go back," she shouts over the music.

"Seems like he should be cleared. He's better than Sticks," I say, watching him. His eyes are hazel, head shaved tight, his jaw square and strong, and his lips, dear God his lips are like pillows.

"You seem to know him," Erin states. "Tell us all about it."

"Long story"—I slam half my beer and look over at her—"one that is not being told here or now."

She doesn't look away, seeming unreceptive to my avoidance.

"If he can't play with his band, why is he playing here tonight?" I ask, hoping to take the conversation back to a safe zone.

"He's on a journey, I think," Natasha says, giving me a smirk.

I look back at the stage and watch him. "A journey," I mumble as I find myself drawn to the man with the sticks in his hand, intense hazel eyes, and an air of anger surrounding him. He is no good for me.

REPLACEMENT
STICKS

When the set I promised Taelyn I would play is finished, I feel anxious, annoyed, and angry. I immediately head out the back and spark up Chilz. Two hits and I'm feeling a little less pissed off and anxious.

"You did well." Masterson holds out his hand for Chilz, and I hand it to him.

"I wasn't feeling it. I played like shit." I shake my head, hoping to erase the entire experience.

"Fuck that! You did damn good," Deeds declares, taking Chilz from "The Master." "Your band was watching."

I look up at him. "Who?"

"Steel Total—"

"But who?"

He looks at me funny, and I realize I'm kind of being a bitch.

"I should go and see 'em. Return Chilz later, but don't you dare lose him."

I walk inside and immediately see Xavier, Taelyn, Billy, and Memphis at the bar. I look toward the door and see fucking Finn walking toward it. Yaya, his woman, looks over her shoulder at me, smiles woefully, and then turns away when Finn opens the door and puts his hand on her back.

"You fucking killed it, man." Memphis pats my back. "Abe, get this man a beer."

I shake my head. "I did okay."

Billy nods. "You didn't drop the stick once."

"How's the grip?" X asks. I know he could tell I didn't give it my all, which immediately makes me defensive.

"Sucks. You know that."

"Better than you were last time I heard you play." He nods and takes a drink. "Do you see your physical therapist outside of the office?" He nods in a direction behind me, and I follow his eyes.

"No," I reply, smirking when I spot her with the chick from her office. I never got a name, but I liked her attitude … and her tits. Her skin is milk chocolate and smooth. I wanted to lick it the first time I saw her. I want to lick it now. Her eyes remind me of a doe— brown and expressive. Her hair is cut into a sassy-do just above the shoulders, but not too short that I couldn't get a good grip on it. She has curves for fucking days and a round, tight ass perfect for bouncing a quarter off of, as some would say. Me? I want my dick slapping that thing. Her tits are full and look soft, just like that body. I'm gonna tap that tonight.

"You sure about that?" Taelyn asks, drawing my attention to her and her smile.

"Yeah, I'm sure." I again look back at them.

Natasha looks up and waves. She has a grin from ear to ear, and I can't help laughing. When she gives me two thumbs up and starts playing air drums, her sexy friend looks at her like she's fucking crazy then starts laughing.

A thousand-watt smile shoots out across the room, and I can't look away. She then looks at me, the smile immediately disappearing. She looks away quickly, and I force myself not to laugh. I know I'm under her skin. The chick *thinks* she hates me, which should be a good reason for me to leave well enough alone, but well, that shit isn't going to fly with me. I see it as a challenge, and I accept it.

I lean over to Abe. "I want a round for that table, and I'll take it over."

When he completes my order, I walk over with the tray of drinks and set it on the table. Then I sit down right next to the hot as fuck, curvy, doe-eyed reason for the half chub in my pants.

"How you doing?" I ask, intentionally invading her personal space.

She nearly jumps out of her seat, but I make sure to plant my good hand firmly on her knee, keeping her in place. She sighs and rolls her eyes, but never once does she push my hand from her knee.

"You," she says trying not to smile.

"Me."

"River!" Natasha practically dives over and hugs me. "You did it."

I regretfully pull my hand off the knee of the girl I'm going to get to know better by the end of the damn night and hug my shit-faced therapist.

"Yeah." I grin.

"Thank you for the drinks. We love them. Best. Drink. Ever!" she yells, giggling.

"Is that so?" I can't help being amused because I see Dr. Natasha weekly now, and this is not the chick I usually see.

"I. Love. This—" She stops when Masterson walks up to the table.

I hear the girl—fuck, what's her name?—next to me laugh.

"Anthony."

"Keanna," he greets, still staring at Natasha.

"You really need to leave it alone," the girl I now know is Keanna warns.

"A challenge is a challenge," he remarks, still staring at Natasha. "Don't you leave until I come back," he tells her, then walks away.

"Oh. O … kay?" Natasha responds, wide-eyed, as Masterson takes the stage.

"Girl, you better run," Keanna warns.

"Boo," a male voice comes from behind me.

"Oh, hell no." Keanna shakes her head.

"You look fine, baby." Some douche she obviously knows slides between us.

"Watch it, motherfucker," I growl.

The motherfucker doesn't watch it. He doesn't do shit but lean in and whisper in her ear.

She doesn't say dick. She stands up, backs away from him, pushes her sleeves up, and turns as if she's going to walk away. However, he grabs her elbow, and she turns before swinging at him, hitting him in the side of the face.

"You keep your filthy hands off me!"

He grabs her elbow and pulls her toward him, yelling, "Who the fuck—"

I tap him on the shoulder, and he turns toward me, glowering.

"The lady said to get your filthy hands—"

48

"Who the hell are you calling a lady?" he sneers. "K is my bitch. Always has been; always will be."

"Get your fucking hand off her," I grit out through clenched teeth, feeling my temperature rising.

Keanna yanks her arm away and snaps her fingers in his face. "Get to steppin'."

He reaches out to grab her hand, but I grip his elbow. He then turns and starts to swing, so I do it first and lunge, knocking him and myself to the floor.

As quickly as it all happens, I am pulled back, and Masterson is jumping off stage and pulling the stupid fuck who doesn't listen all that fucking well off the floor.

"Fucking whore," he yells, pointing at Keanna.

My hand throbs. Belatedly, I realize I hit the fucker with my bad hand.

"What the fuck were you thinking?" X asks, pulling me back.

I look past him at Keanna, who looks shocked.

"Useless fucking slut!" the bastard yells.

"Keanna!" I yell as I am being pulled back. "Need those healing hands, babe, and if you're gonna be a slut, how about you be my slut tonight?!"

"Aw … for fuck's sake, River, that was smooth," X huffs.

"You sure you can handle it?" she yells back all badass like, surprising me.

I snort. "You should ask yourself that question. Let's you and I bounce."

"You do it, and you'll never have this again." The dick, who is still being held back by Masterson, grabs himself.

"Never intended on having it again," she retorts. Then she whispers to Natasha, grabs her bag, and walks toward me.

Fuck. Yes.

Once outside with X and company, who followed us out, I reach back and grab Keanna's hand.

"You need a doctor," Taelyn tells me as X hails a cab.

"Nah, I'm good." I look at Keanna. "Real fucking good."

"You just hit that asshole with your injured hand," Billy snaps at me.

"Not too fucking smart," Memphis chimes in.

"I made a fist." My eyes are still focused on hers. "Progress."

"You really did?" Taelyn asks with a smile.

"Knocked his ass down, too." I look back and nod toward the door. "I'm good. Go back in."

When they don't move, I glare at Memphis, hoping he will get the fucking point. He does immediately.

"Yep, he's all set. Let's get back in there and see if *The Master* needs a hand."

A cab rolls up, and I smile.

"If I get you in the cab, there is no turning back."

"You have any idea what you're up against?" She arches a brow.

"I have more than one idea, and I plan to show you them all." I open the door and nod. "Ladies first."

"You better hope so." She smirks.

I watch her round ass slide into the cab, and then I am behind her like I plan to be as soon as we get to my place.

I start to give the cab driver directions, but she interrupts with hers, then looks at me.

"I am not doing the walk of shame."

"Shame? Leaving my bed would be shameful? You wound me, Keanna."

She grabs my hand and looks at it. "That was stupid, you know — hitting him with an injured hand."

"He grabbed you. Men, real men, don't ever put their hand on a woman ... or a child." I make damn sure she knows I'm serious.

"But your—"

"But nothing," I interrupt, grabbing the back of her head and pulling her toward me. "I want those lips. Now."

She pulls back and shakes her head. "No kissing."

Shocked, I look at her. "Why the hell not?"

"Long story," she says as she runs her hand up my knee and rubs me through my jeans.

"It's a go. Hard as fuck and ready. Lips, Keanna."

I lean in, but she turns her head, so I get her cheek. Good enough.

She smells sexy as hell, like coconut. I lick down her jawline as my hand takes its place on her thigh and moves up. I let my fingers tease her skin just under the hemline of her dress. She likes it. Her hand rubs me a little harder.

"I can't wait to be up in here," I tell her as my fingers rub circles against her soft skin. "I can't wait until my cock meets your pussy." I lean in and nip at her earlobe, and she moans.

She messes with my belt, and I am not ashamed to say I would fuck her in this cab if that's what she wanted, because I damn sure would.

The cab comes to a halt in front of an apartment building, and she slowly pulls back. Her eyes are liquid heat, and I know damn well her pussy is, too.

I pay the cab driver, open the door, slide out, and reach out my hand for her to take.

"Second floor," she tells me in a husky, sexy as hell voice as we walk toward the building.

The building is made of brick and glass, five floors, and I see the hospital in the far distance.

"You work over there?" I ask.

"I'm a nurse, so yes."

"Aw … fuck," I mutter under my breath. "She's a nurse."

"Is that a bad thing?" Obviously, she heard me.

"No, not at all. Hot as hell," I admit.

I follow behind her as we take the stairs. Her ass is round, tight, and I am two seconds from biting it.

Contain the freak. I consider ignoring the fleeting thought. Fuck, I have no idea why it even crossed my mind. This girl doesn't kiss, yet she rubs my cock in public transportation, and I know damn well I could have finger banged her in the cab.

"Ouch," she cries out when I decide, *fuck the thought, I wanna bite the ass*, so I do.

I look up at her as she stands still on the landing, looking down at me.

"I'm seconds away from taking you right here, so let's get inside if that idea doesn't make you as hot and ready as I am."

When she doesn't move, I reach up, but she slaps my hand away and steps down the hall.

"Warning: I have a dog," she says as she fishes through her purse to grab her keys. "Tinker Bell is my girl. She loves me. Step out of line —"

"I'm gonna step," I interrupt, "and I'm not afraid of dogs."

Her hair is in her face, but I see a smile creep across the lips my dick is aching to be in between.

"All right, then." She unlocks the door and steps in. "We have a guest. Behave," she warns, opening the door wider to allow me in.

I take a step back when the hundred plus pound dog barks, and I swear it scowls at me.

"Tink, behave," Keanna warns.

"That's not a fucking dog; that's a bear," I state, looking between the black, long-haired dog and the sexy as hell chick I plan on banging tonight.

"Newfoundland." She smiles as she snaps her finger and points to the ground. The bear sits yet is still giving me that look. "Are you coming in, or has my girl done her job?"

"Is her job to make hard dicks shrivel up and make grown men run?" I ask, holding eye contact with the massive animal.

Keanna laughs. "Sure is. If you get intimidated by her, you sure as hell can't handle me."

I reach out to pat her head. "You and I are gonna make fast friends, Tink. I want your owner so badly even you can't make this boner hide." She snarls at the hand held toward her. "Don't be like that." I squat down, knowing damn well, at this point, I am either fucked or not gonna be. Her ears perk up, and she tilts her head. "Sniff my hand. It's already been on her, and she really wants more. If you and I become friendly, I may buy you a steak or something."

She nudges my outstretched hand with her nose, either deciding she wants to eat it or make friends.

I look up at Keanna, who looks a little surprised. "I'll make nice with your dog just to get to your pussy."

She smirks. "Good to know."

Suddenly, I see a mouth coming at me, and a tongue immediately washes over the entire side of my face.

"Your owner doesn't like kissing, yet you, Tink, nearly slipped me the tongue having known me for seconds." I pet her head, and she pushes against my hand.

When I look up at Keanna again, she narrows her eyes a bit, trying not to smile.

"We good, Tinker Bell?" I ask before standing up and looking at Keanna. "You ready to get naked?"

"Is that foreplay?"

I can't help the laugh rumbling in my chest. "Not even close."

I step around the dog, and she walks around me out of the entryway and toward the living room.

"Bedroom?"

"Would you like a drink?" she evades.

"No." I take a step forward and take her hand. "Let's not waste any more time. You and I both knew this was gonna happen when we met in the doctor's office." I pull her toward me.

"I would have laid you out in lavender if Jordan wasn't there." Her voice falters when my mouth touches her neck.

"Lavender isn't my color," I say before pushing her jacket off her shoulders.

She pulls back a little. "Let me ask you something."

Sighing, I remove my mouth from her sweet smelling skin.

"You ever been with a black woman?"

"Yes," I answer honestly.

"Let me rephrase: have you ever been with a strong, black woman?"

"I've been inside many women, Keanna. Is that gonna be a problem?" I ask, confused because this is far from the norm for me. However, I will tell her exactly who I am in case she doesn't already get it. "I'm not looking for a relationship; I don't take orders in life; I don't follow rules; and I fuck my way."

She looks me up and down. "You fuck me right, understand? I come, you come, you —"

"I can assure you I know *exactly* how to fuck."

Taking Turns

Sweet baby Jesus, this man...This man has confidence in droves. His eyes show no fear, no insecurities, but they make *me* feel both fearful and insecure, two things I will not let him see. Two things that are learned behaviors, behaviors I have made great strides to unlearn.

Self-confidence is sexy.

I am sexy.

"The confidence in your ability is—"

"Hot?" he provides as he pulls his shirt over his head, exposing ink, beautiful, sexy ink that my quivering tongue itches to trace.

I clear the thickness from my throat. "It—"

"Makes you wet?" He kicks his boots off.

"Well, it—"

"Makes it impossible to resist the fucking you've been playing over in your head like your favorite song on repeat?" He unbuttons his jeans and shoves them down. His thick, erect dick springs forward as he steps out of them.

His cock is glorious. It's possibly the eighth wonder of the world. The black-inked tree traveling down his side crosses over to his hip, and the roots kiss the base of his unbelievable length and incredibly thick, mouth-watering goodness.

Don't get me wrong; I have sucked dick — oral is a give and take for me — but my mouth is undeniably watering at the sight of his utter perfection. I am salivating, and my pussy throbs with need.

"That fucking in your mind is not even close to the fucking you are about to receive, Keanna. Take your clothes off. I need my mouth on you." He steps toward me and takes my hand, raises it up, and turns me like a dancing ballerina on top of a childhood jewelry box. Then he pulls me back against him.

"I'm gonna make you come so hard, when you're old and married, you'll finger-fuck yourself to the thought of tonight." His hot breath hits the back of my ear, bringing my body to a new level of awareness.

I swallow quickly, afraid I may drool, which would be an incredible embarrassment.

"Fuck, I can't wait to taste your pussy," he growls as he slowly unzips my dress, kissing down my spine with each inch of flesh he exposes. He is midway down, on his knees, when he pulls my sleeves down. "Arms out."

I do as he asks without hesitation.

"You've got to be fucking kidding me," he growls as my dress hits the floor, pooling at my feet, before he glides his fingers back and forth under my garter belt. "I did not see that coming. Fuck. Thigh highs attached to *this*. Now I'm gonna have to fuck you twice: once in and once out of this sexy as hell get up." He stands up and walks us over to the couch where he bends me over the back of it. "Don't move."

I want to tell him I don't take orders, but right now, I'm willing to take whatever he has to give.

I feel his finger run down the back of my thong before he pushes it to the side.

"I can feel the heat radiating. Now I wanna taste it."

Without warning, he pushes a finger inside of me, and my knees buckle as I cry out.

"I'm gonna fuck you in those boots," he says with a growl as his fingers work their magic in me.

"Yes," I cry out, unashamed.

His fingers pull out unexpectedly, and then I feel his mouth cover me from behind. I feel his tongue roll over my clit with just enough pressure to make me want—no, *need*—more.

He nibbles on me, sucks on me, and I bury my face in the cushion of the couch as my grip on it tightens, crying out as I feel the first wave of an orgasm crash through me.

Both of his hands are on my ass now, spreading me wider as he growls before pushing his tongue deep inside. Savage sounds escape him as he buries his face deeper against me, licking, lapping, sucking me so intensely that I immediately come again.

He continues lapping slowly at me as I come down from the most intense oral encounter I have ever experienced. My body sags against the couch, and his mouth leaves me.

He chuckles before I feel the sting of a hand against my ass.

"Don't get too fucking comfortable. I'm gonna fuck that pussy I just tasted. Then I'm gonna tap that fine, fine ass."

"Like hell—"

I feel his finger push inside me, rendering me speechless.

"Trust me, sexy. I will not" — he pauses and I hear the rip of foil — "disappoint you. You sure as fuck haven't disappointed me, and I haven't even been inside yet."

With that, he pushes into me fully, too fucking fully. I can't even cry out, because I feel like the wind has been knocked out of me.

His body now covers mine as he hisses in my ear, "Don't move. Don't fucking move or I'm gonna come so hard I may rip this tight pussy to shreds." He grinds into me and rotates his hips. "Don't. Fucking. Move."

"I ... I ..."

"Swear to fuck, I need to stretch you out a bit. Then I am gonna fuck you so hard, so deep, so fucking nasty that I'm gonna have to carry your ass to bed to do it again." His deep, dark laugh rumbles through me.

"Holy hell," I moan as he continues rotating his hips, stretching me.

He stills then hisses, "Hell ain't shit. Been there, done that, dethroned the motherfucker. Hang on, sexy." His fingers grip my hips. "When I'm done, you'll be wishing you could go to Hell for a reprieve." He grips behind my knee and pulls my leg up, holding it against the couch as he slams into me.

"Fucking beautiful," he groans. "Never had a pussy that framed me like yours. *Fuck*!" He pounds against me mercilessly, deep, hard, and fast, over and over again until I feel my knee buckle.

His hand squeezes my ass tightly. "Stay with me. Stay. Fucking. With. Me."

The rhythm is almost too much. The places he hits have never been touched. The painful force becomes pleasure as the pace slows and he nearly withdraws, and I ache to be filled again.

When he slams back into me, I swear I see lights, a tunnel. I am sure that I am going to die before he finishes, and if I do, that's fine with me.

"I need to come. Come with me."

"Can't," I pant.

"The fuck you can't." He grinds against me hard, then reaches in front of me and strokes my clit. "Give it to me."

"Oh, oh, god."

"Give. It. To Me," he demands, and I feel him swell inside of me as he pushes his finger hard against me. "Now."

I fall apart at his command, his touch, and I fall in brilliant colors, hearing his groans, grunts, and hisses as he comes. Then he lowers my leg and pulls me up against him.

"Bedroom," he pants. "Lead the way."

My body is still trembling as I walk toward my room.

I point to the door. "Right there. I need to use the bathroom."

I walk in then close the door behind me, lean against it, and try to catch my breath.

"Unreal," I mutter under my breath, still trying to figure out how the hell I just let that happen. "Get it together, girl. Go show him who is boss."

I unzip and step out of my boots, grab a washcloth, and clean the important parts. Then I grab my lavender, silk robe off the back of the bathroom door, wrap it around myself, brush my teeth, and then head out the door.

I walk in my room to find him lying gloriously naked, sprawled out on my bed.

"What took you so long?" He smiles and grabs his dick, stroking it. "I'm ready for round two. How about you take that off and climb on? I wanna see those tits from front row, center."

"Change of plans," I tell him, walking to my dresser and opening the bottom drawer. I turn around and hold up my leopard print cuffs, allowing them to fall out, exposing them to him.

He smiles and shakes his head. "I think I proved out there I don't need to tie you down."

"These are for *me* to tie *you* down. I'm in control this time."

He laughs loudly. "Fuck it. I'm no stranger to cuffs, so let's fucking play. You be the cop. I'll be the criminal." His eyes crease slightly as he sits up, holding out his arms for me.

"That's not how it works. How about you lie back down." He does. "Arms stretched out," I instruct, walking to one side of the bed, where I take one set of cuffs and snap it around his wrist.

He chuckles until I attach it to the bedpost.

"You've done this before, haven't you?" He smirks.

"I've been in bed with a few men, River. Is that gonna be a problem?" I ask the same question he asked me. "I'm not looking for a relationship; I don't take orders in life; I don't follow rules; and I fuck my way."

He shakes his head, repeating what I said to him. "You fuck me right, understand? I come, you come …"

"I can assure you I know exactly how to fuck." I reach across him, taking the other hand more gently than the first. "I'll be careful."

"You be whatever you wanna be. Just be on my dick soon."

"My show, my rules. I don't remember giving you orders out there a few minutes ago."

"Not like you had a choice," he says as I attach the other cuff. "I was owning that hot, little twat."

I stand up and turn my back.

"Where the hell are you going?"

Unable to help myself, I say, "To find a gag."

He bursts into hysterics as I walk over and turn the light off. He doesn't know it, but I am being serious. I really wish he would just stop talking. The sound of his voice, the words that drip sex — and not just sex, more like a mind-blowing, fuck fest — puts me off my game a bit. And right now, I have a point to prove. I will not be one upped in bed. Never have been; never will be.

"Lights on, babe. I wanna see those tits up close and personal."

I turn on the very dim side lamp, then walk to the end of the bed where I crawl up between his open legs and cup his balls in my hand, giving them a tug.

"You like them, don't you?" he asks, spreading his legs wider. "Why don't you give them a lick?"

"My show," I tell him, but damn if I don't want to do just that.

"Of course. My bad."

"You have the right to remain silent." I smirk, leaning over and licking the head of his erection. "Anything you say can and will be used against you —"

"I sure as fuck hope so," he says, thrusting his hips up. "Let's start with mouth and end with pussy, shall we?"

"Don't make me get out my baton," I warn, wrapping my hand around his base and beginning to stroke him slowly up and down.

"Don't threaten me with a good time." His eyes darken as his voice becomes huskier. "But do understand, a bad cop will get it back twice as hard. But a criminal like me—"

"Not when the criminal is cuffed." I stroke him a little faster.

"I have people." He thrusts forward. "Fuck, Keanna. Mouth. I need those lips around my cock, please."

My mouth is already in route, so I continue. I suck him hard and slowly, moving down his shaft until I can't move any lower. I suck as I pump him.

"That's it, baby. Suck that cock. Suck it hard." He grunts. "Take it deeper. Show me what you've got. Show me everything I have coming after fucking that sweet pussy so hard you'll feel it tomorrow, and I'm not even done with you yet."

As my pussy clenches at his threat, I take him deeper and force myself to swallow. I want his cock to remember my mouth as bad as he wants my pussy to remember his dick.

"Fuck, don't do that. I won't last for shit," he grits out through his teeth.

I take it as a challenge.

Faster, deeper, sucking harder, I take more than I thought I could handle and swallow while he is deep in my mouth, milking him.

He twitches, and I taste pre-cum.

He tries to pull back. "Gonna come. Where do you want it?"

I untie my robe and let his heavy cock fall from my lips as I cup my breasts and lean forward, surrounding his dick with them.

"Fuck!" he roars and pulls his good hand hard, breaking the cuff. "Those tits. Those fucking tits." He reaches forward and pushes my hair out of the way to get a better view, thrusting his hips back and forth and fucking my tits as he watches.

I feel the first burst of his cum hit underneath my chin, then a second.

"Fuck, Keanna. Fuck yes!"

When he is finished, he lies back and chuckles.

"Hot as hell. Give me ten minutes and unlock this thing. I need both hands for what I have planned, and it's my fucking turn."

I unlock the cuff and look at his hand. It's scarred and obvious that he's had surgery.

"What happened?" I ask as I place it gently on his chest.

He closes his eyes and smiles. "Karma came knocking, and I was home."

"I'm gonna go wash up." When I stand up off my bed, his cum slides down my throat and between my breasts.

He opens his eyes and shakes his head. "You should really let it dry. My cum looks good on you."

I shake my head and walk to the door.

I hear him sigh then mutter, "Shit's good. You should have swallowed."

I walk in the bathroom, and Tink comes in behind me. She sits and looks up.

"Sorry, girl. What was I thinking?" I wipe my body down with baby wipes and toss them in the trash. Then I grab a pair of yoga pants and a sweatshirt. "Let me go and tell our guest I'll be back after our W-A-L-K."

I walk back in my room to see him still naked, still sprawled out, and I am pretty sure he's asleep.

"Okay, let's go. I don't think he'll even notice we are gone."

After walking Tink, I find he is still out like a light. I am exhausted, so I decide to hell with it and climb in next to him. I roll to my side, my back facing him, and close my eyes, beginning to drift off as I pet Tink, who is sitting next to the bed like she always does when I'm falling asleep.

"Good girl."

I don't know how much time later, I wake to a hellacious hangover and the man next to me sputtering in his sleep. I have no idea what he is saying, but I know it sure as hell isn't a sexy dream. He's angry, his body tense, and he mutters, "Don't. No. Please," before curling into a ball.

"River," I call to him when he continues sputtering.

When he doesn't wake, I reach over and shake him.

"River," I say a little more loudly.

He gasps and sits straight up, causing me to jump.

"Shit," he exclaims when he catches his breath and looks over at me.

"Bad dream?" I ask, trying to act like he didn't just scare the hell out of me.

"Nah." He shakes his head. "My clothes?"

"It's late, just sleep."

"I plan on it, but I need a little aid in doing so." He stands up and walks toward the door. "Keanna?"

"Yes?" I ask, lying back down and covering my head with the pillow.

"Best pussy ever." He chuckles. "I'm coming back for it."

"Hit me up in the morning. I'm going back to sleep."

*****

I wake to Tink whining and my head pounding. I throw my feet over the bed and groan, placing both hands on the side of my face.

"Morning, Tink." I stand up and look back at the bed.

It's empty.

He's gone.

"Must have scared him off with the cuffs." I sigh as I pet Tink. "Damn shame. He was worth a round two."

Tink cocks her head to the side as if she is concerned.

"Don't worry; your mom isn't looking for another man to make her whole. She *is* whole."

STANK
DANKNESS

"Answer your fucking text," I say to my phone, seeing the battery on ten percent. I am seriously too fucking amped up right now to function.

I see the cab coming from down the road and step off the curb, needing to make damn sure the driver sees me.

Fucking Masterson, I think while in the back of the cab.

I pay the cabby and step out of the car in front of my pad.

He better be here.

I walk in and flip on a light. No one's crashed on the couch or passed out on the counter. Fuck, no one has been for a couple months now.

With my accident and Finn being a fucking chicken shit and hiding in pussy at the fucking farm house he bought with said pussy, avoiding this place like the plague, this place is a fucking bore.

I throw my phone onto the charging mat on the kitchen island and look around.

My chest tightens as I make my way through the house. I check everyone's rooms, but no one is around. Hell, Billy isn't even here.

I feel like I am going to explode. There is ringing in my ears, my chest feels tight, and I find it hard to catch my breath.

I walk in my room and open drawers, looking for something to take away the pain, the emptiness, the fullness, the … feelings.

I open a box stashed deep inside the bottom drawer and grab it.

In case of emergency, break the glass. I wrote those words as an inside joke years ago.

I sigh, the pressure in my chest getting harder to bear.

I twist the rubber plunger top off the glass cylinder. The smell is overwhelming, and I inhale deeply. Stank dankness—I fucking love the smell. I also love that, years later, it hasn't dried out completely.

"I was right, Jesse. Preserved to perfection," I say to … no one.

I hold it under my nose and inhale, wishing I could find an air freshener that smelled just like this. A good, smoke-filled room brings a smile to my face. But this, this devil weed as we dubbed it back in that trailer where we first met, was the fucking bomb diggity. No better homegrown ever encountered than this shit.

I pull out one of the two buds crammed inside with crystallized purple hairs, and it's sticky as fuck, almost resin-like.

*****

"You can't take that," she says with an almost grin, which is very unlike the normal, somber expression I have grown accustomed to.

I grab another bud from the candy dish on the makeshift pallet coffee table and shove them both in my pocket. "Tell me again what I can't do."

Her lips purse together as she tries not to smile. "You're gonna smell."

"Good. If I smell like pot and you when I go home, I'll be happy." I pull the blanket up that has fallen down to hide where my hands travel, pushing under her skirt and pulling her legs apart before planting a finger inside her.

Her eyes roll back, and she exhales a deep, little moan as I move around inside her a little bit.

"When?"

"When, what?" I ask, rubbing her insides.

"Do you go home?"

"When she calls," I answer as I drag her hand to the tent my pants are causing.

"Your girlfriend?" she asks, squeezing me hard.

"My mother," I say through my teeth, and she loosens her grip.

"You live with your mom?" she asks, almost grinning again.

I want to tell her of course I do. I'm sixteen years old. But then I imagine she thinks I'm older. They all do. I sprung up six inches in a year, gained thirty pounds of muscle, and am fucking fearless.

"You're wet, Jess," I tell her, trying to change the conversation. "No fucking mom talk. I want you to come on my hand."

"They'll be back. We — "

"Who is they?" I ask, shoving a second finger inside her and wrapping my hand around hers, stroking me faster. "No one but you, me, and the buzz."

The next day, we go into town with Tom-Tom and hit a head shop where I grab a glass cylinder and a bowl she's been staring at – Chilz.

*****

I roll my neck, trying to release the tension that is lessening, but still … fucking Chilz is MIA, and I'm pissed.

How did I forget Chilz? I don't lose Chilz, not anymore, anyway.

I walk out into the kitchen and grab my phone off the charging pad. No message from Masterson, fucker, so I hit him up again.

Call Me.

And … send.

I set the devil bud on the counter and dig through the drawer for some papers. There are none, so I grab a can out of the recycling bin and rinse it out. Then I grab a knife from the butcher block and jab it in the side, making a carb. I dent the can on the top, pokes holes in the dented area, and then set about tearing up the bud.

"What are you doing?"

I look up when Billy walks in, still in last night's clothes.

"Getting ready to cheat on Chilz," I answer, looking back down at the bud.

"You were supposed to keep that shit in your room or outside," he says with a scowl.

"You need to lighten the fuck up." I scowl back at him. "Or maybe you need to get laid."

"I'm all set, thanks." He grabs a bottle of water from the fridge.

"Oooo … Billy got laid." I put the bud on the crushed part of the can, on top of the holes, and grab the lighter from my pocket.

"River." He shakes his head as I inhale a few times, then lift my thumb off the makeshift carb. I inhale deeply and hold it in. "You seriously need to find a new hobby."

I exhale and smile as the taste, smell, and immediate buzz wash over me. "Partake?"

"I'm going to bed, man. It's seven in the morning." He shakes his head as he walks away.

"Would mean a lot to me, man. This shit here is aged like fine wine."

He stops, but he doesn't turn around.

"It would mean a lot to me," I mumble as I walk to my room where I sit on the bed and take another hit, this time longer, harder. When I release my thumb from the carb, I breathe in more deeply, leaning back against the headboard of my king-size, black bed and close my eyes.

I hear a knock and then the door opens.

"Why would it mean a lot to you if I smoked up?" Billy asks.

"Never mind, man. It was stupid," I say, smiling without opening my eyes.

"No, what was stupid is you punching some guy in the face with a hand that is finally healing."

I feel the bed buckle as he sits down.

"He was fucking with the lady," I tell him, lazily handing over the can.

To my surprise, he takes it.

"Who was she?"

"Best pussy I've had in fucking years." I smirk and attempt to open my eyes. Only one cooperates.

He takes the lighter. "I'm not sure why the hell I'm doing this," he says before lighting it up.

"B-man, easy on that. I'm not one to give a fucking warning, but that is some potent shit."

He inhales and coughs immediately.

I can't help chuckling. "Devil weed."

He hands me back the can. "You gonna see her again?"

"Keanna? No, man, I'm not."

"Best pussy in years and you aren't gonna do it again?" he asks, yawning as he crosses his arms and settles back against the headboard.

"No. Told her I would, but I'm not. That shit can become an addiction, and well, let's face it; I already have one or twenty of those."

I hit the can again, then hand it back to Billy. Then I close my eyes and lean back.

"Why not trade one addiction for twenty?" he asks, and I hear him flick the Bic.

"I'd rather take my chances with drugs. They don't need me; I need them. Women, they're way too much trouble."

"Memphis and Finn don't seem to think so."

"Memphis and Finn aren't like me."

"I beg to differ. They're no different, River."

My head is in a funk-a-delic fog. "They're better."

"What's that supposed to mean?"

"They've never killed someone," I mutter right before I pass the fuck out.

*****

I wake up to find Billy next to me, can in hand. I take it out and set it on my nightstand before getting up and walking to the kitchen to see if I left my phone there.

Fucking phones.

I snatch it off the counter and look at it.

There is a message from Masterson.

Just got back to the hotel. Hitting the bed. Long fucking night. Come on over when you get around. Suite 439.

"Thank fuck," I state, holding my hand to my chest.

The Master. I snicker to myself.

Billy walks out of my room, stretching. "The hand?"

"No change." I hold my hand up.

"You played great last night," he mentions, walking over and grabbing a K-cup from the carousel.

"Yeah, well ..." I leave it hanging.

"When are you gonna come back?"

"When I'm healed," I say matter-of-factly.

"So when are you gonna address the real issue?"

"I'm going to therapy —"

"With Finn."

"I don't know what the fuck you're talking about."

"This isn't about your damn hand. It's about Finn and you and that girl —"

"Jesse. Her name was Jesse. She wasn't some random fucking girl." My breath becomes harder to catch.

"Jesse. I'm sorry, man. Didn't mean to imply —"

"She loved him. He was good for her, and I killed her. Kind of fucking hard to fix that shit." It all comes out fast, and I wish I could take it back, but there is something about wishes I learned a long time ago: wishes don't come true for men like me.

"You didn't kill her, River. From what I understand, she was all sorts of fucked up. Mental health—"

"I don't want to talk about her. I don't want to talk about it, Billy." My chest tightens. I feel a burn in it. I need to get fucked up. I need Chilz. "I need to borrow your ride."

"If you're sober, the keys are on the hook by the door," Billy says, picking up his ready cup of coffee.

"Good. I'm gonna shower and jet."

"No smoking before you drive."

"Of course, I would never—"

"While you drive," he continues like I didn't say anything, "or while you are in possession of my vehicle."

"Fine … Mom," I remark, telling him what he wants to hear as I walk toward my room.

*****

"What the hell do you mean she's gone?" I snap at Masterson.

He runs his hand through his hair and shakes his head. "I put it right fucking here by the door so you could grab it."

I take off through the suite, opening bedroom doors, bathroom doors. "This is not fucking happening!"

"Chill the fuck out, man!"

I chuck a couch cushion at him to shut him the fuck up.

"Chill the fuck out? Chill the mother-fuck out! Fuck that!"

"No one is here. The bowl is — "

"Who was here? Names, numbers. Come on, man; think!" I grab him by his black, silky fucking man robe. "Last night's ass? Come on; think!"

"Last night's ass was in no position to take a damn bowl," he growls. "And you are crossing a motherfucking line by grabbing ahold of me like that."

"Who else!" I release him because, if I don't, I'm going to fuck his shit up.

"It's not like I allow an audience. No one else was here." He is as pissed off as I am, or at least, he thinks he is. Then his face scrunches up, and he shakes his head. "My cousin Miguel has a room key."

I don't like that look.

"Would he steal from you?"

"No. But he would from you."

Before I have a chance to react, he turns and walks over to the table.

"Now why the fuck would he steal from me?"

When he doesn't answer, it pisses me off.

"Answer the fucking question, Masterson."

He holds up his phone.

I walk over and read the text out loud.

Did you take the bowl?

His message pops back.

Just delivered it to Keanna. Maybe that bitch can give it to the fucking drummer.

I look at him.

"What the fuck?"

"Keanna and he…" He stops and chuckles when I apparently look confused. "The hot ass you left with last night would be Keanna."

"No shit. Get to the point," I try to get him to hurry along.

"The guy you hit last night was my cousin, Miguel."

"Son of a bitch." I run my hand over my head. "Where does she live?"

"I'll ask." He starts to text.

"Don't fucking tell him I don't remember her address."

*****

Driving to Keanna's place, I am pretty much amped up on 'What the Fuck?'

What the fuck do I say about ditching this morning?

What the fuck do I do when I see her and am instantly hard?

What the fuck is she going to say when I ask if her ex was here with my bowl?

What the fuck are you letting that fucker in here for?

"What the fuck!" I hit the steering wheel.

I park in the front and feed the meter, greedy, little bitch that she is.

I remember the building, the stairway, and biting her ass at the top of the stairs.

I walk up to her door and adjust myself, trying to hide the evidence. I am about ready to knock on the door when I realize this shit is not cool. I mean, I ditched. She's a chick. She's going to think I am a total tool when I show up, asking for a bowl.

"Who the fuck cares?" I murmur to myself, lifting my hand to knock. "You do, dick."

I remember seeing a little corner store. Should I get flowers?

I run down the stairs, fully prepared to get flowers. I mean, I appreciate that ass. Loved it as a matter-a-fact. And we all know how I feel about Chilz. Flowers are totally appropriate, right? Fuck yes, they are.

I grab some flowers and a steak. I promised the dog. At least, I think I did. That will also make points with the ass.

Feed the dog, make nice with the ass, maybe even get a little kitty action.

I am crossing the road, flowers and bag in hand, when I hear brakes squeal to a stop and look left.

I see the bear-dog … Aw, what the fuck is her name?

I see a cop. Then I see teeth. Big, angry bear/dog teeth.

The fucking cop has his hand on his gun.

That shit's not going to happen. I just bought that thing a fucking steak!

"TINK!" I yell. That's her fucking name.

I don't have a fucking dog, so I yell what every chick wants to hear from me, hoping it works.

"Tink, come."

Shattered Glass

After calling Animal Control for the tenth time, I decide it would be best to go and look for her … again.

I look at my face in the mirror for the twentieth time, knowing there isn't shit I can do except fix the smudged mascara underneath my eyes by wiping it away.

I opened the door without thinking. When I saw it was Miguel and noticed the anger in his eyes, I tried to shut it, but he kicked it open and Tink immediately lunged at him. He sidestepped her, and she skid across the floor into the hall. When she turned to come back in, he kicked her, and she yelped. Then he shut the door.

I came at him with everything I had. I landed one kick to the nuts, and he became enraged. I ran to get my phone to call for help, but he threw something glass toward me. It missed my head and hit the wall. Shards of glass flew everywhere, some hitting my face.

"Fuck!" he yelled and started toward me.

"Get out! Get out or I will have you arrested!"

Thankfully, he left.

I feel the burn in my throat again and will myself to get it together.

"No more tears. Nothing good comes from wallowing in shit, Keanna. Get it together."

I walk out of the bathroom to the entry closet where I grab my vest, pull the hood up, and then zip it closed. I push my feet into my brown Uggs and grab my sunglasses off the small, wooden entry table. Then, looking out the peephole, I am immediately pissed at myself for being afraid.

"You may not control all the events that happen to you, but you can decide not to be reduced by them." I use Maya Angelou's words out loud. I let them envelope me and sink in. Then I open the door without fear or self-pity.

I walk down the stairs as quickly as I can, hoping the asshole apartment manager doesn't hear me. I don't want to hear how my dog should be put down, how she bit him, how he hoped I had renter's insurance, or how he may sue me. I just want to find Tink.

I walk out the door to see her and River crossing the street. One of his hands holds a bag in front of her nose and the other has a grip on her collar. For a brief second, I wonder why he's here, but Tink's return is much more important. That and his presence overwhelm me further.

Tears form in my eyes as I watch them. She's okay, and he ... Well, he is a beautiful conundrum of gentleness and hardcore rock and roll, wearing black boots, low-riding black jeans, a charcoal Henley shirt, black vest, black baseball cap, and aviators. He is six feet of sexiness, and he is sinfully delicious. He is crude, the kind of man a good girl should run from, yet they dream about every night. He is lean muscle and badass with no fear at all. He is also the man who curled up naked in my bed this morning and is now bringing my dog home.

I allow myself to keep staring.

"There's your momma, Tink," he says as he steps up on the curb and lets her go.

Tink barks and runs to me, and I fall to my knees, bracing myself for the hit I know damn well she will give.

"You're okay, baby." I feel tears fall as I hug her big, furry neck, and she huffs and whines in my ear. "You're okay."

I glance up as I stand and find River looking at me. I can't see his eyes, but his jaw is set, and the muscles in it are tense.

"Where was she?" I force myself to ask.

He doesn't answer. He reaches out and strokes the pad of his thumb across my face, wiping away tears. I flinch, and his chest expands as he pulls his hand back, taking in a deep breath.

I hate sunglasses. I can't see people's eyes. I can't read what he's thinking when I want to know.

I hang my head, hoping my hair hides my face, as he walks past me and opens the door.

"Let's go, Tink." He nods to the door. "Ladies first."

I walk past him with Tink's collar in my hand and head for the stairs.

Opening the door that I forgot to lock, I feel a hand on my shoulder, stopping me.

He walks in ahead of me and looks around, then waves me in.

He knows.

I take a deep breath and walk in.

"You must be thirsty, girl. Come on," I talk to Tink, ignoring River.

When I walk toward the kitchen then look back, Tink is sitting next to River's feet.

"Tink." I squat down. "Come here, girl."

When she doesn't come, I feel overwhelmed. Therefore, unable to control myself, I cover my face as shame, pain, embarrassment, shock—all of it mixes together and falls out in tear form.

I hear boots, then feel arms surround me as he sinks to the floor and pulls me back between his legs, his arms holding me tight from behind.

"I am strong," I declare with as much strength as I can muster.

"I know you are," he replies gently, evenly, calmly.

"I am."

"No doubt you are." He holds the side of my head and pulls it against his chest.

"I … I kicked him in the balls."

"Who? Who did you kick?"

"My ex."

I feel him tense and hear a rumble in his chest. "Did he … do that to your face?"

"I kicked him."

"Keanna!" he snaps then takes in a deep breath. "I'm gonna—"

"He threw some glass thing at me, said it was yours. I ducked; it shattered." I stop when I think I feel him shaking.

"His address?" he growls.

I pull away and sit up. I don't understand why he wants to know this.

"His address, Keanna? Surely you know where he lives if his dick was inside of you."

He's angry, and after Miguel, it makes me nervous.

"Get out." I try to stand, but he grips me more tightly.

"Hold the fuck up. You want to protect that asshole?"

"No, I want the asshole here to leave."

"Well, just a heads up, I'll get his fucking address whether you give it to me or not."

I bat the tears away and stand up. "Do you have mental issues? I mean, two seconds ago, you were comforting me — you brought flowers, for fuck's sake — and now you want to — "

"He fucking hurt you. If something hurts, stay the fuck away from it. What the fuck is wrong with women?" He lets go of me and stands.

"This is my fault? You can't be serious!"

He shakes his head back and forth. "Look, I have no fucking clue what I'm talking about. I won't even pretend to know what goes on inside a woman's mind."

"Clearly," I retort, walking toward the door.

He looks at the floor then at me. "I'm gonna kick his ass, regardless. Fuck, maybe I'll make it so he can't fucking come back here and mess — "

"Don't do me any favors," I sneer.

I want him gone. I want my head to stop spinning, but most of all, I want peace and quiet. Instead, there's a knock on the door.

River quickly moves in front of me, practically pushing me aside, and flings the door open. "What?"

"Keanna around?"

It's Aaron, the apartment manager, the man Tink supposedly bit when Miguel kicked her out the door. The one who threatened me and wouldn't listen when I told him she was scared.

As River looks back, I hide behind the door and shake my head.

"No," River says without hesitation.

"Well, when she comes back, let her know that the board wants the dog gone. He's dangerous and—"

"She. The dog's a she," River tells him.

"Well, she needs to go now, or I will be getting a lawyer and—"

River shuts the door in his face before he has time to finish.

He looks at me sternly and shrugs. "The kid with the pockmarks says she has to go."

"I heard him!" I yell, feeling my lip quiver. "I fucking heard him."

"Okay, all right. Shit, don't start crying again. I'm sure you can take her to a friend or family or—"

I walk away while he's talking. I can't think when he's around.

He grabs my wrist, stopping me. "Wait."

I have no idea why I stop and look back, but I do.

"What are you gonna do?"

Frustration, anger, and confusion come crashing together in one big explosion.

"I have no idea! None! This … This is all too much." I point at him. "You are too damn much. So if you'd please just leave so I can figure it out without questioning my choices and myself and"—I throw my hands in the air—"everything else, maybe I can come up with a solution!"

"How did Tink get outside?"

He asks the most random questions at the most random times. It doesn't stop the chaos from raining down on me.

I shake my head. "River, please just—"

"How did she get outside? It's an easy question to answer, Keanna."

"He let her out. Actually, he kicked her out, okay? Now could you just leave?"

"You got a phone?" he asks.

"Of course I have a—"

"Give me your digits."

I shake my head while he nods his.

I see his hazel eyes scan the room before he starts walking toward the table. He grabs my phone and then grabs his, punches in something, and then sets it down.

"I have yours, and you have mine. Now the leash thing, and I will take the bear-dog with me."

Stunned, I am at a loss for words. Why? Why would he do that?

"Keanna, I've got the dog. When you figure it out, call me," River says, walking toward me. "The words are thank and you." He waits, and I still say nothing, because he's fucking crazy, fucking insane, but I have no other choice. "And, well, I'm sorry I was a dick. Sort of. But I am gonna make sure that fucker pays for killing Chilz and fucking up your beyond beautiful face." He leans in and gently rubs his lips across my face. "Lock the motherfucking door. Don't let anyone in. And when your brain isn't so twisted up, call me."

"I should thank you." I shake my head. "But who is Chilz?

"My bowl, the one he shattered. It meant a lot to me."

"A bowl meant a lot to you?" I am now pissed again. He makes no sense. He makes me feel like I make no sense.

"Yeah, it did." He looks serious as hell, too.

I close my eyes and try to use every anger management coping skill I ever learned. Then I hear the door shut, and he is gone … with my dog.

*****

Not five minutes after he leaves, my phone chimes; it's Natasha telling me she and Jordan are on their way over.

Shit!

I spend the next five minutes cleaning up broken glass, putting flowers in a vase, and trying my damndest not to lose it again. I can't let them see me weak. I am strong.

Natasha and Jordan have never met the old Keanna, the one who was a skeleton of a woman. The one I swore I left behind when I walked into the gym a few months ago. And a ten-minute scuffle will not undo who I am. Miguel, the man-boy I practically grew up with, will not undo the work I did to make myself who I am today.

There have been momentous moments in my life. I was the first to graduate high school in my family, the only one who didn't get knocked up or knock someone up before high school graduation, the only one who didn't spend at least a year of their life in lock up. I was the first to graduate from college and the first to have a home, albeit an apartment, not shared with family or friends. I am a strong, proud black woman.

Nana, my grandmother, the daughter of a preacher, raised me and my siblings when my parents were gone—my father by choice my mother by circumstance. We were raised with God's love and Maya Angelou's wisdom by a woman who walked the walk and not just talked the talk. She was proud of us, all four of us: my brothers and my sister. She was an amazing woman.

There were no monetary indulgences. She was not materialistic. Even when we had extra, she never spent it on herself. Her treasures were us. Her bounty was her family, and she believed she was blessed beyond belief.

Looking around at my beautiful apartment, yet feeling emptiness inside, gives me a deeper appreciation for her way of living. She was right. Money and things are nothing. Family and love are everything. She never looked at me like I disappointed her. I never knew such a look until Miguel.

I wish you were here to tell me what to do, I think as I drag the broom across the floor, pushing the remaining shards of glass into a dustpan.

I immediately retract that thought. Seeing me struggle would have hurt her and me.

I struggled my whole life with weight, with boys, with friends, with self-esteem. She helped me heal. She helped me realize where the pain came from. It was like she flipped a switch, and when the light came on, everything was clear. I learned I was letting things I could never change hold me back.

My grandmother raised a strong woman who has the skills to bounce back from everything. Then, after I graduated college, she died. It was almost as if she knew I would be okay. Back then, I wasn't, but I am now because it's a choice.

I grab some paper towels, wet them, and then use them to mop up any tiny pieces of glass so that, when Jordan grabs the bin of toys from the closet and drags them out here to play with when they get here, he won't get hurt.

Moments later, the doorbell rings.

As soon as they walk in, I know something is up.

"Grab the toys, Jordan," Natasha instructs, clearly flustered after he gives me a hug. "Mom and Auntie Keanna need to do some girl things."

"Where's Tinker Bell?" Jordan asks, looking around.

"She went with a friend."

"Like a play date?"

I nod, trying not to get choked up.

Natasha senses it and quickly bends down to kiss his head. "Just like a play date." Then she walks over, turns on the television, and puts it on the Discovery Channel, Jordan's favorite. She takes a deep breath, grabs my hand, and whisks me off toward my bedroom. "We're right in here, bud."

"Okay, Mommy!" he calls back as he pulls the bin of toys in front of the TV.

She looks at my unmade bed and then gasps when she looks at the floor.

"What?" I ask, following her eyes to see what she is looking at. "Oh, hell."

I grab a tissue and pick up the knotted off condom that River must have dropped on the floor. Then I quickly walk into the bathroom, drop it in the toilet, and flush it away.

Taking a deep breath, I walk back into the bedroom.

"Spill it," she orders.

"You first," I retort, finally making eye contact with her.

Another gasp and she reaches up to push the hair I styled to hide the worst of my horrible morning's evidence, and the first tear falls.

"Did that asshole do this to you?" she asks with whispered rage. I know she's talking about River.

"No. Of course not," I tell her, pulling my hair back to cover my face.

"Don't you lie for him," she warns, wiping away her own tear. "I knew he was a mess. I never should have let you leave with him. I am so sorry, Keanna. If I wasn't so" — she pauses and blushes furiously — "wrapped up in my own need to escape with that … that Master, I would have never."

"River didn't do it. Miguel did."

"I'll kill him!" she snaps.

"Tell me about Masterson," I encourage, hoping to direct the conversation back to her.

"Did he take Tinker Bell?" she asks.

I am tempted to deflect yet know better. I have watched her with Jordan as he tries to get another piece of candy or watch another ten minutes of a show.

"Fine, we'll talk about me, but understand that moment doesn't define me. And please don't ask again. It's in the past, and the only reason I am gonna tell you is to avoid the UN Summit-like inquiries about the incident."

She sits down and nods, not saying a word as I spill every bit of my morning.

"So, no, River didn't do it. He didn't do anything wrong. He found Tink and returned her, and Aaron was having her evicted, and well, he took her."

"He has your dog?" Natasha gasps.

EAT SHIT

I look over at the passenger seat at the bear-dog named after a tiny, little fairy. Then I look at the blue clock lights, seeing it's only ten in the damn morning.

"I am far too fucking sober for this shit."

We stop at a light, and I am immediately overwhelmed with the feeling of responsibility and the fact that I am in no position to take on...any. *It's a dog, not a girl*, I think. After the accident, driving now fucks with me.

I reach around the bear-dog and grab the seatbelt. When she growls, I growl back, and her ears perk up.

"That's right, Tink; I'm in charge, and you're wearing a fucking seatbelt."

She growls again, so I do, too.

I grab my phone and snap a picture, fully intending on sending it to Keanna, which I do.

There's one problem with sending messages: you can't stop the shit. You can hope like hell it doesn't go through, but almost as if it's a universal law, rule, whatever you want to call it, when you want it to, it doesn't. When you don't want it to, it does.

"What the hell?" I throw the phone down, feeling like a turd, a big, giant turd, because…Why the fuck did I do that?

My phone chimes, and I sigh.

"Stupid fuck," I mutter before grabbing the phone and looking at it. Masterson.

I have never been so happy to get a text from a dude in my life. I'm even happier when I realize I am less than a mile from the fucker who broke Chilz, hurt the girl, and let the bear-dog out, unsupervised.

"What's your take on Miguel, Tink?"

She growls.

"I feel ya. You know what the term 'sick balls, chopper' means?"

She growls again.

"Good. Let's go fuck shit up."

I reach out to pet her, and she growls again. I do it back, and then, using my bad hand, I take a chance with the bear-dog and scratch behind her ears. She fucking loves it, pushing against the hand like a chick thrusts her hips against the finger bang.

"I may not know much, Tink, but I know how to make the bitches happy. Physically, anyway. You and me, we're gonna be best friends. Fuck, I may re-name you Finn. You're kind of grumpy like him. And you and I, we don't have a fucked up past, so we're one step ahead of that shit."

I stop petting her when the light turns green. I look left, then right and do it again. A horn blows behind me, so I give them the one finger salute. Fuckers have no idea what could happen in the blink of an eye. I do, so I wait until they blow it again before I hit the gas.

In front of the house Masterson gave me the address to, I pull over and turn off Billy's Beamer.

Tink starts whining and sniffing.

I never had a dog, but I am pretty damn sure that means she either has to shit or needs to stretch those legs of hers.

"Okay, girl, you've got two minutes, and then I'm gonna head in and take care of business, but ladies first."

I get out and walk around the SUV, open her door, and she hops out. She immediately jets to a patch of grass and cops a squat.

"Damn, girl," I cringe, looking away, trying to give her some privacy. Plus, I don't want to see that shit.

I hear her growl and look back. Her teeth are bared. Immediately, I see exactly what she sees — that fucker walking down the road, pants hanging nearly off his ass, headphones on, and he's texting.

My blood boils. I want to kick his saggy ass for fucking with Keanna and Tink.

What the fuck? Now I have given her a nickname? *You stupid fuck!* I yell at myself.

And Chilz. Chilz is the reason I really want to kick his ass.

He walks by, oblivious, and that's exactly what I do.

I kick his ass, and he falls down, face fucking first.

With Tink's leash wrapped around my wrist, I bound forward and plunge my knee between his shoulder blades and into his back.

"You don't listen well, motherfucker," I say through clenched teeth.

"What the fuck, man! Get the fuck—" He stops and cries out, "Ouch, you fucking bitch!"

I look left to see Tink has his hand between her chompers.

"You better be real nice to her, you little fucking saggy pant worm. You already tried to get rid of her once, and just like me, motherfucker, she's back." I shove his face into the pavement. "You broke something that belongs to me, and you fucking cut up a perfect face today."

"She provoked me, man!" Then and there is when I want to make him stop breathing. Fuck that, jail sucks, but I would rather drag him into Hell.

"Did she tell you how good I licked her sweet, little cunt? How my cock filled her like yours never could? Did she tell you what it was like to have a real man between her legs?"

He cries out, and Tink releases his hand.

"Tink, you nasty, little bitch, we aren't done here," I say, and she grabs his shoe.

"Get that fucking piece of shit away from me!"

"Piece of shit? Piece of shit! I'll show you piece of shit!"

I stand up and grab the back of his fucking hoodie before dragging him back to where the shit actually lies. I throw him down, and he pushes up, but I raise my foot above his head and push him face first in the nice fucking pile Tink left.

"You fucking eat that, motherfucker."

"Fuck!" he cries out, trying to push up again.

I grab my phone as my boot holds his head down in the dog shit and snap a picture.

"You go near her again, and I can promise you that you'll fucking drown in a month's worth of Tink's shit."

I hear a gasp and look up to see two teenage girls turning the corner.

I lift my foot and nod. "Girls, don't ever fall in love with a boy who doesn't even know how to pull up his motherfucking pants."

They nod furiously.

"Let's go, Tink. It fucking smells like shit around here."

*****

I walk in the house, and Billy immediately notices Tink. I planned out what I would say to him the entire ride back. I assumed he would be pissed, but there is no shock or awe on his face. It's kind of disappointing since I kind of get off on that.

"Tink, Billy. Billy, Tink. She's a bitch, so don't try to pet her. She got evicted from her last home because she didn't like the guy who ran the joint, so just a heads up, don't piss her off."

That ought to get him.

"You got a dog?"

"No, man, I got a bear named after a fairy." I don't dare unhook her leash, so she and I stroll over to the cupboard and grab a big ass, metal salad bowl, and I fill it with water.

I set it on the ground, and she immediately starts lapping it up, water splashing everywhere. Billy watches, still no change of facial expression. I know that shit is going to set him off.

"She's a beautiful dog. Please tell me this is a joke," he says, looking up at me.

"No joke."

He nods once, then looks down at her. "When we tour, how are you gonna take care of her?"

"We?" I point between us. "I'm not touring. Remember, I have an injury."

"You were holding that leash tightly when you came in, and you played really well last night, so you're ready to come back."

"The fuck I am," I grumble.

"River, it's time you and Finn mend—"

"Don't start that shit with me today. It hasn't been a good day. Chilz is dead, man." I look at him, seeing some concern. "She's gone. Shattered. It's a bad fucking day. So again, don't start."

"So you replaced a bowl with a dog."

"That's no dog. That's a fucking bear. I didn't replace Chilz. I was helping out a chick who helped me out last night."

He looks at me, shaking his head. "I have to go and get some work done. Please tell me this is some sort of joke."

"I can tell you that, but it would be bullshit. I'm too fucking tired, a little bit emotional, and a whole lot too sober to be awake right now. I'm gonna sleep it off."

"Sleep off what?" he asks, his voice finally showing some pissed off.

"The sobriety and loss." I grab my phone out of my pocket, press the photos, and hand it to him. "The dog and I took care of the issue. Will you put that on the charging pad? My bed is calling my name."

"Our name," he corrects.

"No man, mine."

"You and her." He points to Tink, who doesn't even growl at him as he reaches down and pets her head.

"Tink, what the hell?" I look from her to him. "She likes you."

"Dogs and kids always do."

*****

I wake up to a hot tongue lapping at my face. I roll to my side and put my hand on the owner of the tongue.

"So lucky you're a bear. Nothing with this much hair has ever been in my damn bed before." I open my eyes. "Tink, what the fuck are you doing in my bed?"

She stops licking me immediately, lays her big-ass head on the pillow next to mine, and sighs.

"I gotta piss. Then I gotta sleep. No more tongue fucking my face, either," I grumble as I get up and walk to the bathroom.

She grumbles back.

When I come out, Tink is sitting on the floor, panting, and a very sexy woman is in my room. I smirk when she looks at me.

"What have we here?" I clap my hands and dive on my bed, then pat the spot next to me.

"I don't think so."

"Come on; I never got round two."

Tink starts to get up on my bed, but Keanna gasps and says, "Tinker Bell, get off that bed," so Tink heels.

"Look, babe, I can promise you there are clean sheets, and as you know, I don't go in unwrapped, so — "

"She isn't supposed to be on furniture; she is a dog. She has a pillow bed, and that is unacceptable."

"When she's here, she gets the bed unless, of course, you want in. We'll make room."

"Natasha said she would take her until I find a new place."

"Doc? Wait, do you think I can't handle a fucking dog, babe?" Has to be that because why the fuck wouldn't she want an excuse for another round with me.

"Miguel called," she tells me.

Tink and I both growl.

"He's supposed to stay the fuck away from you," I snap.

"You not only allowed but encouraged the dog to viciously attack his hand?"

"Please, I didn't encourage that. I tried the 'sick balls, chopper' command, but she hasn't learned that one ... yet." I scratch my head. "Did he tell you he was face first in a pile of Tink's finest creation?"

"What?" She almost laughs.

Her near smile makes me chub up a bit. She is wearing sweats—hot pink ones—that I know have some logo splayed across that ass. *Juicy*, I bet, and I know it is. With a matching hoodie, she looks sweet, like candy, and I want to taste her.

I lie back and put my hands behind my head, knowing damn well I am putting it all on display. She's trying her best not to check me out, but it's an epic fail.

"Let's discuss." I pat the bed, and Tink bounds up on it.

"Tink!" she gasps.

"You're pissing your mom off, you sexy beast." I chortle.

Keanna throws her hands in the air. "You certainly are something, you know."

"Yes, I know." I slide over. "We had a shit morning, which ended in a shit conversation. I'm exhausted. I know you must be, too. Keanna"—I sigh—"climb up in here and snuggle in. I will try to keep my hands to myself, which is code for I didn't get a chance to play with those delicious-looking tits last night, and as soon as you fall asleep, I am for sure gonna cop a feel, maybe a lick or two."

"You're serious right now?"

I look down, directing her eyes at my dick. Instead of turned on, she looks annoyed.

Nodding turns into shaking my head. "Of course not." I sit up and grab her hand, yanking her down hard so she falls on me. "But you need sleep and so do I."

"Tink. I need to take care of Tink."

I roll so I am on top of her. "Nap first; Tink later."

*****

Pain soars through my body. I try to fight. I try to scream. I can't breathe.

His hand is covering my mouth, so I bite at his flesh.

I pray for help, pray for my mother, and then, when all hope is gone, I pray, beg, and plead for death.

His movement stops, and his teeth tear into my shoulder as he grunts and shoots off inside of me.

"If you tell her, I'll do the same thing to her. If you tell her, she'll hate you worse than she already does. If you tell her, I'll tell everyone how you begged for it. If you tell her, the whole world will know what a weak, sick, little homo you are."

When he pulls away, I feel like I'm going to be physically sick. I feel like I am going to throw up and shit.

I do both.

"Clean that up now, you little fucking bastard."

For River

"Tink, no!" I yell as she grabs River's hand when he grabs my chest.

River's eyes open wide, mine no doubt just as wide. I want to cry, but I want to make it all stop for him, too. I hate that he hurts, and I hate that he even does it in his sleep. Most of all, I hate that he's ashamed and embarrassed by something he feels he has no control over.

"Fuck," he groans breathlessly as he begins to shift around, looking lost.

"You okay?" I ask as he pulls his hand away.

"Yeah," he mumbles. "Sorry."

The lost look in his eyes is almost more than I can take after hearing his blood-curdling cry while he slept. I want to make it go away.

"Don't be. She shouldn't be on the bed."

He nods then looks me over. "I'm not sure—"

"I'm fine. You didn't do anything wrong."

He looks at me like he's looking deep inside of me. I reach up and cup his chin instinctively to comfort, and a rumble escapes deep from his chest before his lips crash against mine, but I can't give it to him, so I turn my head and give him my neck, instead.

Regardless of the day I have had, regardless of how pissed off I am at him, he needs me. I need this.

He pulls away and locks eyes with me. In his eyes is pain. In his eyes is desire. In his eyes is need.

His jaw pops, and I shake my head. Then his shoulders slump.

He thinks I am rejecting him.

"Don't stop," I say, closing my eyes.

"Tink, down," he barks, and she immediately follows his instruction. His hand cups my chin. "Open your eyes, Keanna." I do. "This isn't gonna be like last night. I'm sober."

I nod.

"It's gonna be hard. It's gonna be nasty. You'll come. But once I'm done fucking you, walking without pain *will* be an issue. You understand?"

I understand. Oh, God, do I understand.

My pussy clenches, my nipples are painfully erect, and he is now standing on the bed, looking down at me with a look that is intimidating as hell as he pulls his black boxer briefs off.

The dead tree with the three crows perched on the flowerless branches tells a story. I know it's a story of pain, hurt, anger, and death. My need to make it go away is almost as demanding as the ache between my legs that needs to be filled by him.

"You clean and safe?"

"Yes."

"You trust that I don't fuck without a condom, but right now, I need to go in bare?"

"Give me your word, and I'll believe you."

His head cocks to the side like he doesn't understand.

"I believe you." It's reckless, irrational. I don't understand it, but I believe him, one hundred percent.

He reaches down and grabs the waistband of my sweats, ripping them down along with the thong underneath them. He throws them across the room and falls to his knees between my legs.

"Ass up." He cups my ass in his hands and lifts before pushing his face between my legs, licking, nipping, sucking, nibbling at me like a man possessed.

His five o'clock shadow rubs my thighs, his focus now centered. His tongue pushes inside me as he licks deeper and deeper. A finger then pushes in harshly as he sucks so hard on my clit my legs give way without notice. I think I am going to die from pain. No, pleasure. No, both.

"Oh, god," I cry out, covering my head with a pillow.

The pillow gets torn from my hands, and he pulls my body to the end of the bed. Then he kneels on the ground and pushes another finger in me. I nearly come off the bed, looking into the eyes of a man who may very possibly be mad.

"No more. Oh, please," I cry as my orgasm rips through me like a tornado of ecstasy and stupor.

He lets go, then pulls my legs up, holding my ankle against his shoulder as he sucks on it. I am unaware of anything else except for the electrical pulses coursing through me.

I feel his broad head against my opening, and without notice, he pushes inside me as he cries out, "Fuck!"

He stills, grunts, and hisses as I feel the pain and pleasure dance deeper inside than ever before.

"Dear god!" I call out, my back arching, causing my body to impale itself farther on the rock hard cock of a man whose warning was nothing compared to his delivery.

He pulls my other ankle up so my legs are parallel to his shoulders then begins delivering punishing thrust after punishing thrust.

My body betrays me as I feel the buildup of another orgasm, one I am sure will push me over the ends of the earth. Then he stops and pushes my legs forward so that my knees are nearly touching my ears.

Without pulling out, he puts one foot on the bed then the other. He then quickly unzips my hoodie without any effort from me and peels it off. He pushes one arm then another out of the tank top and pushes it down just below my bra before releasing the bra's front clasp. My breasts spill out as he grabs them harshly, pushing them together and using his finger and thumb to pinch my already painfully erect nipples.

His eyes flicker in sadistic delight as he looks into mine. "Tell me to stop."

"No," comes out from deep inside of me.

I am immediately regretful when he hammers his cock into my pussy like a madman.

"Your pussy—fuck, Keanna. Your pussy was made for my cock. So wet, so hot, so greedy, so fucking tight."

I open my mouth to respond, but nothing intelligible comes out.

He doesn't stop, not for a second. He doesn't break stride, and he is not showing any signs of doing so any time soon.

I close my eyes and take the pounding he promised, the one I agreed to. Thrust after thrust, climax after climax, I take it because nothing else has ever brought me to the place River James is taking me now. A place where I feel like I am having a near out-of-body experience.

I feel him twitch inside of me before his cum bursts in hot, powerful jets as he grunts out my name.

He lowers my legs, and his body crashes down on mine. While he pants, almost in sync with me, I throw my arms over his shoulder, fearing if he gets up and pulls out too soon, I may possibly split in half.

His body tenses, but I don't move. Then, when his breath becomes shallower, he pushes himself up and looks into my eyes.

I see regret immediately.

"Talk to me," I say as evenly as I can while holding his shoulders.

His eyes narrow slightly. "About what?"

"About your dream. Your nightmare, River. You can tell me who hurt you and —"

His body is off mine in less than a heartbeat.

"I have no idea what the fuck you're talking about."

I pull my tank top up and sit, cringing at the rawness I feel between my legs. "Twice now, I have woken up to —"

"It's called sobriety, Keanna. Some people are more fucked up when they're fucked up. For me, it's the opposite." He walks into the bathroom, and I watch as he cleans himself off with a washcloth.

"River, I don't believe —"

"That's enough!" He looks angry, sounds angry; he is angry. "I have shit to do, and you have to take Tink to Doc's house. Thanks for taking me raw. Been years. Thoroughly enjoyed your hot, little cunt." He pulls a sweatshirt on and walks to the door. "Maybe I'll see you around."

Then he is gone.

After hearing him beg someone in his sleep to stop hurting him, I can't in good conscience push him any harder. Having just met him, regardless of the feelings I have already allowed to take hold, it's not my place.

*****

After washing up and dressing, I walk out of River's room to find another man, a tall, dark-blond, very much a boy next-door type of guy, standing at the counter. I recognize him from Natasha's office.

He pushes a cup of coffee forward. "Cream and sugar?"

"I'm fine, thank you," I say awkwardly.

"Will you join me for just a couple minutes?"

I am embarrassed and unsure of what to expect, but I walk over to the huge island that divides the living area and kitchen and sit.

"River just left."

I nod. "I'm aware. I am gonna take Tink and leave now, too."

"He's"—he pauses and runs his hand over his head—"a mess."

"I sensed that, too."

"He isn't normally. I mean, he is, but in a much different way."

I don't interrupt. I let him talk. I want to know more.

He continues, "He's always funny, constant jokes. He walks a line between wrong and criminal. I have only seen him pissed off at Finn, and that's a long story, but I understand both sides and don't even fully know them. My point is, he likes you, but he sure as hell is trying not to." He shakes his head. "I don't understand it."

My eyes focus on the floor. It's obvious River is as much a mystery to his friends as he is to me.

"He likes the dog, too."

"Yeah, well" — I look up at him — "I love the dog. She has gotten me through some times, you know."

"Miguel?"

I quickly look up at him. "How do you know about him?" I know by the look on his face it came out defensively.

"When River left just now, he said, *she's not to be around Miguel. Tell her that.*"

I know I should be angry. I should be so angry, but no one, not one person, has ever stuck up for me.

"Well, I—"

"He said you should stay here until you can take the dog home. I mean, you're more than welcome, but—"

"No, absolutely not. I am fine." I already want to save him when I know it's impossible for someone to do that. He has to do it himself.

"I don't think you are," Billy replies, straightening his stance. "Piecing things together, this Miguel is the man who hurt you, messed with the dog, and broke River's beloved bowl. I will have to agree with River on this: until you are sure you're gonna be okay, then—"

"I'm actually going to stay with my friend. She agreed to take Tinker Bell in and then asked if I wanted to stay. And, well, I do. At least for a couple days."

He looks relieved and nods.

"But I was thinking …" I clear my throat and take a deep breath. "Do you think maybe Tink could stay here for a couple of days? If she is any trouble, then I will immediately come and get her."

"For River," he whispers, seeming to know what I am thinking.

I shrug. "I just think—"

"No need to explain. I agree."

With that, Billy helps me get her cage and food in the house.

WRONG FUCKING HIGH

I hop out of the cab, fully intending to go into the bar and score something a fuck of a lot harsher than pot. I'm not sure I will ever smoke again. Nah, scratch that. I have the other bud. Devil weed is on reserve.

I need her out of my mind 'cause, let's be real here: *it's not her; it's me*, definitely pertains to the situation, and I'm not being topped by a chick ... ever.

An emergency stash of vintage, voodoo buzz-be-had.

Why the fuck didn't I just do that? Why the fuck didn't I just grab the can that will never replace Chilz yet will have to work, because well, fucking Chilz is dead? Fucking dead.

But I have the purple-haired, stank dankness.

I scratch my head. I have no fucking clue if I really want to get some shit to shoot up in my veins that I know damn well will make it all go the fuck away or if I want to go home and suck the can.

I stand on the sidewalk, looking up, wondering what the fuck I'm going to do, and then I spot something across the road. It's shiny, yellow, has four wheels, it's not a taxi cab, and it needs to be mine.

I walk across the road, horns blaring, but I don't give a shit. I flip them off and keep on walking.

I look at the sign on the glass building: Jersey Shore Auto. Then I walk in, pushing my sunglasses up on my head.

A woman comes over and smiles, asking, "How can I help you?"

"I can think of lots of ways, but let's start with the canary yellow Range Rover out there."

She blushes. "It's a 2016 Range Rover hybrid."

"I'll take it."

She looks me up and down, and not in the way that I am accustomed to. She is trying to figure out if I can afford the thing.

"It's a ninety thousand dollar vehicle, Mr....?"

"I'm guessing, since you didn't stop at my dick while eye-balling me, you weren't telling me your silky, little, high-end panties are ready to be pushed to the side so I can show you a good time, and you're trying to figure out if I can afford it." I nod.

"I can assure you I can." I reach in my pocket and pull out my wallet, taking out the folded up insurance check from the accident and handing it to her.

"Fifty grand. I'll sign the check over." Then I pull out my credit card. "Put the rest on this."

"Mr ...?" She looks at the card, but I beat her to it.

"River. My name is River James. I don't have a whole lot of time, so let's get this done, shall we?"

"You do know it's a Saturday night?"

"Yes, and tomorrow is Sunday. The next day is Monday, and so on and so forth."

She smirks and nods. "Let's go and see what we can do."

While the paperwork is being processed by the finance guy who seems kind of pissed that he has to do his fucking job at eight o'clock on a Saturday night, Tani, the sales lady, asks if I want a test drive. And fuck yes, I do.

I'm on a new sort of high right now, a high like the vagina that pushed me into the world used to get when she was shoe shopping.

She tosses me the keys, and I hop in the driver's seat while she slides her narrow, little ass in the passenger seat.

"The vehicle is equipped with Bluetooth everything. Your phone can be synced so your calls and music can be played right here from the steering wheel." She reaches across and brushes her perky, little tits against my arm while her ass is in the air so I see the lacy tops of her thigh-highs against her pale, white skin.

"How does the seat adjust?"

She points to the side. "Right over there."

Once I reach down and hit the switch, the back goes down.

"You wanna help me out?"

She swallows and leans all the way over, ass high in the air, and all I keep picturing is how she could easily suck my cock while I am driving my new ride around.

"Back farther?" she asks, leaning up and giving me a bird's eye view of her tits.

"All the way. I'm not a small man." I wink, and she bites her lip.

When she gets the seat to move back, she looks up. "Is that good?"

"Could be better," I say, looking down at my dick.

Her eyes follow mine, and she licks her lips.

"How about we drive around for a bit, you sync my phone, and maybe I'll let you cop a feel?"

"I don't know what you're talking about," she responds coyly.

"Let's not play games here. You're looking at my dick like it's a present under a fucking tree that you might want to open on Christmas Eve. You don't want to get caught. I will assure you that this zipper goes up the same way it goes down. No one will ever know that the naughty, little Tani decided to peek and see what was inside. Your pretty, little panties are getting all sorts of wet right now, and I have to tell you, going home tonight and finger fucking yourself to the thought of what may be tucked inside the denim will be nothing like finger fucking yourself to the thought of the real thing."

I hand her the phone. "Sync this while you toy with this." I take her hand and rub it up and down my half–chubbed, denim-clad cock and then let go. She doesn't move her hand.

"Is this push button?"

She nods, looking like she is questioning herself.

"It's a dick, a perfect dick. I won't tell a soul if you wanna play with it a while."

I drive.

She plays.

Feels good.

Could be better.

I'm not going there, so I will stick with the feeling good shit.

When I pull into the dealership, I see a vehicle that looks familiar, but there is no way in hell it could be.

I drive around to the back and throw her in park.

"Seat down and spread 'em."

She complies.

I reached between her legs and shove two fingers inside her wet pussy. No need for a build up; she's already soaking wet.

"You're gonna come soon."

"I-I … Oh, God!"

"Mouth over here. Finish me off."

She is a hot, little piece of ass. Not my favorite type, not much of a body, but she has been working the D for fifteen minutes, so she deserves this.

Thankfully, she is vocal. Something all chicks should know: If you suck in the sack or aren't blessed with a natural sexual prowess, be loud and talk a little dirty. It works for us.

When I rub her insides and thumb her clit with one hand, her pussy clenches around my fingers. I rub and tap at her G-spot, and she cries out with her mouth full of cock.

Some girls know how to suck a dick. This one doesn't. In order to get there, I have to basically do it myself. I hold the back of her head down as I thrust in and out of her mouth, still banging away at the G until I come.

She sits up as soon as I release her head. "I-I—"

"You good?" I ask.

She nods.

"Cool. Phone synced?"

She shakes her head.

"Think you could do that?" I ask as I reach over and use her skirt to wipe off my fingers.

She looks at me, stunned, then nods her head.

I almost feel like a dick, but she was the one bent over the console, so I let it roll off my back. What the fuck do I care? She came.

I pull around the front and hop out, her still toying with my phone. I walk around to open her door and have to bite my tongue when I see a little of me on her chin.

I reach over and wipe it off. "You need to fix that hair, girl. Straighten the skirt and —"

"You've got to be kidding me," I hear from behind me, and I know immediately who it is.

"What the fuck are you doing here?" I ask as I turn around to see Finn.

"Got a call that you were spending a shit-ton of money."

"Why the fuck did they call …?" I pause and shake my head.

" 'Cause my name is on the account."

"Oh, yes, the responsible one," I huff, walking past him.

"Fuck you," he mutters under his breath.

I stop immediately, turn around, and want to punch him in the smug-ass, bearded mug.

"I have to sign if you're really gonna buy this fucking thing," he tells me.

"Un-fucking-believable," I huff as I throw the door open and walk in. I don't hold it open for him, either.

I hear his boots behind me. "You're the motherfucker who set the limit. I don't wanna be around your ass any more than you wanna be around me."

"That's getting changed on Monday."

"Good," he grumbles, walking into the finance office.

I see Sonya and her boy off to the side of the office. She looks up from the tablet he is playing at and smiles. "How are you, River?"

"Just great," I answer as I sit down.

I hear Finn growl something, and as much as I hate the fucker, I know I'm being a dick.

"Hey, Noah. What's up, little man?" I smile. It's not the kid's fault Finn is a fucking self-righteous prick.

"Hi, Uncle River." He smiles and waves.

Both Finn and I look at him, and Sonya gives him an apologetic smile. I take some sick satisfaction in that shit, smiling back at him. A big ha-fucking-ha smile.

Finn's hands grip the arms of the chair more tightly, and yes, fucking pride swells in my chest. I hope he thinks about me fucking Jesse as much as I thought about him fucking her back when I found out about him. Then I hope he wonders if I want to bang Yaya.

"You should come by and check out the ocean in the winter, Noah. Have your mom bring you by when he's at work." I thumb toward Finn.

"But then you'll be at work," Noah says with a shrug.

"No, kiddo, not true. I'll be home. I'll give your mother my digits, and the three of us can set something up."

He looks at his mother, confused, while Finn glares at me. "Ease off the kid."

"I've had a bad fucking day; back off me."

"Yeah, I saw bad day all over that chick."

"Chilz is dead, man. Don't fucking stand on your high horse and look down on me. You fucking win, okay? You fucking win."

He looks away when the finance guy comes back in and sits down.

"Everything checked out. Not an easy task on a weekend. Congratulations, Mr. James, you are the proud owner of a beautiful vehicle."

*****

When my phone rings, I look around the car, trying to figure out how to answer the damned thing. I pull over because I have no clue, and I honestly don't need to be fucking distracted while driving.

Seeing it's Billy, I answer my actual phone instead of trying to figure out the damn car system.

"She left three hours ago. You coming back or staying out?"

"You staying in?" I ask.

"Yeah. Apparently, you invited some people over tonight for a party." He sounds irritated.

"I don't recall," I respond because I don't.

"I ordered pizza and wings. We have the fridge keg, and it's full. I have no desire to entertain, so could you get back here?"

"Sure thing. See you in twenty minutes."

I hang up with him and grab the card Tani gave me. She answers immediately.

"Hey, will you give me a quick tutorial on how to answer the phone?"

She giggles.

I wasn't even being funny, but ... whatever.

*****

When I walk in, I see the bear on the leather sofa. I'm shocked.

Billy walks over. "I said it was all right. She —"

118

"She here?" I stare at the bear-dog, who is the queen of the couch. No one is sitting next to her, and I can't blame them. She is pretty fucking anti-social.

"No. Keanna needed a couple days. I told her Tinker Bell could stay."

"You told her that?" I don't really mean to come off like an ass, and I'm not really sure why I do.

"She's a nice woman."

I scratch my head. "You fuck her?"

"No," he answers, staring at me. "She's pretty fucking awesome, though."

"Yeah, well, I fucked her ... twice. Keep that in mind." I walk away, leaving him standing there. "Tink, come."

I walk through the crowd of about twenty all scattered away from the couch.

"Tink, you're gonna have to crash in here." I open my bedroom door and nod for her to go in.

She sits and looks away.

"You serious?"

She doesn't budge, so I step in and call her again.

"Tink, come on. Babe, it's been a fuck of a day, and I really need you to cooperate."

She yawns then gets her big, old butt up and walks in, taking her sweet damn time.

I step to the door, and she growls, stopping me.

She's eyeballing me, giving me that look bitches give.

"You don't own me." I snort, and her ears perk up. "I'm gonna shower. You ... I don't know ... make yourself comfortable."

After a shower and a long talk with myself about how I will not have a repeat of a day like this, I towel off. Then I stand in front of the mirror and try to talk myself into shaving, but I decide, fuck it.

I don't have a clue what has been up with me for the past almost twenty-four hours, but I refuse to think it has something to do with the doe-eyed chick, despite the fact that my dick springs up with just the thought of her.

I am not cut out to lead a band, let alone think for one second that I will ever have normal. I don't even want to tap in and try normal. I would rather sit back, tap us in from behind, and get the ass that wants me, not Steel Total Destruction, because they have no clue who I am.

I won't kid myself. I'm not like them. I'm just the drummer, and I like it like that.

I brush my teeth, towel off my hair a little more, and then walk out into my bedroom where I see Tink gnawing on something, and not just something …

"Tink!" I yell, reaching down and grabbing the shredded plunger next to the fucking glass tube labeled, '*In case of emergency, break the glass.*'

Fuck! Son of a bitch.

I pry open her mouth but don't see shit.

"You fucking kidding me, Tink!" I let go and sit back. "What the fuck? What the fucking fuck?"

Awe hell no, not on my watch. What the fuck am I saying, it is my watch.

I stand up, tighten the towel around my waist, and run out of the room.

"Billy!"

Everyone looks at me.

"Jesus Christ, River," he huffs. "Clothes!"

"Need you in here bad, man."

He stops dead in his tracks and looks around. "No."

"It's Tink. She's … She's … Well … Seriously, man, come on!" I finally huff out.

120

I see Tani. I almost forgot I invited her when she helped me set up the phone again. Shit. Then I see Finn and Sonya. I can't deal with this shit right now!

I walk in my room, grab a pair of gray sweats, and pull them on.

"What the hell is going on?" Billy finally follows me in.

"Shut the damn door," I order. "She ate the Devil weed."

"She, what?" he gasps, shutting the door.

"The emergency stash, she ate the whole bud. No idea how she got her big, old tongue in that thing, but she fucking did. Now what are we gonna do?"

"Get her to a vet!"

"And say what, man?" I have no clue what I would say to the vet and even less of a clue what I would say to Keanna.

"What's going on?" Memphis walks in, shutting the door behind him.

"Tink's a fucking pot head," I half growl, giving her a dirty look.

She pushes up off the ground and walks toward Memphis.

"She bite?"

"Fuck yes, she does. She's a bitch!" I yell at her because, one, she is a bitch, and two, I am so pissed at her right now. She ate my weed! She ate it! And now — well, what the hell is going to happen to her?

She pushes up against Memphis, and he pets her. "Big baby is what she is." He chuckles. "All sorts of fucked up, aren't you? You are a beautiful, sexy bitch."

"Shit's not funny. We need a vet! If something happens to her, well ..." I stop when there is a knock on my door and then it opens.

Finn walks in. "All cool in here?"

"What the fuck?" I snarl.

"River's new bitch ate his weed," Memphis lets out a snicker as he continues petting Tink.

"You fed your dog weed?" Finn gasps, then immediately follows up with, "Why the hell would *you* get a dog?"

"Fuck you!" I point at him. "Fuck you. And why the hell are *you* having a kid? Oh, wait, 'cause you didn't pull out. Seems like one would learn."

He takes a threatening step toward me, and I beckon him with my hands. "Come and get some. That would make this fucked up day worth it."

Tink attempts to growl, but then I swear she smiles. Fucking dog.

Billy steps between us. "Enough! You two need to sort your shit and stop the fucking childish behavior. River, I'm calling Keanna—"

"The fuck you are." Memphis still hasn't stopped laughing, but he's now thumbing through his phone. "Here. See?" He holds out his phone. "She's gonna be fine, just high as hell for a while."

Tastes good, doesn't she?

"I can't believe you left Tink for him." Natasha yawns.

It's after ten o'clock on a Saturday night, and we are two single women camped out in her bed, wearing fleece pajama pants, eating popcorn, and half watching *The Longest Ride*.

"You've said that a few times." I shake my head. "I told you, she's temperamental, and I don't trust her around Jordan."

"And you now have an excuse to swing by the beach house and see the sexy drummer of STD." She giggles.

"Yeah, well, it's really not like that at all." I won't go into detail about what I witnessed or overheard while a grown man was sleeping.

Feeling a wave of nausea wash over me, I change the subject. "So how about you spill the beans about Masterson?"

She looks down, shaking her head. "I prefer to talk about you."

"Not fair. You know Mr. James and I got nasty, and you haven't even told me about 'The Master'." I air quote his stage name.

"We didn't have sex," she says, reaching over and grabbing her tea.

"You are so full of shit." I grin, lying back against the headboard.

"I'm very serious." She shakes her head again. "The man — well, he's different."

"You couldn't tell that by looking at him? He looks like someone who gets off on — " I stop when she looks at me out of the corner of her eyes. "Oh, hells no. Tell me he hurt you, and I swear I'll cut him."

"He didn't hurt me. He ... he just ... He's different," she nearly stutters.

"You know there is nothing you could tell me that would make me judge you, right?"

She nods, then covers her face. "He has got to think I'm absolutely insane!"

I am stunned as she starts laughing hysterically.

"Natasha?"

"I started crying when things got hot and heavy, just before ... Well, you know. I started crying." She continues laughing while I sit, dumbfounded and unable to form a word. She then uncovers her face. "The hottest guy I have ever laid eyes on, and I cry. What the fuck is wrong with me?" Her laughter stops, and then she looks devastated.

"Nothing's wrong with you. Not one thing, babe. You just aren't ready."

"My ex has been locked up for two years. He has seven still to go. I *never* want him back. I need to move on."

"I know," I console, pulling her into a hug. "It will happen when and with whom it is supposed to."

*****

124

She is asleep when I walk out and grab my phone off the counter. A message from an unknown number is on my lock screen.

Keanna, Tink's kind of fucked up. R.J.

I hit call, and no one answers. I give it the time it takes to put on my boots and coat and head out to my car that is covered with ice to get a return call, a message, anything that tells me more about what is happening with my dog. When it doesn't happen, I hop in and start it up. Then I grab the ice scraper.

Ten minutes later, I am heading to the beach ... in a January ice storm.

I park up the road since there are cars lining both sides of the street. It's obvious there is a party, and I am going to feel like a complete ass walking in there, dressed the way I am.

I quickly decide that it matters not. Tink is fucked up. What does that even mean?

I knock, but no one answers, so I decide to walk in.

There are about twenty-five people in the living area. I spot River immediately, shirtless and in sweat pants. Apparently, I'm not the only one underdressed. At least I'm wearing a damn shirt, though. Evidently, he doesn't have to, since a little blonde is draped over him like an overpriced outlet find.

I feel a little bit more than a pang of jealousy. Maybe it's because I'm a little bit — no, a lot pissed off.

I stomp off my boots and look around for Tink. I see Billy walking out of River's bedroom, and he looks up and sees me. His eyes widen, and then he looks around until he finds what he's looking for — River.

I don't want him to know I'm here, though, so I quickly make my way over to Billy.

"Is Tink in there?" I point to the door.

"Yes, but ... um ... but ..."

I don't wait for him to continue. I push past him and open the door to find Tink on the bed again.

"Tink, down."

Her ears perk up briefly, but she doesn't even lift her head.

I sit down next to her and pet her. "You okay?"

"She's high as hell." I look up to see River walking in.

"What?" I snap.

"Not my fault. She found a bud and ate it." His brows furrow and he shrugs. "We looked it up online, and she's fine, just fucked up."

"How did she get pot?"

"I was showering and came out, then saw the empty container and no pot."

"How much?" I grab my phone out of my pocket and hit up Google.

"One bud," he answers, sitting on the other side of her. "Good shit, too."

He is making a joke, and I'm pissed.

Tink shifts to her side, her head on his leg, looking up at him.

"Good shit. Bad dog," he scolds her as he pets her. "Very bad dog."

"You need fucking help, you know," I whisper, scolding him.

He looks at me, a devilish grin spreading across his face. "You wanna give me some help, Keanna?"

"I wanna kick your ass is what I want to do." I stand up. "Tink, come on, girl."

River sighs, looking up at me. "She's fucked up. Let her sleep it off. She'll be fine."

The door opens, and the blonde walks in. "Oh, I'm sorry."

River sighs, yet says nothing.

"Can I talk to you for a minute?" the blonde asks.

He stands up and turns his back to her. "Gotta take a piss."

"Okay, I'll just wait here," she calls after him.

When the bathroom door is shut, she says, "Hi, I'm Tani. I met River today when he bought a new Range Rover."

I'm not in the mood to chat. My dog is fucked up; the guy I fucked last night and this morning is a complete mess of a man yet doesn't seem to give a shit; and tonight's ho is trying to chat it up with me.

"Oh, are you two together?"

"No," I answer, petting Tink.

"Oh, good." She walks over and smiles. "That would have been weird. I mean, he and I ... you know..." She stops, and I look up at her. She's grinning from ear to ear. "We kind of hooked up today, and I'm pretty sure he's interested in ... more."

"*More*?" I half-laugh. "More what?"

"Well, between you and I"—she starts to sit down, but Tink growls, giving me hope that she is not fucking brain damaged and keeping the little Barbie off the bed.

Tani steps back. "More than just a quick blow job in his vehicle. I mean, that's unlike me, totally unlike me, but he invited me here tonight so ..." She giggles again. "More."

"River is not looking for a relationship." I half-laugh again, sounding fake to my own ears. "He's looking for girls like you to give him the high of a release."

"Really? And you know this because you've *'been there, done that'*?" She chuckles mockingly.

I look up at her and shake my head. "You really wanna step off."

"Maybe you should leave. He clearly wants me here, but you—"

"Bitch, how did I taste? When your skanky, little ass was blowing him like a whore in his vehicle, how did I taste? I can assure you, I get mine before any man gets theirs."

"How dare you call me a skank!"

"Bitch, please, let's not pretend you're not."

I am fully intending on continuing when the light from the bathroom shines into the bedroom, and a very smug-looking River stands in the doorway.

"Do you own a fucking shirt?!" I scream at him.

"Damn, Keanna," he remarks as he walks toward me as if he has a purpose.

"You can stop right there. I'm not interested in-in … anything you have to offer. You two would do well to walk out the door and find another room. Until I can get her"—I point to Tink—"out of here, I'm not going anywhere."

"Isn't she sexy?" River smirks at Tani, who gasps. He has that look in his eye, like a child who knows damn well he's about to do or say something incredibly wrong, and I brace myself for it. "Tastes good, too, doesn't she?"

She turns all red. "I can't believe you. You … Wow, just wow."

"Incredible, aren't I?" River replies smugly.

She turns on her heels, ones no woman should wear on a January day in New Jersey, and walks out of his room, slamming the door behind her.

He's such an ass, a complete and total ass.

"You're something; that's for damn sure," I mutter out loud, still thinking to myself.

"I like the way you taste, the way your tight, little cunt hugs my cock, and — "

"Please just leave. If you hurry, you can catch up with her and still get laid tonight."

He looks at me like I offended him. Then he opens the French doors and walks out of the opposite door she left from.

"Tink, sweetie, I know you're not feeling all that well, but we need to go."

The bedroom door opens, and a man with a beard and a dark-haired woman walk in, holding hands. He looks pissed. She looks at him and smiles, then looks at me.

"Hi, I'm Sonya. Is River around?"

I point to the French doors. "He just walked out there."

"Sorry if we're interrupting something," she says to me, then looks up at the bearded man. "It's time, Finn."

He takes her chin in his hand and lifts it. "This is for you."

"This is for us," she corrects, taking his free hand and placing it on her stomach. "We never look back again."

He leans in and takes her mouth possessively. I look away.

When the man I now know as Finn walks out the door, Sonya looks at me and smiles.

"I'm sorry. I didn't catch your name."

The way she speaks is almost forced, like her confidence is man-made and not something she was born and raised with.

I immediately answer. "I'm Keanna."

"A friend of River's?" she asks, sitting on the other side of Tink and petting her.

Tink sighs.

"Well, aren't you the sweetest?" Sonya smiles at Tink.

"She's not normally, but apparently, she ate some of River's pot," I inform her, shaking my head.

Sonya giggles and covers her mouth. "I'm sorry. It's not funny." She leans her head to the side, studying me. "How well do you know River?"

When I take too long to answer, she reaches over and grabs my hand.

"I see."

"See what?" I ask.

"It'll be okay."

I have no idea what she thinks she knows, but I want to know what it is. "What will be okay?"

She shrugs. "I guess it's all in what you can handle. I like him. I see good in him. I — "

"Fuck you! Fuck you, Finn!"

Sonya and I both look at the French doors that are partially open.

"No, fuck *you*. This ends now! I get pressure from the band, pressure from Sonya … This shit between us gets buried now!" Finn's deep voice growls at River.

"Buried like Jesse?"

"Just fucking like her!" Finn snaps.

"Nah, fuck that. Fuck you, and fuck that. Face me like a man, Beckett. You want an end? You want a fucking end! You want that easy out; that's what you fucking want? I've lived with this shit for years. I've kept it all fucking bottled up so you, the fucking good guy, could shine, and you fucking *shined*! You're still shining, motherfucker. Gonna be a daddy and all."

"You fucking watch it, River. You fucking watch your—"

Sonya and I both jump up and run to the door when we hear punches being thrown, finding them on the snow-covered deck in a tangle of fists and fury.

"Finn!" Sonya yells, stepping toward them.

I hold my hand in front of her. "Let them go."

"What!" She gulps.

"Your man is fine. Let them go." I watch as Finn holds River's left wrist, not allowing for any punches to be thrown with it.

"What about River?" she asks, gripping my hand.

"Let him work through it."

Within seconds, they are both on their feet, and both have bloodied noses.

Finn pulls his hand back, shoves it in his jeans, and pulls out something shiny.

"This was hers. Take it." He shoves his hand forward. "I don't need it."

"And I fucking do?!" River shouts, looking like he has been slapped.

"I don't fucking know if you do. Sonya thinks ..." Finn stops and shoves his hand through his hair. "She thinks it'll help."

I don't know why, but I squeeze her hand.

She looks up at me, gives me a sad smile, and whispers, "Sorry."

"For …?" I whisper back.

"Because I know what the two of you are facing. I promise you'll get through it."

"Oh, no. You're reading this all wrong." I shake my head.

"Uh-huh." She gives my hand a final squeeze, then walks toward them.

She stops between Finn and River and hugs River. "It's a new year. Happy birthday, River." Then she turns to Finn and takes his hand.

When they walk away, I stay, watching River who has his hand to his side, his right hand gripping whatever Finn gave him so tightly I swear I feel my heart being strangled.

I am fully dressed, yet my teeth are chattering. I should go inside, but no one deserves to be alone when they are hurting, especially on their birthday.

He may not know it, but I am a stupid girl, and like so many others just like me, I am wildly attracted to broken boys. There isn't a boy I have met who is more broken than River James, though.

I can be his friend. I *will* be his friend because he was one to me when I needed it the most.

When I walk through the dust of icy snow on the deck in my socks and stand beside him, he inhales a deep breath, but he doesn't look at me. I reach out and take his hand, holding it lightly. He then exhales slowly and looks up at the clear, winter sky. Slowly, I feel him grip my hand back.

I don't know how long we stand there, but it's long enough that I can't feel my feet and am shivering.

He looks over, his bloodshot, hazel eyes looking me over. "I need to fuck you."

I should be offended. I should, but because I am about to become River James's friend, I laugh out loud.

When he scowls, I laugh harder and pull my hand away to cover my mouth. Then he starts laughing, too, and it's a beautiful sound.

"Laugh it up all you want." He shoves the shiny object in his pocket, then grabs me around the waist, lifts me up, and hoists me over his shoulder.

He walks toward the door with me laughing even harder now. Then I feel his hand slap my ass, and I yelp. His hand covers the spot and begins rubbing it.

"Don't laugh at a man when he says he needs to be inside your pussy, Keanna." He flops me down on the bed, then walks back and shuts the door.

"Not gonna happen," I tell him. "If you wanna fuck someone, go find the Barbie who sucked you off a few hours ago."

"Jealous?" he asks. The look in his eyes is that of raw hunger as he starts to climb toward me from the bottom of the bed.

I scoot up to the headboard and quickly place my soaking wet, cold feet on his chest, stopping him. "No."

"Holy fuck, babe!" He stops his ascent and grabs my ankle, then immediately starts kissing my foot.

"River James, I am pissed that my dog is high. I am pissed that you sent me a message that my dog is messed up, then didn't answer your calls or texts when I replied. And although I am not jealous, I would be lying if I wasn't thoroughly disgusted that you allowed that little skank to"—I stop because I need to keep this light and friendly. After all, I am going to be his friend—"taste my pussy by way of your dick. I'm pissed that, as your self-delegated, new friend, you treated me like shit today."

"Did you just friend-zone me?" He stills, no longer kissing my foot.

"The way I see it, you have ass on speed dial. What you really need is a friend. So, yes, I certainly did."

"Tink, she just friend-zoned me."

Tink opens one eye and closes it quickly.

"I'll take friends with beni's."

"Sorry, bud, this ass doesn't share. Although, after the really-get-to-know-River phase of this friendship, maybe then the benefits can happen. Just so long as you don't mind that what's good for the goose is good for the gander."

"I'll agree with everything you say so long as I can lick your pussy whenever I want."

"After the get-to-know-each-other phase, I may allow it."

"Allow it?" His eyebrows shoot up. "You'll be begging for it."

I look him straight in the eye. "As long as you're okay with me getting it licked elsewhere, too."

His eyes widen. "You seriously don't think anyone else could eat that pussy like I can, do you? I am a master pussy connoisseur. I know everything about pussy and how to eat it."

"Goose." I point at him. "Gander." I point at myself.

Understanding fills his eyes. "Because of that chick?"

I shrug, then nod once.

"Son of a bitch," is all he says.

LONG,
HARD,
AND ROUGH

There comes a time in every man's life when they would sell their soul to the devil for just a taste of a pussy as smooth and sweet as Keanna's. Meatloaf sang it best. Fucked up or not, I remember that he was praying for the end of time after promising something to a girl in order to tap her ass.

"I can guarantee I'll never see that chick again. Fuck, I can't even remember her name."

Keanna smiles at me, yet shakes her head.

I flop down face first and groan, then feel her nails skate over my scalp. It feels good, so I stay just like I am: face first, cock impaling the mattress while she rubs the wrong damn head.

I hear the door open, and she stops.

"He okay?" It's Billy.

When he closes the door behind him, I know this is to mute the noise from our "guests."

"I'm pretty sure he'll be fine," Keanna whispers.

"What the hell happened between him and Finn?"

"I was in here with Finn's girlfriend, so I'm not sure."

I know that's some bullshit, but fuck if I'm going to correct it. I kind of dig that she isn't saying shit.

"It's his birthday," Billy explains with obvious concern in his voice. "He's twenty-four today."

"Someone should make him a cake," she says quietly.

I want to tell her I would rather eat pussy, but I don't want Billy to push the discussion of Finn and my … *issues*.

"You … um … staying over?"

Billy cracks me up. *Smooth, man, smooth.*

"To keep an eye on Tink," she answers.

"And him?"

That-a-boy, Billy, I think.

"I'm pretty sure we're gonna be friends, so yeah, him, too." She uses a gentle tone.

"Good. You're a good person, Keanna. If he gets to be too much to handle, let me know."

And now I want to kick Billy's ass. But as soon as he leaves, her hand returns to the back of my head, and her nails skate gently against my scalp.

I am almost asleep when she stops. The bed rises when she gets up, and I feel her untie my boots, then pull them off.

"I don't know what happened to you, River, but I hope you'll let me or someone else inside enough to trust them someday so it doesn't hurt you so damn much."

I push myself up once I hear a door shut. I see the bathroom light through the small gap under the door and know she's in there, wondering what the fuck is up with me.

I pull out the top drawer to my dresser and grab the baggie I got today off one of the guests. Then I grab the one-hitter I took from the same bastard, shove my feet in my slides, and walk outside and onto the deck.

I pull the lighter out of my pants pocket and shake it next to my ear. It's full. I will have to remember to thank Sonya, because I know for damn sure Finn didn't do it.

I look at the Zippo and see a faint marking: Yin and Yang—light and dark. Him and me. It wasn't done by a shop or at the hand of an artist; it is nowhere near professional. I know it was her. I feel it.

I bring the lighter to my lips and hold it there. "I'm so fucking sorry, Jesse. I'm so fucking sorry."

I hold the packed one hitter between my lips and inhale. I let the burn consume me, holding it in as long as I can. Then I do it all over again.

When I feel the cloud fog my brain, I feel content in knowing I will sleep tonight without incident.

I turn to head back in and see Keanna leaning against the open doorway, her arms crossed over her body, her head lying against the door jamb, and the moonlight framing her lush curves.

"Keanna." I stop because I have no idea what the fuck to say to her. She's not looking at me like Jesse did, like I am the only person on Earth who could make her smile. She isn't looking at me like all the women lined up after a show for a chance to fuck a rock star. She's looking at me like an angel, like someone who sees me, the real me, and isn't running the fuck away.

She holds her hand out. "It's cold out, River. Come inside."

I walk toward her outstretched hand and take it.

Once inside, she shuts the door, and I begin. "Keanna—"

"It's been a long day, a rough day." She turns to look at me. "You should sleep. And because your birthday is technically tomorrow and I am sure your friends have plans for you, I think you should rest."

I'm glad she interrupted, because I'm not sure what I was going to say. But right now, I know what I want.

"You staying?"

She nods. "Yeah, I have to make sure Tink is okay."

"Right. Tink." I kick my slides off, then drop my sweats.

"Jesus, River, a little modesty," she exclaims as she takes off her hoodie and slides in the bed.

"I sleep nude," I inform her, walking over to the bed. "Scoot."

She smirks. "Nice try, champ. Other side."

"But Tink," I argue, hoping maybe Keanna is fucked up, too, but I know better. Of course she's not. That's too bad, too.

"She's in the middle of the bed, bud." She pulls the covers up, concealing the tank top that her tits are using to play peek-a-boo with me.

"Fine." I get in the bed. "But if you were a friend, you would seriously want to smother me with those perfect fucking tits of yours."

"Smother?" She is clearly amused at my fuck up.

"Snuggle. I said snuggle."

"No. No, you didn't."

I look at Tink. "You think she needs to go out?"

Keanna sits up and pets her. "You need to go potty, Tinker Bell?"

Tink covers her nose.

I look at Keanna. "Did you see that, or am I seeing shit?"

Keanna smiles and shakes her head. "I saw it." She leans over and kisses Tink on the top of her head. "Let me know if you have to, okay, girl?" She rubs her head like she did mine, and I am suddenly jealous of a bear-dog.

I finally lie down, muttering, "Friends."

She lies back down and rolls to her side so she's looking at me. "Could you use another?"

I roll to my side and face her. "You sure that's what you want?"

"I want honesty. I wanna know you," she says, which immediately makes me tense. "I want you to trust me, River James."

"I want you, Keanna ..." I pause, having no clue what her last name is.

She smiles. Fucking perfect teeth.

"Sutton." She holds out her hand for me to shake, and I do, but I don't let go.

"Trust isn't something I do," I admit.

"Not an easy thing to give when you — " She stops and looks away. "When you haven't been given a lot of reason to trust people."

I try to pull my hand back, but she holds on firmly.

"Please don't," she begs. "Please tell me what happened."

I shake my head. "If you want a friendship, you don't ask that again."

I'm starting to sit up when she asks, "Who is Jesse?"

I don't want to talk about Jesse, either. I don't want to talk about the past. Still, at least that's all she is asking of me.

I lie back down. "Jesse … well, I — "

"You and Finn were both in love with her?"

I shrug. "Maybe. I mean, what does a sixteen-year-old kid really know about love?"

"Right," she says as her thumb runs across my knuckles.

"I met her at a party. We were fucked up. The next morning, her foster family came, and she got taken back. We stayed in touch over the phone, and one of her friends with a license helped us hook up when we needed to see each other."

"Did you know Finn?"

"No. No, I didn't. I knew she had a boyfriend. I knew he was straight laced, judgey, and she was a fucking mess. She was like me. Just like me."

"She was funny?"

"No! Hell, she didn't even smile unless I was making jokes. She begged for jokes."

Keanna reaches over and touches my chest. "The Joker?"

I hold my hand over hers. "Yeah."

"She made you smile."

"She made me a lot of things." I shake my head. "Stupid being one."

"Stupid?"

"Yeah. Well, I think so. She got pregnant. Then she got dead."

"I'm really sorry." She props her head on her hand and looks at me.

"Fuck, I have no idea why it's so fucking easy to spill this shit to you."

"It's not me, River. From what I have been able to piece together, you have an amazing career because you're extremely talented. There was an accident, a secret revealed, and everything changed. So now you are running in the opposite direction because you, River James, think that Finn …?" I nod at her questioning his name, mesmerized by the insight she has. And being high as hell, I allow the truth to unfold. The buzz numbs the pain of the truth, always has. "Because Finn Beckett is better than you?"

I don't answer right away. I don't say shit while I look into her light brown eyes. Then I tell her, "The dark and the light."

"You made her laugh. Are you sure you're the dark?"

"Oh, I'm the dark. I gave her the cash she used to buy the drugs that she OD'd on … Or she got so fucked up she drowned at her foster family's home on April fifth."

"Not your fault. It was her choice, River. You were kids." I sit up, and she grabs my hand, stopping me, "Don't go."

"I can't do this. Fucked up or not, I can't do this." I try to get up, but she doesn't let go. "If you're gonna keep me in this bed, you better give me a damn good reason to stay." I look back at her.

"Like what? Let you fuck me after" — she swallows hard — "the Barbie?"

I nod. "Gotta give me something."

"Like what?"

"Something personal, something fucked up and embarrassing, and … I don't know, Keanna, but I just gave you a shitload of way too much, and you're giving me sympathy doe eyes, and of course I wanna fuck you. Jesus, Keanna."

"And I don't want to feel used," she says, dropping her eyes.

"You know damn well I'll get you there first." I have no idea why I am reminding her of this.

She knows.

She. Knows.

She smiles, yet her clear, white eyes get a little misty. "My embarrassing moment … If that's what you need, then fine." She takes a deep breath. "I suspected Miguel was cheating on me for a couple years. Hell, I saw him tripping over himself over some dumb, little, stick-thin Barbie bitch my last semester of nursing school, but I ignored it because I had to get through finals. I had to graduate because my grandmother was so damn proud that her granddaughter was getting her bachelor's and becoming a nurse. So, as much as I would love nothing more than to get naked and sweaty with you, there is no way in hell I will allow myself to feel second best to another skank again."

"Okay, okay. But—"

"No buts," she demands, standing up from the bed.

"Look, if it means anything, if you were around, I would have much rather come in your mouth."

"You really are an ass; you know that?" She shakes her head as she walks quickly into the bathroom and shuts the door.

I look down at Tink, who is looking up at me. "Don't look at me like that. I have no fucking clue how to deal with a woman like her."

I get up and head to the bathroom door, knocking once before pushing it open.

She's using my damn toothbrush!

"Why wouldn't you kiss me?"

"Really?"

"Yes, really," I say, grabbing my toothbrush out of her hand, licking it, and then handing it back. "My mouth was on it before you put it in your mouth, too, so don't look at me like I'm crazy."

"You, you—"

"Just answer the question. Why wouldn't you kiss me?"

"It's more intimate than a one-night stand." She grabs the washcloth and runs it over her face.

"It was a night and a day," I argue.

"It was—" She spits the toothpaste out, and for some fucking reason, that's hot to me. "It is *still* a rough couple of days."

"You know my shit now, Keanna; how much more intimate can that be? I mean, I can fuck whomever I want, but trusting you with all that shit out there? That was fucking intimate, so stop fucking with me and give me those lips."

"You'll stop trying to fuck me if I kiss you?"

"Is this a game?" I ask because I am so fucking confused. Where did she come up with that?

"No, it's not a game."

"Then what is it?" I wonder.

"Well, hell if I know!" She throws her hands up.

"Trust is given, taken, and then pissed on in ten minutes," I tell her.

"All because I won't fuck you?" She seems to be getting pissed, but fuck, so am I.

"Hell, you won't even kiss me."

I scratch my head and ponder the thought while she continues washing her face.

I look up when she sets the washcloth down and reaches toward my face. I think shit's going down. Shit I need to go down is going down.

She cups my chin and pulls my face down. "You still have blood on your nose," she says sorrowfully. "Let me."

She grabs the washcloth that's sitting next to the sink, the one she used to wash her face, and wipes under and around my nose softly, gently, and fuck if that doesn't do something to me.

"Now let me see your hand."

I give her the good one, but she shakes her head, so I give her the one with all the scars. She turns my palm facing down.

"All this talk about grip and being able to make a fist doesn't mean you're supposed to fight all the time to test your recovery." She places my hand under the faucet, rubbing over it, moving it all around, making a fist while she washes it. "It's not your grip River. It's your wrist."

I nod since it's true.

"Have you told Natasha?"

"No."

"Why?"

I shrug.

"Because you're afraid you'll be ready faster and have to face him?"

I shrug again.

"Well, the way I see it, he tried to make amends today."

"Because she made him," I point out as she massages my wrist.

"You give the woman too much credit. We can't make men do or be anything. People can't really make people do anything. We can just suggest, support, and help."

"You give men a lot more credit than they deserve," I inform her, shaking my head. "If you're the owner of a hot, little twat with an ounce of kindness and confidence, you can rule the world."

She smiles at me and shakes her head.

"What?"

"Women can fake confidence just like they can fake an orgasm." She turns off the water and grabs a towel, drying my hand off.

I reach out and push her hair away from her face. She has little cuts that are now exposed without her makeup on.

"That motherfucker made you fake orgasm and marked up your face. He shouldn't be breathing."

"Like I said, today was a rough day."

I lean in and kiss her cheek, which she allows.

"As much as I want those lips, I won't push anymore," I promise. "I am a selfish fuck, Keanna. I don't know what kind of friend I can actually be to you."

She looks up at me and nods. "One day at a time."

I take her hand this time, not because I know it's the right thing to do, but because it feels right. We then walk to the bed, and Tink is off of it now. We both look around to find her next to the glass door, her face and body squished against it, holding her up.

I chuckle, and Keanna lets go of my hand and almost skips to her. When she squats down and hugs her, Tink leans into the hug, and they both fall over. It's kind of beautiful.

Keanna giggles as Tink buries her nose into her neck. I grab my phone and take a picture.

I get lost in it, lost in an exchange that is nothing but the real thing. The woman is happy, the dog feels loved, and—

"A little help here," Keanna says, still giggling.

"Shit, sorry." I toss my phone on the bed and grab Tink, pulling her upright. "You gotta take a piss?" I hold her collar while reaching down for Keanna's hand. She takes it, and I pull her up.

"Thank you, kind sir." She snorts and then lets go to open the door. "Come on, Tinker Bell; let's go potty."

Tink pushes herself up on all fours, and it clearly takes some effort. Then Keanna steps into my boots and walks out the door.

I find my slides and shove my feet in them before walking out behind them.

Tink starts licking the deck, gobbling up some of the snow.

"I'll go and get her bowl."

"Water bowl." Keanna reiterates.

"Right." I nod and start to turn toward the room.

"Pants!" Keanna giggles, and I stop dead and look back.

The light surrounds her again, and I am so fucking painfully aware of how drawn to her I am.

"You're so fucking beautiful, Keanna. So fucking beautiful."

She looks like she is about to cry.

"Sorry, babe, but it's the truth." I grab a pair of shorts out of my dresser and throw them on. "Tink gets water; what do you want?"

I look back to see she is still looking at me the same way.

She swallows down some sort of emotion and whispers, "The same."

Birthday Knots And Cake

Tinker Bell falls asleep with her nose next to the shallow, stainless steel bowl River brought in as a water dish.

"Should I put her on the bed?" he asks, looking at her. "She can't be comfortable."

"She's a dog, River." I smile. "And she's high. She probably doesn't care where she is sleeping or how uncomfortable she is."

"No shit, right?" He smiles and nods, crossing his arms over his bare chest. "I've slept in worse places."

"Haven't we all?"

He drags his hands over his head, then walks over and grabs a pillow and the throw from the end of the bed.

"Are you sleeping down there with her?" I ask, almost immediately regretting it. I mean, it's pretty ballsy to think he wouldn't expect *me* to. "I mean, I could."

He doesn't bat an eye at what I said. He kneels down next to her, lifts her head, and places it on the pillow, and then covers her up with the blanket.

"You think she'll be too warm?"

"No. She's right next to the door. It's colder down there."

"Do you think she'll be too cold?" he asks, putting his hand on the glass.

"No, Goldilocks. I think she'll be just right."

"Who the hell is Goldilocks?" he asks as he stands up.

"*Goldilocks and the Three Bears*? A childhood fairytale? You know, like the kind your mom read to you at bedtime?"

He just looks at me and shakes his head. "No one read to me at bedtime."

Immediately, I want to know how that is possible.

"Did you …? I mean, were you … poor?"

"Fuck no." He chuckles uncomfortably. "I was privileged."

"Oh." I want to ask a million questions, but I feel like he might get upset, angry, and we have made progress tonight.

He jumps in the middle of the bed and pats both sides of him. "Which side, Keanna Sutton?"

I look at him and shake my head.

"Look, as much as I wanna be inside you, I want you to get some sleep, too. I will behave."

I kick off his boots and climb in. "This side. That way, if she wakes up in the middle of the night, I'll hear her."

He covers me up, tucking me in tightly, and then kisses my scratches before lying down on his back.

"You want me to tell you about *Goldilocks and the Three Bears*?"

He glances over and smiles. "That would be cool."

As I tell him all about the little girl who was lost in the woods and finds a cottage, tries out three chairs, three different porridges, and then three beds until she finds the one that is just right, I lightly scratch his hair with one hand, and he holds the other against his chest.

When I know he's asleep, I look at the alarm clock on the dresser. It's three in the morning.

"Happy birthday, River James." I bend down and brush my lips against his, careful not to wake him up.

*****

I wake to soft whimpers and small movement.

When I open my eyes and my ears have the time to adjust to my surroundings, I realize it's him again.

"Get the fuck off me. No, don't. No," he mumbles as he thrashes under the covers like he is trying to fight something.

It's the same way I woke yesterday after our nap. I don't want the same thing to happen, and I know I should leave him alone, but it hurts my heart to see him suffering.

"River, it's okay," I whisper gently, sitting up. "River." I take his hand in mine, and he immediately pulls it away as if I hurt him. His movements get angrier, but then he curls up again, and I swear, in the darkness, I hear him cry.

I wait it out, continuing to watch him as he falls back to sleep. I lie back down and put my hand on his head, rubbing his scalp with my nails.

"Keanna," he mumbles in a whisper. Then his body uncurls, and his breath evens out as he rolls to his back. Through the moon's light coming through the window, he looks peaceful.

I lie closer to him, knowing his nightmare has subsided, and he rolls to his side, trying to get comfortable. His head lies against my chest, his arm snaking around my waist, and he sighs as he finds peace and comfort in a warm body.

After a day like yesterday, it feels so odd that I would be able to sleep without wonder or worry that my ex would try to come after me … again. I eventually doze off, feeling safe and protected by a man who became an unlikely hero to me today.

*****

I wake again to River practically on top of me. The hand that was around my waist is now on my boob, his nose buried in my neck, and his knee is snug against my lady parts.

I want to be annoyed. I'm tired and have had little to no sleep, and my dog is still sleeping. But as I glance down at him, knowing what I now know about the sexiest drummer in the world, I could stay here all day.

I haven't had a weekend off since I took the job in the pediatric wing, so this is just fine with me. Plus, I start my job at the center, Monday with a seven to three job, Monday through Friday. Life is about to change.

"Morning," he grumbles, squeezing my boob. "I pick this bed, these pillows, and—"

I smack his hand away, and he looks up at me with shiny, clear, hazel eyes; a devilish grin. He lays his head back down, then lazily moves his hand down my body until it comes to rest on my hip. I feel him relax.

"Happy birthday, Riv—"

He pulls me up and on top of him, and I squeal in horror and delight.

"It is now." He chuckles.

I look down at a much different River than I saw last night or yesterday morning.

"Did you sleep well?" he asks as his hands grip my hips.

"Yes. And you?" Immediately I regret asking the question, and I see his eyes squint for a second, recognizing my regret.

"Not sure. I was asleep, but I woke up really fucking well."

I lean down and cup his face. Then I rub his stubble. "You look amazing in the morning."

"And how do I feel?" He gives a sleepy, sexy smile.

I reach up and touch his forehead. "Fine."

He snickers. "I'm talking about the nine inches pressing against your pussy."

Before I have a chance to hit him, my phone goes off. I lean over to grab it, climbing off him to see it's Natasha.

"Oh, shit, I never even left a note," I grumble, hopping off the bed.

"Hey," I answer, and Tink sits up when she hears me. "Sorry. Tink had an issue, and I needed to come. You were asleep."

Tink walks to the door and starts to whine. I look back and smile at River, pointing to his boots, asking his permission to wear them. He nods, stands up, yawns, and stretches.

"Damn," I remark as I open the French doors to let Tink out.

"Damn, what?" Natasha asks.

"Nothing," I answer.

"Spill it," she whispers.

I know leaving her was wrong, but I did make sure she was asleep. Still, I feel I have to give her something, and River can't hear me.

"River James in ball shorts and morning wood, dayum."

She laughs, and I do, too.

"Did you get some more last night?"

"No, not even the tip." I giggle as I grab Tink's collar and drag her to the steps when she starts to squat to pee on the deck … again.

"What? Why?" she gasps.

"Long story, no time. Tink, come on; I am freezing," I say as I try warming my body by jumping up and down.

I look back to find a very amused-looking River standing in the doorway.

What? I mouth.

"*River James in ball shorts and morning wood, dayum,*" he mocks, using some sort of chick voice. My jaw drops, and he grins. "It's my birthday, babe; why not come and give me some?"

"Call the car sales girl," I retort smugly, then turn around so he can't see the fact that I am incredibly embarrassed that he heard me.

"The what?" Natasha asks.

"Nothing, nothing. Do you know how freaking cold it is outside?"

"Go inside. I've got this," River says from behind me.

I turn around and look at him. "You're half naked. At least I have a tank top and sweats on."

"You see how hot I am?" He winks. "Go inside. I wouldn't want you to get a chest cold, babe."

"Did he just call you babe?" Natasha asks.

"Yeah." I walk past River and mouth *thank you*.

Once in the bathroom, I shut the door behind me. "I've had to pee for fifteen minutes, so I'm gonna mute you."

"Wait, what?" She laughs. "We use public bathrooms together, stall by stall, and you're gonna mute me?"

"True." I shove down my pants and undies, then hover over the toilet.

"So, are you two …?" She waits for me to reply.

"Friends," I answer.

"Really, 'cause you've never stayed two nights in a row anywhere," she remarks with a little bent-nosed tone.

"I'll stay tonight with you." I wipe and flush the toilet.

"You promise?"

"Wait, what day is it?"

She snickers. "It's Sunday."

"Right, new job tomorrow."

"Weekends off." She seems more excited than me.

"Except for the per diem hours I pick up," I remind her as I towel off my hands and walk to the door. "If I wanna buy a house, I need a fat down payment."

"Keanna!" River yells as he runs in from the deck. "We've got a fucking problem!"

He throws a sweatshirt at me and grabs one for himself.

"What is it? Tink?"

"Yeah, I'm gonna kill the motherfucker!"

"What's happening?" Natasha asks, practically screaming in my ear.

"Call you back!" I toss the phone and pull the sweatshirt on.

"I'm gonna kill you, fucker!" I hear River's voice boom, and I run outside.

I run down the beach toward River, not seeing Tink.

"Get your fucking dog, you stupid fuck!" he yells at a man with a cane.

"River! No!" When I get closer, I can see around River. "Oh, my god!"

"Brando, come!" the older man calls his dog.

I start to run toward them, but River grabs the back of my shirt.

"You don't wanna get between that."

"Tink!" I yell as I fight to pull away from him. He wraps an arm around my waist, pulls me tight, and lifts me up as I fight to get loose.

"How many fucking times have I told you that fucking asshole dog needs to be on a leash?"

"How many times have I told you he's my seeing eye dog?!" the man yells back at River.

"You are really damn lucky she's here, or I would bust that fucking cane over your damn head. I mean, for fuck's sake, if your ass was blind enough to depend on a dog to lead you, you'd be balls deep in Tink right now."

"River!" I yell at him.

"What fucking guy drives a car yet needs a seeing eye dog? The fucking thing shits all over the beach, and his royal blindness leaves those logs everywhere."

"How dare you talk about my disability like that."

"Oh, fuck you," River snaps at him.

I hear hysterical laughter coming down the beach from behind us.

"Fucking Memphis," River grumbles, turning around and finally letting my feet touch the ground. As soon as he lets go, I run to Tink. "Goddammit, Keanna."

I grab Tink's collar and pull her. "Come on, Tinker Bell!"

The white German Shepard snarls and snaps at me.

"Fuck you! Fuck you ... you ... bastard! You bite me, and I will bite you back."

River grabs ahold of him and yanks him back. "The fuck?"

Through his hysterical laughter, Memphis says, "No use, man. They're stuck!"

"They're what?!" I yell at him.

"Sorry, Keanna, but it's called tying or knotting or something." He covers his mouth, trying to contain his laughter. "Until he's done, they're stuck. Not a damn thing you can do about it."

"Oh, my god." I cover my face.

"You serious?" River snaps at him.

"Serious as shit, man. It can kill a dog to tear them apart, so don't do it," Memphis informs, trying to hide his grin. "Happened to our dog growing up, right on the front lawn."

River steps back and starts to storm toward the old man. He pushes his finger within inches of his face. "That fucking dog hurts Tink, and I will shoot him, then poke your motherfucking eyes out, make sure you can't see. Then you'll get a real fucking guide dog and not a rapist, fecalpheliac—"

"River!" I yell as I make my way toward him and grab his elbow. "Don't. Just don't."

"Fucking worthless, motherfucking, lying, cesspool sucking, bottom feeding—"

"River!" I scream in his face. "Enough!"

He looks at me, veins bulging out of his neck. He is red, so red. His eyes are cloudy, and his hand shakes. The rage inside him comes from a place deeper than an old man and the pervert dog.

I grab his hand and hold it tightly. "There is nothing we can do."

His jaw clenches, and its muscles pop out as he scowls at me.

"There is nothing we can do," I repeat.

I can't bear to watch him anymore. I can't handle the fact that there is nothing I can do about Tinker Bell without causing more harm than good, so I turn away from him and walk away.

I don't get far before Billy reaches out and grabs my hand. "Sorry, Keanna."

I nod and walk toward the water.

"You pissed at me?" I hear River yell from behind me.

I close my eyes and shake my head as I hear him getting closer and closer.

"I'll rip him apart."

"I don't doubt you would," I say as he stands in front of me, pulls the hood up over my head, and holds both sides while looking into my eyes.

"If you asked me to, I would. If Tink asked me to, I would."

I nod.

"I'm fucking this friendship up pretty badly, huh?" he asks as he strokes his thumb over my scrapes.

"No, River, you're not."

"I got your dog high."

"My dog got herself high, and clearly she was fine this morning," I say, not only to put things in perspective for him, but to remind myself not to put blame on him. Hell, I left her here.

"I was watching over her when she got fucking nailed by the shit-bag." He stops, and his jaw starts flexing again.

I reach around his hands that are still gripping the hood of the sweatshirt I'm wearing and pull his hood up. I look at him as intensely as he's looking at me and say, "I let her out. You were worried about me being cold."

His eyes narrow. "Yeah, I was, wasn't I?"

I nod. "You're a good guy, River."

"Don't kid yourself, Keanna. I'm just a drummer."

I smile as he pulls me closer to him.

"Now, today is my fucking birthday, and you're spending it with me."

"Is that so?"

"It is."

I let go of him because my hands are freezing. I shove them in the front pocket of the hoodie, and then he pulls me into a hug.

"I do have a request, though."

"What's that?" I ask as I breathe in his scent and take in his warmth.

"Don't get too close with Billy. He is the only single one here besides me, and he's a friend, so I wouldn't want to have to kick his ass."

"Yeah, okay."

He is quiet as he rubs his hands up and down my back, keeping me warm as his chin rests on my head.

"And that's a wrap." I hear Memphis hoot. "Come on, you little whore. One night with STD and you get all fucked up and laid. I bet your momma won't want you to hang out with us too much."

FUCKING ART

Keanna is in the shower. She wanted to leave and get some clothes and shit, but somehow, I convinced her to stay, giving her a long-sleeved STD T-shirt and a pair of jogging pants. She tried to argue that my friends would think she didn't own any clothes, and I tried to convince her that she shouldn't.

When she comes out of the bathroom, it's obvious she found a pair of scissors because the shirt's collar is gone, and the shirt is hanging off her shoulder, exposing her black bra strap.

When she asks for a bag to put her dirty clothes in, I grab one and come back in, holding it open and watching as she drops her clothes from last night into it.

"Are you commando right now?" I ask after seeing the lacey, little black bootie shorts drop in.

She rolls her eyes and just shakes her head.

"You know, for the rest of the day, I'm gonna be hard as hell now, right?"

She slaps my chest before taking the bag and dropping it by the bedroom door.

"You coming?" she asks as she opens the door.

"I could be," I grumble. "I'm gonna take a shower. You should go out and make sure Tink doesn't tear anyone apart. Although, I'm not gonna lie; she looks a hell of a lot more relaxed than she did yesterday."

"I bet she is." Then she walks out.

In the bathroom, I stand in front of the mirror, staring at my reflection and looking for the "I don't care" in my eyes. I don't see it. I'm not sure I want to. Being present isn't so bad. Christ, what is she doing to me?

I have always been intrigued by strong women. I can safely assume it's because of the lack of knowing any for most of my life. First, my mother, then Jesse and then every groupie who gave it up eagerly to get my attention, which is not at all as appealing as it may seem.

Keanna scares the hell out of me. She's strong, yet vulnerable and soft. She's seen shit that no one else has, yet she is still here.

I briefly question her sanity and then chuckle at myself. Who the fuck am I to question anything?

I'm just a drummer.

But before that, I was far worse off than I am now.

I hold my hand up and look at the scars, then make a fist, a tight fist, and swivel my wrist. It's tight, but after Keanna was messing with it last night, it felt looser, better.

I look at my eyes. They're clear, and so is my head for the first time in years.

I'm undecided whether I like it or hate it.

When I walk out of the bathroom, Keanna is back in my room, sitting on the floor next to Tink and petting her with one hand while flipping through her phone with the other.

"She okay?" I ask as I pull some clothes out of the dresser.

"She's fine, I guess. I just hope she didn't get …" She pauses and shakes her head.

"Get what?" I ask as I step into my jeans.

"Pregnant," she answers, closing her eyes and resting her head against the wall.

"Oh, shit, I never even thought about that." I throw my shirt on and sit on the other side of Tink.

"Neither did I, but Natasha did. Now I'm stressing."

"Don't they have the morning after pills for dogs?" I ask.

She looks over at me. "She is only a year old. I should have gotten her fixed. I just didn't think about it. And no, I'm not giving her any more drugs."

There is a knock on the door, and it opens.

"Timer thing is going off," Billy informs.

"Thank you." Keanna pushes up off the floor. "You wanna come out, Tink?"

She pushes up on all fours and follows Keanna.

I stand up and follow them to the kitchen where Keanna bends over to open the oven, taking out something … a fucking cake. She sets it on the counter, then looks up at me.

I can't help smiling as I point to myself.

"Hope you like chocolate."

"Fucking love chocolate." I lick my lips and wag my eyebrows at her.

She smiles and shakes her head, something she only seems to do at me.

"Frosting preference?"

"Your cum," I answer honestly.

She looks around, then looks relieved that no one heard me.

"What?"

"*What?*" she mocks, shaking her head once again. "Can I get a real answer?"

"I fucking love chocolate."

She nods, taking a deep breath. "Why don't you go and hang out with your friends and let me see what I can find in this big, old kitchen that clearly doesn't get used enough."

"Tales is coming over soon," Memphis shouts over. "If you need anything, she'll grab it." He stops and grins widely. "We're having fucking cake, man!"

"I can run to the store. I want to make you dinner."

"I wanna make *you* my dinner," I tell her, letting her know I'm a starving man.

She points to the cake. "This—" The oven alarm goes off again, and she opens it up before pulling out another cake. This one is a yellow cake. She sets it on a plate, then wipes her hands off. "I need to go to the store."

I stand up off the stool. "I'll go with you."

"No. Go and relax with your friends."

"I like my newest friend better." I pout, but she looks determined. I sigh, pouting my lip out even more. "Take my ride, then."

"The blowjob mobile?" she sneers, walking toward the door.

"My. New. Ride." I grab the keys off the hook and throw on a pair of shoes. "I'll start her up for you."

"I can take mine."

"It's my birthday. I want you to drive my—"

"Ride. Yeah, sure."

*****

After she leaves, I sit on the couch, and Billy and Memphis stop talking and stare at me. I try to ignore it and call to Tink, who sits at my feet and looks up at me.

"Fuck," I whisper, wondering what the hell is wrong with me. I pull her head on my lap and lean back.

"What's going on with you, man?" Memphis chuckles. "You've got a girl, a kid"—he points to Tink—"and do I hear wedding bells?"

Before I have a chance to answer, the gates of Hell open via the front door, and in blows Finn.

"Am I late?" He stomps his feet off, then walks over, plopping down on the couch opposite me.

"No, man, we haven't started yet," Billy says, pulling out his nerd pad, and sits back. "We have a tour schedule."

I start to stand, but Memphis clamps his paw on my leg. "You need to stay for this. It's our band, all four of us."

Finn's eyes lock on mine.

"What?" I bark.

"When are you gonna grow the hell up?" he snaps back.

"I don't know, oh, bearded wonder, maybe when I get a girl knocked up and have to."

"You motherfucker!" he snarls.

"Okay. Enough!" Billy yells. "You two need to fix this shit. Leave the past behind for the sake of this band."

I look at Billy and Memphis. "I say you stick with replacement sticks."

"Not the same," Finn grumbles, and I look at him. "He's good, but for the sake of the band, I'm willing to move forward."

"Just move forward." I chuckle darkly.

"Look, someone pointed out to me that—"

"Sonya," I interject.

"Yes, fucking Sonya," he snaps.

"So this is all for her? Nothing about the fact that I hid it all, marinated in the hell of knowing, and—"

"Don't wanna discuss it, River; you hear me? I'm moving forward. If you wanna continue soaking up the poison, feel free. I have a family now, a future, and—"

"I'm not saying I'm ready to come back, but if I have to sit through this, I don't wanna hear his fucking mouth."

"Bottom line, man," Memphis starts, looking at me, "you had enough love and respect for him to keep it all to yourself. It was your choice to do that. This is just a phase, so let's breeze past it. Everything will work out just fine."

A fucking phase, I think to myself.

The door opens, and X and Taelyn walk in.

"Sorry we're late. The roads were atrocious," Taelyn says as Xavier bends down to help her take off her boots. "Happy birthday, River!"

She steps out of both boots, then comes over and gives me a hug, handing me an envelope. She stands back, smiling from ear to ear.

"Come on; open it!"

I open the envelope and see the tour schedule. I look up at her and just stare.

"It's time."

I look at the guys, who are all looking at me.

"We need you; you need us. Let's go rock them the only way STD can ... with MFRB."

I look at Memphis, confused.

He explains, "Memphis, Finn, River, and Billy."

Xavier sits down next to me. "No other way. Your band brothers know it and so do you."

"You fuckers ambushed me via Taelyn on my *birthday*."

"Hell yes, we did." Memphis smirks. "We need the double peddle, peddler, the high hat humping, tom-tom tapping, fucking maniac with us."

I can't help chuckling at Memphis's asinine way with words. "I'm just a drummer, man. I'm just a drummer."

"There's something else in there," Taelyn redirects me to the envelope.

"More birthday joy?" I reply, rolling my eyes. I pull out a plane ticket to LA.

"We're going to California, leaving tomorrow, to make our very first STD video."

"You serious?" I ask.

"Hell yes, she's serious." Xavier grins widely. "We should've done that from day one, but shit happened so fast."

"Okay," I answer, and the whole room falls silent. "Give me a minute."

I stand up and walk into my room.

"Happy fucking birthday," I say to myself as I open the nightstand drawer and pull out the can. I pack it up and sit on the end of my bed, then hit the can twice before I feel the calm I crave.

Finn walks in my room and shuts the door behind him.

"Shit needs to stop, River."

"What?" I hit the can again.

"I'm not gonna pretend to know what the fuck goes on in your head, but Sonya said some shit that made sense, and I know you lost her, too."

"Easy for you, isn't it?"

"Nothing was fucking easy about Jesse. Nothing was easy about watching her get fucked up and looking completely empty and then trying to bring her back to reality."

"Maybe her reality was not something she could face, Finn. Maybe she needed to forget about her fucked up life. Maybe, instead of trying to fix her, you shouldn't have promised her she would be fucking fine. You should have tried to understand why the fuck she wasn't. Maybe, just maybe, her past, her pain needed to be totally forgotten in order for her to be happy."

"I was sixteen years old, thrown in foster care after watching my mother burn down the only home I ever knew."

I look up at him, not really wanting to see his tits that are apparently growing as a side-effect of *love*, but allowing him to speak.

"My mother was a meth head with no respect for her husband or her child. What the fuck did I know?"

"Not a damn thing." I point to the door. "You and I, we don't have heart to heart chats and expose our vaginas to one another. You and I jam and party. We're good-time friends, and you know what, man? Good-time friends are a dime a dozen. I don't need one. We work together; that's it."

He nods. "Well, just so you know, over the past few months, I have looked into your past, trying my best to excuse away your fuck ups, and there isn't shit, man: Jesse and a divorce; that's it. Move the fuck on."

"You don't know dick about me. And you have no fucking right to look into my past. Get the fuck out!" I scream.

The door swings open, and Keanna and Sonya walk in together.

"What is going on?" Keanna asks.

"He's an entitled prick," Finn hisses. "I tried, just like I promised, but he … He doesn't want to change. He's gonna kill himself."

I hear the impact of her hand meeting his face before I see it.

"You leave him alone!"

Holy fucking shit! She hit him!

She covers her mouth and looks at me, horrified.

"We're out," Finn says, taking Sonya's hand. "Because I don't hit bitches."

"Finn," Sonya scolds him.

Before the door shuts, I take her hands and hold them against my heart.

"I'm so sorry."

I don't say a word. I have no idea what to say.

She tries to pull away. "I'm gonna get going."

"Where are we going?"

"No, it's your birthday, and I just — "

"*My* birthday. I'll spend it the way I want. Where are we going?"

"No." She shakes her head, trying to pull away. "I had no right to do that. I had no right to — "

The door opens again, and Sonya walks in and shuts it behind her.

Keanna's eyes flood with tears. "I'm so, so sorry."

Sonya gives her a sad look and a kind nod, then looks at me. "It took a lot out of him to get to where he is right now and even more to open up to you, River. He did it because he wants the same for you. He wants you to heal."

"I don't need his forgiveness or understanding," I retort.

She sighs. "Maybe he needs yours." Then she looks at Keanna. "Offer still stands. If Tink needs a place to stay until you find a new place, we have plenty of room."

"The dog stays here."

Sonya looks back at me. "You're leaving tomorrow."

Fuck.

"She stays with the dog here."

Keanna looks at me and shakes her head while Sonya smiles, then turns and walks out the door.

"I can't stay here," Keanna gasps.

"Tink needs a place, and you need to be with her, so you stay here."

"River, I—"

"No. Just shut it down, turn it off, do whatever it takes to stop you from telling me no. It makes perfect sense. I'll be gone for a week. It'll give you time to look for a place and relax. It also has a kickass security system. You'll be safe."

"I need to leave," she says, shaking her head again.

"I need you to stay. I don't know why, but I really need it."

"I really need to know why," she says, stepping back.

Uncomfortable at the depth of this conversation, I look away. What the hell am I thinking?

"Okay," she finally concedes.

I can't help smiling at the small victory. I still don't know what the fucking game is, but I will take this win.

"One more birthday request?"

"Sure," she whispers, looking up at me.

"Give me those fucking lips."

Drunk and Irrational

"If I give you that, you have to trust me with more." I look up and see the hurt in his eyes. It penetrates my heart.

I close my eyes, contemplating what to say to make it better for him.

I feel his breath coming closer, and before I have a chance to change my mind, his low, husky voice whispers, "Open your eyes." His hands are on each side of my face, his thumbs stroking my jaw slowly, lightly, and intoxicatingly.

I force my eyes to open slowly because the heat I feel building in my toes, crawling up my body, is so incredibly hot I feel like I may be blinded by what I see.

"I've wanted this since seeing you in the doctor's office. I just didn't realize how damn badly until the other night. And now, Keanna—beautiful, sexy, Keanna—your lips are already like an addiction, and I haven't even gotten to them yet."

He runs his lips and tongue up my jaw as he angles my head, giving him better access to my flesh, flesh that is tingling in the wake of his kisses. My skin begs for his lips to return, but the untouched skin begs for it even more.

"River." My breath hitches.

"Shh," he whispers against my ear, his thumb tracing my lip. And then, eyes wide open, his beautifully full lips touch mine.

The connection is electric and magnetic. I can't pull away. I don't want to pull away.

He grips the nape of my neck and wraps his other arm around me, pulling me to him completely, while I place my hands on his hips, bracing myself for the inevitable fall.

I love and hate the feeling of the fall that comes with a kiss like this. Its wait is painful, its touch one hundred ten percent pleasurable, but the aftereffect is the shattering of one heart. It's horrible and wonderful. It's giving a part of you away that you will never get back and taking a promise that will ultimately be broken, yet deeper than any other sexual connection.

A kiss ultimately means more.

Dear god, what am I thinking?

I don't even want to be the stupid girl who's waiting and wanting more.

His tongue slowly traces the seam of my lips before slowly pushing in. His groan calls to my moan, his tongue stroking mine and mine his. Then his body shifts, and I feel his erection against my stomach. I shift, causing our bodies to connect, to become so close I feel like I am inside of him and he is inside of me.

The intensity builds slowly and then all at once as he takes both sides of my face in his hands again, and the kiss deepens. He again angles my head upward, and I grip his shoulders for fear I may fall. He then pushes me back against the wall, his knee between my legs. One hand leaves my face, and he shoves it down the front of the sweatpants.

"River," I gasp as his forehead touches mine.

He stalls momentarily, and I search his eyes for something ... more, but I don't know what.

"I'm ... I'm."

"Soaked," he growls as his fingers find evidence of exactly what his kiss has done to me. "Fucking hot."

Embarrassed and on edge, I rest my forehead on his shoulder as his finger slowly enters me. I thrust my hips forward unintentionally, and he pushes his knee up snugly against me as he drags his finger out of my pussy, grips my hips, and rocks me on his knee.

"Don't," I beg, but his mouth covers mine, his tongue shoving in without permission as he continues rocking my hips against him until I feel my orgasm coming strong. Then he pulls back, panting, and looks into my eyes.

"Take it, babe. Fucking take it," he demands.

I wrap my arms around his shoulders and hold him tightly as I come, riding his knee.

One knock on the door and it opens.

"Dude, come on," Memphis yells in and then I hear the door shut behind him.

"I'm gonna start locking that fucking door," River whispers in my ear before grabbing my face and kissing me quickly, then rubbing his lips across my forehead. "Best birthday present ever."

"How was that a gift for you?" I ask, leaning back against the wall.

"You gave me something I've been craving, and it more than exceeded any expectation I had. Perfect."

He looks down, and I close my eyes. Then I hear him laugh, and I look up, embarrassed and uncomfortable.

"Oh, no, you don't." He chuckles.

"Don't, what?"

"Get all stuck in your head. You may have come without my dick or mouth on you, but you weren't alone. I fucking came in my pants."

I look down and gasp. "Oh, my god."

"Hey, don't look at me like that. It was all your fault." He kisses me hard again, then steps back. "I've gotta get cleaned up." He steps away, then turns back. His brows furrow as he shakes his head and motions between us. "What the fuck is this?"

"Friends," I answer weakly.

He gives one nod, then turns around and walks into the bathroom.

I immediately straighten myself up the best I can before walking out of his room, unsure if it would be more awkward to face his friends or him. Right now, I choose his friends.

"I'm Taelyn," the redhead from Natasha's office says, walking briskly over to me with her hand outstretched.

I shake her hand. "I remember you."

"It's so nice to see you again," she says with a little bit too much excitement and emphasis on the "again."

"You, too." I smile, watching her look at me, appraising me.

"So you—"

"Have a cake to finish," I say, which makes her laugh. "Sorry, I hate how awkward this is."

"You need help?" Sonya asks. I am surprised she's still here.

"I'm sorry," I say, looking away. "I ... um ... I've got it." I hurry toward the kitchen and open the fridge.

Billy comes over. "Let me know what you need."

"Meat tenderizer, cutting board, sauce pan."

He puts his hand on my shoulder, and I look at him.

He smiles. "How about a drink?"

"How about two?" I smile back.

After grabbing me all the things I asked for, he walks away.

I feel eyes on me, and I hate it. I glance up once and make eye contact with Finn, the man I slapped in the face. He doesn't look away, doesn't look angry, doesn't look anything, but I know he is trying to figure me out. And hell, if he can shine some light on what is going on with me, I'd thank him.

Billy walks out and sets a glass of wine on the counter in front of me, and I thank him before taking the chicken breasts out and I begin to tenderize them with complete focus. I have such focus that I don't see River walks out until he is standing beside me, and I feel the weight of his eyes on me.

"River."

"Keanna." A pause. "Can I help you?"

"You can go" — I point to the living room — "and hang out with them and let me get to work."

"What are you making?" He leans forward and places his elbows on the counter. "Besides me hard again."

I look up, hoping no one is looking at us, and he laughs before walking away.

I turn the stovetop on to boil the water for the pasta, which keeps my eyes focused away from the group of men and women in the living room who are surely wondering what the hell I am still doing here. Hell, I'm wondering what I'm doing here and why he wants me here. I want to be his friend; I want him to trust me, but for what?

Out of the corner of my eye, I see River squat down and pet Tinker Bell. Her tail thumps on the ground a few times, and I feel immediate guilt about leaving her here and about staying with her last night instead of leaving.

River then moves and sits next to Taelyn, who is smirking at him as he whispers something in her ear, making her laugh. I am suddenly jealous of their interaction with him.

Jealousy is an emotion, a feeling I despise. It weakens us, makes us feel less than. I'm not less than.

I am thankful the water is rumbling behind me so that I can turn around.

I put the pasta in the boiling water, then go back to tenderizing the chicken breasts, breading them and frying them for just a few seconds.

When the pasta is done, I use the strainer that Billy set out for me. I have a hunch that he does most of the cooking around here. He seems like a great guy.

When the Chicken Parmesan is in the oven, I'm setting out to frost the cake when Sonya walks in with Memphis's girl they call Tales. They both grab the ingredients to make the Caesar salad while I busy myself with the cake, hoping the idea in my head actually ends up being the final project.

"Are you making a drum?" Tales asks with a sweet smile.

I glance up and smile back. "I'm trying."

"The drumsticks?" Sonya asks.

"I still need to get those done. Thank you for the reminder."

"I put the bag in Finn's old room, right next to River's. We can make sure he doesn't see you slip in there," she tells me sweetly.

"I appreciate it." I see Sonya filling my glass and shake my head. "Thank you."

"Trust me; I'd be joining you if I wasn't pregnant."

I look up at her. "You're pregnant? I mean, I thought maybe, but you aren't showing."

"Lucky, I guess. The baby is due at the end of July."

"Finn's baby?" I ask, and she nods. "The man I —"

"Yes." She chuckles then jokes, "He's still here, isn't he?"

"He must hate me," I mutter as I spread the frosting on the vanilla layer of the cake.

"Not at all, and neither do I. River's never had a female … um … hang out for very long," she whispers.

"Well, I think River and I are gonna be good friends."

"I hope so," Tales says, rolling her eyes. "God, the women they attract are complete and total sleazebags."

I can't help snickering. "So what does that make them?"

Tales giggles. "Reformed man-whores."

"It takes a strong woman to end up with one of these guys." I look up to see Taelyn sitting down across the island from me. "I just hope you like him as much as he seems to like you."

"We're friends," I comment, looking away briefly.

"Perfect. That's a good place to start," Taelyn quips.

Start? What makes her think this is anything more than a friendship or a fling?

I look down at my cute, little drum cake and write River's name in script below *Happy Birthday*. Then I set it to the side, and all three swoon over it. I laugh, thanking them, and then ask Sonya which room is Finn's.

Once inside, I get to work on the sticks I bought to add the finishing touch to his cake.

When I walk out, River spots me. "You done, Betty?"

I nod and smile.

"Good. Come and chill."

He has obviously had a couple drinks, probably smoked some while in his room, but he looks relaxed and happy, so who am I to judge a friend?

When dinner is over and the table is cleaned off, River, Memphis, Finn, Billy, Xavier, and their women are still at the table, talking about the tour. I'm thankful Sonya went to the store with me, or I wouldn't have known more people were coming. River isn't saying much. It's clear that both Tales and Sonya, whom some of them call Yaya, work for the band; both will be traveling to California with them.

River's phone rings, but he hits ignore. It's the third time he's done it.

"Dude, is that your mom?" Memphis asks.

He shrugs. "Yeah."

I can't help giving his knee a squeeze under the table. He doesn't even look at me, though.

"She's called, like, a hundred times."

"So?" he says.

Memphis grins. "Well, she did push you out of her snatch."

"For fuck's sake, Memphis," Xavier groans, running his hand through his hair. "Seriously, he mellows out, and you just keep getting more out of control."

Feeling a little insecure about River completely ignoring my gesture, I stand up to get the cake. Feeling more insecure, I stick the drumsticks into the cake that I decorated like a sixteen-year-old girl crushing on her favorite drummer.

"I've got the ice cream," Sonya speaks up from behind me.

"Thank you."

After putting the candles in the cake, we walk over to River, and Memphis, the band's front man, starts singing, "Come as you are, as you were / As I want you to be." The rest of them continue singing the Nirvana song. It's not an uplifting song, but the grin that creeps up on his face tells me he likes it a lot.

I set the cake in front of River, and he looks up and smiles. It's a much different smile, a shyer smile than he gave the others while they sang.

He mouths, "*Thank you*," then closes his eyes and blows out the candles.

He pulls out the drumsticks and reads them aloud. "*I'm just a drummer*" — he shakes his head — "*one who holds it all together.*"

Everyone laughs, including him, but I don't. I know that's the drummer's job, and whether he believes it or not, tonight makes it apparent. The band knows they can't do it without him.

When he blew out his candles, I made a wish for him. The wish was for him to see the value he holds.

He pulls out the other stick and reads it. "*I don't take orders; I don't follow rules; and I —* "

I reach out and cover his mouth without even thinking, and he pulls my hand away.

"What?"

Memphis snorts. "Oh, come on; now we have to hear it."

I close my eyes and wait for it.

"Nah." River laughs, and I open my eyes, shocked. "This is mine." He nips at my hand. "All. Fucking. Mine."

He then gets up quickly and walks to his room, drumsticks in hand, and when he comes back out just as quickly, they aren't with him.

Relief rolls over me. I give him a smile that I know is exaggerated because of the amount of wine I drank. Then I nod and cut the cake while Sonya begins to scoop the ice cream.

As soon as the cake is eaten, everyone leaves to pack for their trip.

Tomorrow, at noon, Steel Total Destruction hits LA to make their first music video.

I have a killer buzz and am completely exhausted, so I excuse myself and start to go to his room, but he catches my hips from behind.

"We need to take a ride."

"What? To where?"

He turns me around and kisses me with a quick peck, "Your place to pack some bags." Then he kisses me with something more urgent.

"We've been drinking," I remind him.

"Billy hasn't, and he's gonna drive."

"I can go in the morning before —"

"No. Nope. Fuck that. Miguel got to you there, and that's not gonna fucking happen again." His thumb rubs over my cheek. "Not while I'm here and certainly not while I'm gone." He reaches behind me and squeezes my ass. "You feel me?"

I nod, that stupid drunk girl grin making another appearance. "Okay."

"That's right it's okay," he says, narrowing his eyes. "Because I'm just a drummer."

"You're a good man." I nod to him.

He closes his eyes, shakes his head, and looks up. "No. No, I'm not."

"Right. You're awful, you're a horrible lay, and you can't kiss for beans." I tick off my fingers.

His eyes fly open. He looks pissed then starts laughing a deep, dark laugh, taking my hand. "Billy, let's roll."

"Now?"

"Hell, yes. I have something that's gonna need my attention as soon as the packing is done."

"Practice?" Billy asks hopefully.

I can't help giggling when River tugs my hand sharply.

"No need to practice what's already fucking perfect."

Outside at the car, River gets in the back seat.

"What do I look like, a chauffeur?" Billy grins.

"Just turn up the tunes and drive, man. It's my motherfucking birthday," River jokes.

I laugh until his eyes turn to me.

"You should not be laughing, young lady. I am gonna put a hurt on your pussy, making it impossible for you to walk without thinking I'm still all up in there while I'm gone. Hell, I might even fuck you so hard you'll be begging me to stay away when I come back for you. And, Keanna, I don't make idle threats or promises I can't keep. Fuck, I don't make promises at all, but I just did, so make no mistake, I'm fucking you tonight ... my way."

I have no words. All I can do is form an O with my mouth.

He laughs as he sits back and leans his head against the headrest.

*****

We walk out of the apartment to find Aaron, the manager, standing there.

He hands me an envelope. "A bill ... from my doctor."

River drops the two bags in his hands and grabs the envelope before I can, crinkling it up and pushing it toward him. "Open your fucking mouth."

"Aw, for fuck's sake," Billy grumbles, dropping the bags he is carrying.

"I said, open your motherfucking mouth!"

"Let's go!" Billy hands River the bags he dropped.

"You're lucky it's not me and you alone in a fucking alley," River sneers. "Consider this notice: she won't be back."

"What about her stuff, the keys?" Aaron calls after us as we walk away.

"It will be taken care of," Billy answers.

"You have ten days," he calls out.

"Okay, Aaron," I finally say. "Okay."

"Don't you ever cower," River orders as he wraps his arm around me after hefting two bags into the trunk. "Confidence is so fucking sexy on you. Keeps the bad guys away."

"I'm strong," I defend myself. "But you make me feel — "

He stops and spins me around to face him. "I make you feel like what?"

When I don't answer, because I know better than to allow that feeling to seep in, he shakes me.

"I make you feel like fucking what, Keanna?!"

His behavior is irrational, and I am tipsy, so I step back too fast and trip.

Billy catches me. "Easy, River."

"Get your fucking hands off her," he snarls at him, then turns to me. "I make you feel like what?!"

Billy grabs my arm and pushes me gently toward the vehicle. He opens the passenger side door and orders, "Get in."

I do, watching as River walks around in circles, sputtering. I can't hear what he is saying, but I see Billy grab his collar and shake him. Then River grabs his.

I feel overwhelmed and drunk, and I am so mad at myself. I feel tears fill my eyes, and I will them away. At least, I think I do. I cover my face when the back hatch gets opened and the lights in the vehicle come on.

"You don't need to step in between anything I ever have going on. You understand, Billy?!"

"You don't need to fuck up something that could be a damn good thing in your life, River."

"Good things don't happen to bad boys," he retorts.

As the door shuts, the teardrops fall.

How the hell did I let all this happen?

FRIENDSHIP, FLING, OR FUCK

I focus on the beat I'm playing on the leather seat. I am pissed. I want to know what exactly it is I make her feel like, but Billy had to butt in.

I stare out the window, avoiding looking at her. I can't anymore, anyway. Her face is covered and shoulders slumped forward. Why? What the hell happened?

Not a word is said the entire way back to the house. When we pull in, Billy hops out and grabs a couple bags.

When Keanna gets out, she tells him that she'll get them, whispering that she is going to put them in her car.

I am amped up, drunk, and slightly stoned, so I grab her, throw her over my shoulder, and carry her inside with Billy telling me what an asshole I am the entire time.

She doesn't say shit; she doesn't try to escape.

Once inside, I set her on her feet and brace for her to blow up at me.

She doesn't. She simply walks past me, taking bear-dog's leash off the coat rack and attaching it to her collar before taking her out through the dining area patio door.

"You gonna make that right?" Billy snaps at me.

I ignore him, grabbing her bags from his hand and walking them into my room. Then I go outside and grab the rest of her shit that Billy doesn't already have in his hands and shove it in my room before snatching the ones he carries in and throwing them in my room, too.

"You think you can handle yourself?" he snaps.

"I got hot and ready pussy. The only one who will be handling themselves is you!"

"Nice, River." He shakes his head and walks toward his room.

When the door opens and she and Tink walk in, she scowls at me as she calls out, "Thank you, Billy."

"Anytime, Keanna, anytime." He closes his bedroom door.

I walk over and unleash Tink. She takes the leash and hangs it up, not saying shit to me as she walks right by, opens the bedroom door, and snaps her fingers.

Tink walks in, and she shuts my bedroom door behind her. Then I hear a click.

"Aw, fuck no. Fuck. No."

I walk over and try the door. Yep, it's locked. I bang on it a few times, but she doesn't open it. I bang harder, and then I hear her unlock the door. She opens it just a crack and looks up at me.

"Two words; that's all I want from you right now," she snaps with a very pissed off expression on her face.

"Get. Naked," I smart back with a level of pissed off that matches hers.

"Try again." Ooo, she is full of anger.

"I'm gonna fu—"

"Two words, River James. Two. And you better make them count." She is talking to me like I'm a fucking child.

"You better think about—" I stop when the door shuts in my face, and I hear the click of the lock again. "You better fucking think about this, Keanna!" I kick the door. "I could fucking break this door down."

"But you won't!" she yells back.

"Tell me not to," I dare.

"You won't," she says more quietly.

I turn around and nudge it with my back. I want to kick it in, punch it in. I want in my fucking room!

I slide down the door and sit on my ass against it. I want to, but I won't, because a light bulb goes off in my head.

"I'm fucking sorry!"

The door opens, and I fall back, flat on the ground.

"That was three, but it'll work."

I sit up. "You fucking kidding me?"

She gives me a look that says she isn't. Then she turns and climbs up in the bed. She rolls to her side, her back toward me.

I shut the door, and yes, I fucking lock it. Then I strip naked, walk around the bed, open the nightstand, and grab the can.

She looks up at me and sighs as she sits up. "Please, just don't. Just don't tonight. You'll be gone for a week and tonight …" She stops, shrugs her shoulders, and looks up at me. "Just don't."

"Then you tell me what I make you feel," I snap.

187

She closes her eyes, lifts her chin up, and whispers, "You make me feel weak."

I don't know what to say. If I say what I'm thinking, I am bound to get booted out of my own damn bedroom again by a woman who's usually confident. Then there is the way she carries herself, the way she loves that damn bear-dog, and the way she has been a friend to me, not because I'm River James the drummer, but because, for some fucked up reason, she likes me.

I set the can down and sit next to her on the bed.

Her posture is unchanged and exuding a false confidence that I still find sexy.

"If I tell you it sickens me to hear that because there is nothing, and I mean nothing, I find sexier than a confident, strong woman, I will hurt you and push you away. If I tell you that, for some reason, that makes me astoundingly happy, I'm an asshole because it gives me the fucked up feeling that you actually trust me. But fuck it; I feel both," I tell her, looking down.

"It sickens me," she admits, a small smile crossing her lips briefly. "I was never gonna allow that to happen again."

In that sad smile, I see more than I deserve to see, more than I can handle seeing. I need to make it go the fuck away. I look at the clock. Eleven ten p.m.

"It's still my birthday. Either I get high on weed, or I get high on you." I'm hoping for the latter, so I immediately take her face in my hands and kiss her hard.

"This is a bad idea," she says on a whimper when I finally pull back, giving her less than half a second to either say fuck off and die or allow it to happen.

"It may be a bad idea, but it's gonna be one hell of a good time," I say before lifting the shirt.

She lifts up her arms, and I pull it off. Immediately, my mouth covers her dark brown nipples, sucking, pulling, tugging with my teeth. Her back arches, pushing against me, her hands gripping the back of my head and pulling me in even closer. I push her back so she is lying on the bed, then pull the sweats off, exposing her bare pussy.

I fuck my way, and right now, I need it. She does, too.

Once I pull her back up and onto my lap, she wraps her legs around me as I reach between us and drag my cock slowly up and down her wet pussy, coating it with her need. Then she inches closer, and I push forward inside her hot, little cunt that hugs me tight.

"Fuck … yes," I hiss, right before ramming it fully inside her.

I lean back, wanting to see her when she is still breathless and full of my cock. Then I lean forward and lick my lips before pulling her nipple into my mouth while pinching the other between my fingers and thrusting in and out of her pussy.

My mouth can't get enough; my fingers can't, either, and my cock is aching to go off, but that's not the way I roll. Therefore, I flip her on her back, still fully inside her, and pull her to the edge of the bed where I step off it as I raise one leg up to my shoulder.

"I love the way your cunt looks around my cock," I grunt as I push in her hard. "Black." I trace her outer lips with my finger, then suck the juices off. "Pink." I trace my finger around her inner lips and hood, then push my finger in her mouth, hooking it as she sucks fiercely on it. "White," I groan as I thrust in and out over and over as hard and deep as I can possibly go. "Fucking art," I moan out as I continue fucking her hard and fast, listening to her pleasure-filled cries and watching my dick move in and out of the pussy I batter, keeping a promise to a girl and to myself that she is going to feel me. All. Week. Long.

I pull out fully, then push in harshly until her eyes roll back in her head. I do it again and again and again until she comes, her pussy clenching and quaking around me as she cries out my name.

I still and close my eyes, trying to control the raging need to come inside her, but I'm nowhere near being done.

When her eyes flutter open, I look into them. "I just rocked your fucking world."

She nods slowly.

"Now roll the fuck over so I can make good on my promise to shatter it."

Her eyes widen and her lips part, but she doesn't move, so I roll her over and thrust in hard, knocking the wind out of her. I grip her hips and pull her back until her feet touch the floor, and then I kick them wider apart.

I grab her ass and squeeze. "I fucking love this ass." I spread it wide and thrust as my thumb brushes over her tight, little hole.

She looks back at me over her shoulder, her eyes widening as I continue applying pressure with my thumb.

"Tell me no."

She arches her ass up, telling me the total opposite of no non-verbally.

I stop and pound away at her pussy savagely, calling her to come again. Then I pull out quickly, knowing I am going to come if I don't, but I'm not that much of a dick that I want to leave her hanging, which is a first for me.

I shove two fingers in hard, rotating my wrist so I can thumb her clit, allowing her to fall apart on my hand.

Her face sinks into the mattress as she pants.

I love how she looks after she comes.

Satisfied.

I love how she looks with my cock in her pussy.

Sated.

She almost catches her breath when I stop fingering her.

I watch as she sinks farther into the mattress, so relaxed.

Unsuspecting.

She thinks she's done.

Not even fucking close.

I push my cock in again, harder this time.

"Christ, River," she gasps.

"No, babe, not even fucking close."

I wrap my hands around her hair and pull her up, forcing my cock even farther inside.

She gasps and looks at me over her shoulder. "River," she whimpers.

"Your pussy is soaked and hot, and my cock is almost bursting apart because I need to come so fucking badly it almost hurts. My balls are achingly tight, and this, Keanna, my strong, sexy siren"—I thrust in hard as I tighten my grip on her hair—"is just beginning."

"I can't," she gasps.

"Lucky for you, I fucking can, and I will."

"Oh, god," she cries as I fuck her hard and wild.

I can feel her knees shaking, threatening to give out, so I slap her ass hard, then squeeze.

"Stay right the fuck here with me, Keanna. Be my high."

"Yes," she cries as I batter her twat some more. "Oh, god, yes."

It's after midnight, and she is still bent over my bed. I let her rest with her face in the mattress, my dick still in her pussy.

"I've come in your pussy. I want that ass this time," I growl as my fascination with her tight, little, puckered hole grows.

She mumbles something inaudible as I slowly pull out, dragging my cock up and down her seam, lubricating her with her pussy juices.

"Tell me no," I command as I push the tip of my finger in her ass and plunge my cock in her pussy again.

She doesn't say shit but my name.

I let the saliva fall from my mouth onto her ass, and then I pull out, not wanting to come yet, and dip my head down.

"I'm craving the taste of your pussy," I tell her right before running my tongue up and down her seam the entire way.

"River ..." Her cheeks clench, but I pull them apart. "You shouldn't."

I lap at her. "Tell me no," I growl as my tongue taps against her hole.

"It's ... just not right," she gasps.

"I've eaten chicken nuggets before, babe. This right here" — I lick around her — "is pretty fucking okay."

"Dear god," she mumbles, her back arching.

She's fully relaxed.

"Ever done this before?"

"No," she pants.

"Fuck. Me." I lick her more harshly.

Need — nothing but need to be the first consumes me. Her body language tells me unequivocally she wants it.

"Tell me no," I repeat.

"I can't!" she cries into the duvet.

I line up the head of my cock to her ass, then warn her one more time, "Tell me don't."

"I won't." She pushes against me.

I pause because there can be no mistaken communication here, not with her.

"Get high on me, River. Take me with you."

"Thank the fucking stars," I hiss as I push against her, into her.

I stop when I feel her body clench. Then she lifts on her elbows and looks back at me. When I rock in a little more, her mouth opens slightly, and her eyes flutter, yet don't close.

"Fuck," I groan as I feel the fire building in my balls.

I reach in front of her and rub her clit, tap it, and then press it down. I want this to be good for her. I want it to be so fucking good.

When she cries out, I go all in.

"Oh, my god," comes out in a moan as I push in all the way, needing to be deep inside when my cum spurts off inside her.

"*Fuck!*" I growl when it does.

I lean over in relief and push my face between her shoulders.

"You good?" I pant as I drag my lips across her skin.

"Um, yeah ... Yeah, I'm good." She sounds unsure. I don't like that one bit.

"Lips. Gimme."

I kiss her softly because she deserves that after what she just gave up ... to me.

I pull out slowly as I kiss her even more slowly.

"Incredible," I sigh as I roll to my back and look at her.

She nods and gets up, dragging the blanket with her as she walks into the bathroom.

When she comes out, I stand up and walk over, kiss her forehead, and point to the bathroom. "Be right back."

I take a quick shower, washing my hair, my face, my dick — twice. Fuck, I already want more. When I come out, she is already sound asleep.

I lie down next to her and pull her onto me.

"I have five hours before I have to be up." She whines.

"You can sleep after work all damn week, right here while I'm gone. Tonight, I need to make you come ... all night long."

She nods and lays her head on my chest.

My dick is hard. She smells good, and I know she tastes even better than she smells. She's also exhausted and a nurse who has to help people and shit. All I have to do is get up, get on a plane, and sleep for at least six hours.

I look at my clock. It's almost one in the morning. Birthday is over. Best one yet.

I'm so fucking tired, but I need to smoke. Yet I don't want to get up, don't want to move her, or wake her. I will give it five minutes.

What happened?

I wake again to soft whimpers and small movement.

"Get the fuck off me," he mumbles. "No. Don't. No."

He mumbles as he thrashes under the covers, just like the last time. I don't want the same thing to happen, and I know I should leave him alone, but it doesn't hurt my heart anymore, not after three nights of assuming what I see so clearly now. It wrecks me.

"River." I grab his hand and squeeze. "River, wake up. Please wake up."

As his eyes open, he looks shocked, stunned, and then angry.

In my state of exhaustion, I plead with him, "Don't do that, not after tonight."

He closes his eyes tightly, and I lean over and kiss him. I kiss him hard like he kisses me. I rub my tongue against his lips and hear a groan. Then I kiss down his neck, across his chest, down his side, and from hip to hip.

In the moonlight, I see the tree tattoo, and I kiss it, as well, all the way up and all the way down to the roots.

He draws in a sharp breath as if I may have injured him, but I know it was not me who did this to him. It was not me who causes him pain. And it is not my responsibility to take it away, either. Regardless, I can't help myself.

Before gripping the base of his cock and licking up the underside of it, I run my tongue around his wide head, then flick across it. His hand grips my hair almost painfully as I wet my lips and slide my mouth down him.

His hips thrust forward, and I nearly choke, but I don't care. I willingly allow him to take what he wants.

He guides my head up and down, up and down, faster, deeper, harder. When I pull away, he hisses, but then I grip his base and stroke him up and down as his grip on my hair loosens. Still, his thrusts don't become any less harsh.

I suck, hollowing my cheeks, and he thrusts as our rhythm syncs. He then reaches behind me, stroking me with his finger as I stroke him with my hand. His hips thrust, and mine grind against his touch. He pushes his finger inside, and I take him as far as I can until I nearly gag myself.

I feel another finger. He is now sitting up, pushing in farther and thrusting faster, and then I feel it—the burn.

His thumb presses against my clit, and I come, crying out. He pushes my head down, his cock deep in my throat, and then he comes in my mouth.

When he pulls his hand away and lies back down, I continue sucking until I no longer feel the hot jets of his cum going off. Then I lick him clean and kiss him gently over and over until the waves of sensation stop rippling between my legs, and his breath evens out.

I lie my head across his stomach, his cock still in my hand, and try to steady my breathing.

Without notice, I feel tears burning my eyes. Unfortunately, he feels them, too.

"Are you crying?" he asks, pulling me up and taking my face in his hands.

"No," I lie.

He wipes away my tears and pulls me securely against him, holding me closer than he did the night before. "Why?"

"I don't know."

"Bullshit, Keanna. Why?"

"Whoever ... Whoever hurt you —"

"Don't," he half-growls, half-pleas.

"I hate them. I hate them for hurting you. I hate Jesse, and I hate ..." I stop because I can't think of what he called him in his sleep. Then I remember. "I hate Henry."

He doesn't let go, but his body tenses up. I feel something shift.

"Don't ever say that name again."

"River —"

"Don't, Keanna. Just don't."

"You need to talk about it."

"To whom? The woman my cum has filled every orifice of? To the girl I wanna feel strong for?"

"If you don't feel comfortable talking to me, then —"

"Then, what?! Talk to my ex-best friend?! A shrink?!"

"Please, River, please don't push me away." I sit up as he slides out from under me. "I already know. I have heard your cries. Your pain has torn me up inside. It made me stay when I should have left a hundred times."

"That's fucking great. That's just fucking great. So what was that, a pity blow job?" he huffs. "Was earlier pity anal?! I'm not your fucking problem, Keanna."

"You're my friend."

"Is that so?" he huffs as he pulls on a pair of sweats. "How many friends have come in your ass and mouth? You know what? I don't wanna fucking know." He grabs a pillow and starts toward the door.

"Please don't," I practically beg.

"Have a nice week, Keanna." He walks out the door, shutting it behind him.

I wipe the tears, now flowing down my face and look at the clock. It's four-thirty in the morning. I can't go to Natasha's now, but I can't stay here, either. What choice do I have, though?

*****

At six-thirty in the morning, I stand at the door, trying to muster up enough courage to walk out and face him. Instead, I close my eyes and lay my head against the door.

I feel like shit, I'm exhausted, and the bags under my eyes are evidence of the weekend I had.

River made good on his promise. My body feels bruised inside and out, and not just the parts he physically touched. My heart is bruised, too.

Finally, I open the door, lift my chin, and walk out.

Billy is standing at the counter. He pushes a cup of coffee toward me. "Roadie."

"I appreciate it."

I glance around, then and see River in a corner. His eyes are dark, and not just the pupils; around them, they look dark, too. He looks at me expressionless, and I immediately see something recognizable in them.

I look back at Billy, who shakes his head.

"He's-he's ...?"

"Messed up?" He nods. "Pretty badly, too."

Controlling myself is no longer even an option. I storm toward River, place both hands on the chair's arms, and look him square in the eyes.

"Look at me," I snap, unable to control my rage. "Look. At. Me!"

He doesn't move.

"What did you do?!"

"Keanna," Billy says quietly from behind me.

"What did he do?!" I am shaking when I look at Billy.

"He did what River always does. He got fucked up, and no one knows on what."

I turn back and face River. "You selfish, self-centered fool! Does no one matter but you?" I want to hit him. "Answer me, dammit!"

"Fuck. You," is all he says in a forced voice.

"No. Nuh-uh, fuck *you*. Fuck you, River James! Fuck. You!"

Billy grabs me from behind and holds me back.

"Fuck you!" I pull myself free and turn to Billy. "When he comes out of this, *if* he comes out of this, tell him the girl who once was his friend is no longer. I will not watch another person I care about kill themselves. I will not!"

"I'm so sorry, Keanna," Billy whispers, guilt in his eyes.

I take a few deep breaths and push away the tears. "I can't be late for my first day at my new job. I'll grab Tink when I'm done." I bat away a few tears that manage to spill. "Get him some help. Please, get him some help."

"I'll let you know when he—"

"No. No, I don't wanna know. I don't wanna know anymore." I turn and look at River again. "I let you get high on me, and I wasn't enough. I am fucking strong, and this"—I point between us—"friendship or fling is over."

*****

After working eight hours and picking up Tink and her things from the beach house, I knock on Natasha's door.

When she opens it, I smile. "Want a couple guests?"

"I thought—"

"Plans change, and I really don't wanna talk about it, Natasha, because I have gone nine hours and forty-five minutes holding myself together like a trooper. I'm gonna make sure Jordan gets the same smiling Auntie Keanna as he always gets, and then, as soon as he's asleep, I am gonna curl up in your spare bedroom bed and cry myself to sleep. When I wake up, I don't ever wanna talk about it again."

Understanding seeps through her expression, and she nods. Half a second later, Jordan is dragging me to his room to show me all the new cars he got for Christmas. I sit next to him on the floor for an hour, holding a large, red, plastic bin from his shelf, handing him one car at a time as he lines them up, row after row, sorted by style and color.

When Natasha calls him for dinner, he jumps up. "Let's go, Keanna."

I go through the motions, pushing my meal around my plate, listening to Jordan talk about school, and watching Natasha try her best to act like she is unaffected by me.

After Jordan eats, we watch TV, snuggled up on the couch. Then he takes a bath and finally goes to bed. It seems thoughtless of me to think that, but considering the day's events, I let myself off the hook.

"You wanna talk?" Natasha asks, leaning into the spare room.

I look at her and smile, albeit forced, but she seems to understand. She is understanding. She's Natasha.

"Not now, maybe not ever, but I hope you know I'm grateful you're in my life." My voice cracks.

She holds her hand to her chest as if she can feel my pain. "I wish you would talk to me. It helps, you know." Before I have a chance to say anything, she holds up her finger. "One sec. I let Tinker Bell outside; let me let her in."

In a flash, she is gone, and before I have time to come up with an excuse not to talk, she is back.

Seeing Tink bound into the bedroom and jump on the spare bed without an invitation does me in.

I am crying again and hugging her tightly around her neck.

Natasha sits on the other side of her and pets her as she says, "Talk to me, Keanna."

"I am a shitty dog mom," I sob out after not so carefully considering what I'm going to say.

"No, it wasn't your fault that she has a nose for … marijuana." The ways she says it makes me laugh. Then she laughs.

I am crying and laughing, and Natasha looks wigged out for about two seconds.

"That's only the half of it," I tell her, looking over Tink's head at her.

"Oh, okay?"

And then I just can't stop the words from falling out at mach ten.

"I should have taken Tink to the vet. I mean, she is my responsibility. What if she died? What if she died and I could have stopped it, but was so ... stupid? Who believes a bunch of rock stars who use Google as a way to research the effect pot has on a dog? I'm a fucking nurse; I know better. I know—"

"Typically, people ingesting pot plants don't get high. It's the heat that triggers—"

"I don't need you to make me feel better, Natasha. I was wrong. And to top it off, the next morning ... The next morning, I let her out to go to the bathroom, and then—well, you were on the phone, so you know."

"No, not really. You hung up and—"

"See, I'm a shitty friend, too. I—"

"No, you're not." She chuckles softly. "But you can tell me now."

"Right. Well, I came in because he said he'd watch her. Here I am, thinking he was being sweet, and then ... Well, then when I hung up with you, I ran outside, and there was my sweet Tink getting nailed by a bastard's German Shepherd with a gangster name, named by a man who is fake blind, and River was gonna kick his ass. A blind man, Natasha! Who threatens a blind man?"

"Well, apparently he's faking blindness, and who the hell does *that*?" She shakes her head, suppressing a smile. "Back to Tink's, um ... you mean, like—"

"Fucked. Doggie style. And do you know dogs 'knot?' There was no way to break that up. Fucking males, all of them!" I stop and wipe my eyes. "So Tink got high and fucked at the ripe old age of one, because her mother is a bigger piece of shit than mine was. I mean, at least mine didn't have drugs lying around and get me raped. She just sat in a corner, drooling and staring at a wall until she just didn't wake up one day."

As soon as the words come out of my mouth, I cover it. I close my eyes, shielding myself from looking at Natasha who is shocked, stunned, and now aware of my past.

After a few quiet, awkward moments, she breaks the silence.

"My ex is in prison. There is no judgment here."

I look up at her and nod. "I know. God, I'm sorry."

"Don't be sorry. I mean, some people are given a million and one chances to get it right and fail. He was one of them. I was hoping River was not."

"I was so stupid. I mean, I was so ready to have just a fling, a fuck, a—"

"What happened?"

I look down. I can't tell her everything. I can't, because for some reason, I feel like it would be a betrayal. Therefore, I give her what I can, knowing she will know the significance of it.

"I kissed him."

GOING TO
CALIFORNIA

After Keanna leaves, Billy flips his shit on me. I let him go on and on for as long as I can handle before telling him to fuck off and walking into my room where I lie on the bed and can smell her on the pillows.

I immediately get up and tear the sheets from my bed, then flip the mattress off it. Then I lie on the box spring, face down, and fall asleep.

When I wake to my phone's alarm, I get up, shower, pack a bag, and walk out to the living room where the entire band, Nickie D, Taelyn, and Xavier stand, staring at me.

No one says shit.

I see Tink sitting on the couch, looking at me. I swear she is disappointed as hell, and that hurts worse than the thought of disappointing any of the people around me.

"Come." I snap my finger, and she hops down, following me outside.

Once I shut the door behind me, I squat down and pat her head. "She's a good girl, Tink, but she makes stupid choices, like trusting me to be able to take care of you. I mean, what the fuck was she thinking? I'm just a fucking drummer."

Tink looks the other way.

"Yeah, well, now that you're grown, you need to step up and take care of her. She thinks she's strong, but I'm pretty sure I did some damage." I look down at her as she gets up and walks off the porch and does her business. I grab the pooper-scooper that Billy or Keanna must have put out here, scoop up the shit, and toss it at the fucking deck next door.

I can't help laughing at myself when it lands on the last step at the neighbor's.

"Tink, did you see that? I bet that fucker sees it, too. Let's just hope he steps in it first."

I stay out there as she walks around, sniffing, while I am freezing my ass off.

When she comes back up the stairs, I squat down again. "I like you, Tink."

*****

Xavier and Taelyn are in the seats next to me on the plane. Xavier's mom, Josephina, her man, Thomas, and X and Taelyn's baby, Patrick, are in the row behind us. Nick, Billy, Memphis, Finn, Sonya, her kid, Noah, and Tales are close by, too.

I have slept off and on the entire non-stop flight from Newark. When I couldn't sleep, I pretended to be.

I heard them talking about me more than once. None said shit to my face, though, and it's a good thing. I'm not in the fucking mood. Billy is lucky he didn't get a fist in the face this morning. He's lucky I was too *fucked up*.

As we circle the runway at LAX and wait for our turn to land, I watch the clouds, envying them. That type of high—to feel nothing, think nothing, be ... nothing but air and tiny droplets of water and ice floating high above the earth, hurt by and hurting nothing ... that kind of high would be the ultimate.

There are many other types of highs. Some good, like my favorite--the suppression of anxiety and anger—are basically an escape from the past, present, and future. They're what I have chased for years. Then highs are followed by lows. Sometimes, you come down nice and easy. Other times, you feel like you dropped ten stories face first onto cement, and nothing can take away the pain ... except for your next high.

Allowing yourself to get high comes with risks. Death is a risk, which usually makes people decide to "Just say no."

The fear of death never made me even hesitate to smoke something, take a pill, and in the darkest of days, shoot shit in my veins. This morning's high, though, scared the hell out of me. For the first time since I was in that shitty-ass trailer where I met Jesse, I am determined to try to stay away from getting that high ever again.

The plane slowly descends, and as quickly as it does, the reality of the low settles in the pit of my stomach.

As soon as we walk out through the security gates, it's like a scene from some fucking Hollywood evening news program. Except, we aren't celebrities, and this shit doesn't happen unless we are at a show.

Flashes come from all around us, and reporters ask us questions. I just pull my shades down over my eyes and pop my ear buds in my ears while the rest of my party scurries to get to the closest exit.

I take my time because fuck that hiding shit. I see their mouths move, asking questions, while the flashes continue to pop from the cameras as I walk through the ten to fifteen reporters and cameramen who have some serious fucking personal space issues, making me walk around them. Then I finally get outside where I see everyone loading into two SUVs.

Billy yells to me, "Let's roll!"

I'm heading toward him when I feel one of my ear buds pop out. I turn to see one of the cameramen pulling his hand back.

"You're lucky this is on tape, man, or I would fucking nail you in the face," I snap.

"Let's go, River!" Nick yells.

"You're the drummer for STD." A little, platinum blonde shoves a mic in my face.

"No, ma'am, I'm the ghost of Kurt Cobain." I turn, flipping them off as Nick pulls me into the SUV.

Once seated, I look around and almost get out. Finn, Memphis, Billy, Nick, and Xavier are all staring at me.

"I think I'd rather sit at the kiddy table." I reach for the door handle just as the SUV jets.

I sit back and close my eyes, but the combined weight of their stares is so heavy I can't ignore it.

"Welcome to Cali. Anyone have a smoke?"

"You stopped smoking," Billy points out. "After the accident, you quit."

"No, I didn't quit. I forgot. Now I need a damn cigarette. Have the driver stop and —"

"Why the fuck would you start again?" Memphis asks.

"Because he's an addict," Finn grumbles.

"And you're a fucking grease monkey's kid from bum-fuck, Ohio," I snap.

"Never tried to hide my past," he hisses.

"Let's talk about the dead girl, shall we?" I clap my hands together and sit forward. "I'm sure you've painted me as the piece of shit in the situation, so let's just put it out there."

"Fine. You gave her a bunch of cash to terminate a fucking pregnancy, and she used it to buy enough crack to kill a horse. Instead, she had one hell of a party in the bathroom with five kids downstairs, eating breakfast, and then drowned!" Finn roars.

"Right, 'cause you tried to get her to keep a kid she had no fucking business having and pushed her to run right the fuck to me 'cause your pompous ass wouldn't help her terminate the fucking unwanted pregnancy!" I yell back at him.

"Whose kid was it?" Memphis asks like he's just sitting on the couch, watching Jerry fucking Springer.

"Who the hell knows!" I yell.

"I think that you were all very young and—"

"Billy, just shut the fuck up," I bark.

"You know, River, you should take it easy. No one here is pointing fingers or placing blame except the two of you," Xavier says, and I know damn well it's some shit Taelyn has said that stuck with him.

"No one but him." I point at Finn.

"Or you, asshole." Finn points back.

"You two need to grow the fuck up!" Billy screams above us. "I let my dog out to piss when I was fourteen, and she got hit by a car. Dead. Killed right in front of me." Leave it to Billy to say some stupid shit like that. "But I forgave myself. The two of you need to pass the dish of forgiveness to each other—"

"Did you just say 'dish of forgiveness'?" Memphis quips, trying not to laugh.

"Yes, I said, dish of forgiveness," he snaps at Memphis.

"Is that like …?" Memphis stops when Xavier elbows him in the side. "Don't bruise the goods, man."

"Keep in mind that this week is about your rise to the top. We're filming "Surface to Soul," your song that hit number one and stayed there for two months. This is about you as a band. Luckily, there are no camera crews here right now, but there will be a crew at the house we rented, and we are gonna be one, big, happy fucking family."

"What? We're staying in the same fucking house?" I gape.

"One, big, happy fucking family," Finn sighs out.

"Unreal," I mumble.

"It was in that envelope Taelyn gave you," Xavier points out.

"We were sidetracked." Memphis smirks. "That's like a dish of pussy you shouldn't pass between friends."

Xavier elbows him, yet laughs in spite of his attempt not to.

We pull up to a gate, and the driver punches in a code. The gate opens, and then we drive up the driveway to a house straight out of MTV's *Cribs*.

"Sweet, huh?" Xavier winks. "Six bedrooms, a pool inside and out, kickass outside living space, and bathtubs that you can live in."

"Fuck in." Finn smirks.

"Fuckin' live in." Memphis turns to me. "How bad did you piss off Billy today? You two might ..." He leaves it hanging.

"I'll just show Tales what a real dick looks like, and she'll come running now that her training dick has her broken in."

"I will fucking cut you in your sleep if you say that shit again," Memphis growls.

I look at Finn, wanting to say some shit to him, too.

"I won't wait until you're asleep," Finn says, arching his eyebrow.

I lock eyes with him when the vehicle stops. Billy, Xavier, and Memphis all jump out and slam the doors behind them, leaving me and Finn alone together.

"Hold up," Finn says as I reach for the door handle.

"Nah, man." I half-laugh at his bullshit.

"I made a promise to a girl that I would tell you she read Jesse's diary from cover to cover a few years ago and then again after the accident. The lighter was a fucking peace offering. I had it shoved in a box. Forgot about it. Sonya suggested it. I had my mom's, too. It felt good to get rid of it, so I thought maybe you could do the same."

I pause and look down.

"I know how you met. You were her light knight. She was all fucking over the place, man. It had nothing to do with me and nothing to do with you."

He sighs, rubbing a hand in his beard. "Sonya talked to mine and Jesse's old foster parents, and Sally, our foster mother, confirmed what Sonya suspected — Jesse was mentally ill before you or I came into her life. She was abused as a kid, which probably fucked her up even worse.

"I am pissed beyond reason that you never told me. It feels like this whole thing between us was built on a fucking lie, but I will not let it fuck me up anymore. And, River, I'm not passing a fucking dish of imaginary forgiveness, but I am saying, whatever reason you had for keeping it from me" — he shrugs — "I'm sure it was solid."

The air between us becomes a little lighter, but... "I'm still fucking pissed. I'm not a hundred percent sure why, but pissed is a safe place for me to be."

"I'm not trying to one-up Billy's epic fucking moment, but hate, pissed, anger, it hurts man, and I don't wanna hurt anymore." He leans forward and opens the door. When he gets out, he looks back. "I don't want you to, either."

"You getting a blow job from your girl for that?" I ask.

He smirks and nods. "I better get anal."

I stay in the car for a minute, thinking of how I'm pretty sure that shit is over. I'm hoping like hell I can someday give him the same peace he just gave me, but I really have no idea how to fucking do that.

When I get out and walk up the front steps, Josephina Steel opens the door.

"Twenty minutes till a home cooked meal; don't be late."

I lean forward and kiss her cheek, and she laughs and points to the other.

"If you're going to do it, do it right."

I kiss her other cheek. "Better?"

"I don't know, River." She smiles. "But I hope so. Life is too short."

Before thinking, I open my mouth. "What do you know?"

She looks at me sternly. "Everything."

"You team River or Finn?" I ask, half-joking.

"Do you need me on your team?"

"Hell yes, I do." I again try to play it off as a joke because I see Xavier watching our interaction.

"You just fucked up," Xavier warns.

"Oh, no, he did not. He just made a very wise choice," Josephina says to him, then looks back at me. "Keep in mind that I raised four boys who all thought they wanted to be badasses, and look at them now. My boys are men."

"And still badasses." X looks at me. "Told you my momma was the best, man." He kisses his mom on the head. "Kitchen, Momma Joe. Your youngest, sexiest man is starving."

She laughs as she walks away.

*****

Everyone is in bed when the driver finally comes back with a pack of smokes. I'm outside, sitting under the veranda, watching a movie—*Soaked in Bleach*. It's a conspiracy story about the death of a man I have idolized my entire life, his music ever present in the highest of highs and the lowest of lows in my life.

I look over when the door opens to see Finn.

He points to my smoke. "Can I bum one?"

"Want something stronger?" I ask, knowing I need to chill the hell out. He lost her, too. He lost Jesse, and he's now fine. I know we are different in a way he will never understand, but I am going to fucking try.

His eyes narrow. "You got something stronger?"

"You sure you wouldn't get your ass kicked?"

He sits down and grabs the pack of Camel lights. "I still sneak one of these now and then." He narrows his eyes at me. "Don't tell my woman."

"You on a leash now?" I ask before taking a drag.

"Hell no, I'm right where I wanna be."

He lights a cigarette and takes a drag, sitting back in the chair. He blows out the smoke and glances over at me. "I thought you would never watch this shit."

"Conspiracy theory," I reply, then take another drag.

"Maybe, but if the shit's true, that cunt deserves to be given the same treatment."

"He died a few years before my dad left my mom for his second wife." I laugh. "Mother loved his music. Then she didn't. I never stopped."

"Yeah?" He asks, putting out his cigarette, and I nod. "Fucked up."

"The same day as Jesse," I remark.

He lowers his head and nods once. "I never even put that together. Too pissed at her, I suppose."

"Yeah." I lean forward and put my smoke out.

"I'm the one who found her," he mumbles, "the one who pulled her out of the tub."

Nausea washes through me, but I swallow it back.

"How'd you find out?"

"Tom-Tom," I answer, running my hands over my head. "The next day."

Neither of us say a word as Cobain's music surrounds us. We simply sit in silence, watching the end of the docudrama.

When Finn turns off the TV, he leans forward and looks at me. "Fucking cold out here."

"Supposed to be about sixty-five the rest of the week. Hell of a lot better than New Jersey," I remark, just making small talk about the weather.

Finn points to the pool. "See that spot beyond the pool, just past the hot tub?"

"The gazebo?"

He nods. "I keep picturing Sonya in white right there."

"You mean, getting married?" He's definitely whipped. Good for him. He got a second chance. The better men always do.

He nods. "I'm so fucking lucky it was her and not some crazy-ass chick like Cobain ended up with." He glances over at me, and I nod.

"Do it."

"I would, you know." He smirks.

"Would or will?" I ask, fucking with him.

"Can you see me in a monkey suit, standing up there?" He chuckles.

I nod. "Yeah, I can. She's tits, man."

"Everyone's already here," he suggests, looking toward the pool.

"Your old man?" I ask, wondering if he's coming around now, being a fucking father, and if Finn is allowing it.

"He could be on a plane in a couple hours," Finn answers, and I know it's going to happen.

"Fuck it; do it. Well, unless she wants the whole church and friends and —"

"Nah, she wants what I want: her, Noah, and me."

I stand up and slap his back. "Do it."

He stands up, too, and looks at me, then back toward the pool. "You willing to wear a monkey suit and stand there with me?"

I'm shocked. I look around, but there is no one coming outside.

"You talking to me?" I point to myself.

"Yeah, I absolutely am talking to you. Almost seven fucking years." He shakes his head.

"Shit's like common law in some states," I joke.

He shoves his hands in the pockets of his sweatpants. "Is that a yes?"

"Yeah, it's definitely a yes." I can't help smiling. "Fuck yes."

"Good. I want it to be a surprise. After the circus rolls out, we just say yeah, make it legal before the …" He stops and gives me a sideways glance.

I clap him on the back again. "You'll be a damn good father, Finn."

He nods. "She and I, we're fucking solid."

"So we're planning a wedding now? Holy fuck, a few hours ago, I wanted to fucking rip the beard off." I laugh, and so does he.

"Beard envy. How about you just grow your own?"

"Did that once. Got busted," I joke.

*****

Two days fly by. I have either been standing where the photographers tell me to or trying to hide from the fuckers. It's intense.

"I fucking need to catch a buzz," I grumble as I climb out of the pool, only to be met by the stare of Momma Joe.

"A towel is what you need, River." She raises her eyebrows and hands me one.

"Thank you, beautiful Josephina." I smile as big as I can at her.

She palms my face. "My pleasure, son."

When she walks away, I stand, trying to wrap my head around what she just said, *son,* and how, for the first time in more years than I can remember, it doesn't make me angry when Momma Joe says it, even though I always hated hearing that.

I feel a hand clasp my shoulder. "You asked for it," X-man reprimands. "Now I have to tell you that she is tough as nails, man. Teaching the Tango to a tiger in Tuscany would be easier than getting her off your back. It's just never gonna happen. You literally opened the door and walked into it, but if you break her heart, I will break your neck, brother."

I take a minute to allow the weight of that responsibility to sink in.

Not bad. Not bad at all.

*****

Tonight, we are putting on a private show. Apparently, invites were sent out to winners of an online contest Yaya came up with. Two hundred people will be here, watching us play poolside.

It's fucking cold as hell out, but we are having a fucking Hollywood-style pool party, including industrial strength heaters that are apparently going to heat the outside.

Insane as hell, but mixed in with the winners, are pretty big names in the radio industry and cable music stations.

"Yaya's genius in full bloom." I wink at her, and she smiles and looks for Finn, who looks proud as hell of the chick he and I have been sneaking around behind the back of.

"She's more than just a genius, much more," Finn says, wrapping his arm around her shoulder and pulling her against him.

"Oh, yeah? Care to share?" I tease.

"She's fucking mine." He narrows his eyes, and she sighs.

Drunk Dialed

It's Thursday: four days since I started a new job and four days since I have been able to sleep without being awakened, picturing him in pain.

I've considered just caffeinating the hell out of myself so that I don't sleep, but to work here in the drug and alcohol rehabilitation center, I can't do that. It would go against what I am … against.

"Glady," I say to the receptionist as I walk out from the back office, "you need anything before I leave?"

"Drugs," she whispers, and I laugh.

"Looks like no intakes tonight. That's good news, right?" I wink.

"No intakes because we are at max capacity." She smiles. "Not bad for me, but for anyone who needs it right now and we have to turn them away, not such good news, right?"

"I suppose not, but how about we both make a pact to focus on the ones here right now?"

"I hear you, honey child. I hear you."

"Goodnight. If you need anything, give me a call," I tell her.

"You aren't on call."

I am strong and resourceful. I am here to help others, and in doing so, I help myself.

I am the daughter of an addict who died because she could not overcome an addiction. A strong woman raised me, and that woman grew me to become and overcome.

I hold my chin high, and in the darkest of times, I make myself hold it higher. I am not unbreakable, but I am shatterproof.

No person in the universe decides who I will be, just me.

"You have a heart as big as the ocean, Keanna. Never let anyone drain you completely, but don't turn your back when they need to borrow your heart, your strength, your kindness."

I miss you so much, Grandma Martha. I miss so very much, I think as my eyes fill once again while I make my way to my car after work.

I head straight to the gym, needing to exhaust myself. I need to make myself so sore, so tired that, when I fall asleep, I don't think of him.

When I return to Natasha's, I plug my phone into the charger. It's dead from listening to my music on repeat for two hours.

"Dinner's ready, Auntie Keanna." Jordan runs to the door and slides across the hardwood in his socks with Tink running behind him and skidding to a stop right before taking me out.

I give him a hug then kiss his head. "I need a shower. Do I have time?"

"You gonna have to do your hair and stuff?" he asks, putting his hands on his hips.

I smile. "Do I ever not do my hair and stuff?"

"Then I'm waiting, too." He crosses his arms in front of his chest.

"You think you're grown or something?" I give him some attitude right back. "Hey, Natasha, I'm gonna shower."

"Sounds good," she yells to me from the kitchen.

*****

Jordan is in bed, and Natasha and I are sitting on the couch with a glass of wine. She turns on the TV for background noise, hiding our conversation from young ears in the room at the top of the stairs.

"Where's Tink?" Natasha asks, stretching her neck and yawning.

"Perched at the top of the stairs outside Jordan's room." I nod up the stairs. "Where she is every night and every morning." I laugh. "Where have you been?"

She sighs. "I have no idea. How the hell did I miss that?"

"In your defense, she comes down and pretends to sleep next to my bed until I fall asleep. When I wake up, she's gone."

Natasha laughs. "She's changed." Then she looks at me and cringes. "Sorry. I wasn't—"

"She got high and laid. How could she not change?" I force a laugh since I don't want her to feel bad. I know it wasn't her intention to bring up last weekend. "You know, I have to say I feel like a complete idiot. How did I not know he was as messed up as he is? I mean, I'm trained to know when someone has a problem."

"How would you have known? It was like a freaking whirlwind of a weekend." She shakes her head. "I mean, three days with a rock star, Keanna. Women dream of a weekend like that. Hell, I would have left with him, but I am … was … well, am technically still his doctor, and *I* had no idea he was like that."

I hear music coming from the TV, and we both look.

"Oh, my God," she whispers.

In sixty-inch, high definition glory, I see Memphis Black standing under a million, white, twinkling lights, microphone in hand, singing a song I know I have heard a million times but never once put two and two together.

"Holy shit," I whisper as I watch it all unfold in front of me.

Finn is playing bass, Billy on acoustic, and River — Oh, God, River — is playing the drums. I want to close my eyes, look away, but I can't. I see the sticks in his hand, the ones I gave him, and have to physically hold my hand over my chest because I am so afraid it may beat its way out.

He's shirtless, hasn't shaved — I mean, he isn't like Finn, but he has more than a five o'clock shadow going on.

"Look at that ink," Natasha gasps.

I give her a sideways glance.

"I'll turn it off."

"Don't you dare," I say or growl, rather, because she looks at me like she may be intimidated.

Look at it? I licked it, I think, my mouth drying up.

I take a big gulp of my wine, finishing the glass.

"Pause it." I jump up and run to the kitchen to grab the bottle.

When I come back, she has not only paused but rewound it.

I fill our glasses, and we sit and watch it all over again.

Awaken beast, you took my all.
Taboo desires, burn out of control.
Intoxicated youth, a troubled teen.
Still both inside, eternal flames.
Surface to soul.

But I'm chasing the light,
Chasing my goal,
Chasing the girl who owns my soul.
Chasing the night,
Chasing the score,
Chasing the need to rock this floor.
I'm missing you. Oo-oo-oo
I'm missing you. Oo-oo-oo

Chasing my dream.
You chase the same.
We're chasing away the fucking game.
Chasing the right.
Chasing the wrong.
Chasing the words to write your song.

I'm missing you. Oo-oo-oo.
I'm missing you. Oo-oo-oo.

Down on my knees, I beg you now.
I can't let go. I don't know how.
A tender heart, a taken toll.
What was surface took my soul.
Surface to soul.

But I'm chasing the light,
Chasing my goal,
Chasing the girl who owns my soul,
Chasing the night,
Chasing the score,
Chasing the need to rock this floor.
I'm missing you. Oo-oo-oo.
I'm missing you. Oo-oo-oo.

Chasing my dream.
You chase the same.
We're chasing away the fucking game.
Chasing the right,
Chasing the wrong,
Chasing the words to write your song.

I'm missing you. Oo-oo-oo.

"Sweet baby Jesus," Natasha sighs as she leans back.

"Again," I demand, filling my glass for the third time.

"You sure?"

"Yes. Yes, I am."

This time, I watch him, only him.

"He looks good, even has some color. Dirty white boy," I grumble the last part under my breath.

Natasha snickers. "Isn't that a song?"

"It should be his theme song. That dirty"—I pause and sigh—"sexy, nasty, but so fucking good with his mouth, his hands, and he is … hung. *God*, Tasha, he is like really hung."

"Like a black man?" she asks in all her white girl glory.

I can't help laughing.

"Rewind it."

"You sure?"

"Yes. Yes, I'm very sure." I fill my glass again and sit back, curling my feet underneath myself.

I look up when I see Tink coming down the stairs. She sits in front of me and looks at the TV.

"Seriously, Tink?"

"The bitches all like him." Natasha busts out laughing.

"Stupid, stupid bitches." I shake my head. "And look at them all: tan, little, California, bikini-clad, fake tittied—"

"Wow, Keanna." Natasha shakes her head at me, chuckling.

"Sorry," I huff. "No. No, I'm not. I should tweet what I said to the car sales whore."

"Which was …?"

"How did I taste?" I answer.

Her jaw drops open. "You had a threesome?"

"Oh, dear god, no." I shake my head, and instead of filling my empty glass, I decide to just drink from the bottle. "It's a long story."

"Long like his dick?"

We start laughing immediately.

"One more time. And, Natasha?"

"Yeah?"

"Please don't let me tweet that."

"I won't."

I grab my phone and take a picture of Tink the traitor watching her human crush.

"And don't let me send that."

"I would never."

"He looks good, right?" I ask as we watch it 'one more time.'

"Do you want me to say no? I will. I will say no. His six-pack could be an eight, and he looks horrible with a tan and that nasty stubble." She sets her empty wine glass down on the coffee table. "I can say any woman who even considers a gang bang with the entire STD band is out of their damn mind. Would that help?"

I shake my head. "Watch his wrist. Do you think he—"

"Jerks off a lot? Hell yes, he does," she slurs. "Stupid, sexy boy."

I look over at her, seeing she is clearly buzzing and crushing on the band, the entire band.

She looks at me. "They're all dirty pigs." The P in pigs is way over-pronounced.

At that, I laugh, and she rewinds it.

Three more times and we are singing along with the lyrics. Four more times and I am using my fingers, tapping along with his beat. Five more times and another bottle of wine goes back and forth between two friends. Then I pull up Tink's picture, and somehow, someway, I push send.

"Shit! Shit, shit, shit!" I exclaim and throw the phone down.

"What does all that shit mean?" Natasha asks, her voice thick from the amount of wine we have consumed.

"It means you are a horrible babysitter. I sent him the picture of Tink!"

"No," she gasps.

"Yes!" I curl up into a ball.

She grabs my phone. "You are so fucking lucky."

I snatch the phone away. "Why?"

"It didn't go through. Now make sure you don't try again."

RETRIBUTION

I can't get her fucking face, her fucking image, the sound of her moans and cries out of my head. Hands down, it was the best piece of ass I have ever had: spank bank numero uno, a Christ heist, an ass that's defiantly been sitting in sugar, fucking ultimate onion. It almost brings me to tears to think about not having it again … almost.

That shit is done. She's lucky, too, because sometimes, you *like* someone enough to leave them alone. She will be just fucking fine.

I have been sober now for four days. I haven't touched shit except a cigarette, a couple of beers, and my cock. So the high I am depending on is relaxation, relationship mending between me and my band, and the release I find in the shower.

"Fuck," I hiss as I jack myself faster and tighten my hold on my cock. I lean my head on my forearm that's against the shower wall as the water beats down on me. I close my eyes as I feel the slight tinge of pain that comes before I unload, and my cum hits the shower wall. "Fuck!"

I get out, grab a towel, and I'm ready for a fucking nap, not the circus tonight promises to bring.

"One down," I tell myself, drying off my dick. "Now to continue mending fences."

I convinced myself that it's Momma Joe's fault. Yeah, that's what I call her now, and she calls me son.

I get dressed in shorts and a sweatshirt, because even though we are going to be faking summer tonight, it's a bit nippley here.

As I jog down the stairs, I hear the sound of the snare. Someone is beating the drums. I stop at the end of the stairs, immediately recognizing the beat.

" 'Voodoo' by Godsmack," I say as I walk in and see Xavier beating the hell out of the drums, baby Patrick attached to him in one of those baby carrying things, holding my sticks.

Xavier stops playing and looks at me as he stands up. "Wanna play something for me?"

I shrug. "I'm better than you."

He laughs. "You think so? Try doing it with a kid attached to you, smartass."

"You gonna let me wear the kid?"

He looks at me, studying me. I made a deal with his wife, or more accurately, she said a long time ago that I couldn't hold him if I wasn't sober. I know he's thinking about that now.

"Yeah." He unsnaps the contraption and takes Patrick out, then starts to hand him off to me, but stops. "Don't fucking drop him."

I nod and take him.

"Bang-bang," Patrick says, grabbing my face.

"So they've been talking about me behind my back, huh, little guy?" I laugh, which makes him laugh, too. "Little guy, I'm kind of digging you right now."

Taelyn comes in and stops dead in her tracks. She smiles when I wink at her.

"This kid here is tits, T. Can you imagine the one we'd have?" I remark, looking at X-man.

"You're only standing because my son is in your hands," Xavier growls at me.

"I know, man. I know."

Xavier hooks me up in the baby BDSM gear, then puts Patrick in. It feels fucked up, yet pretty cool. Then I sit at the drums with a kid attached to me and tap in while he swings my sticks around as he laughs when he makes contact with anything, including my head.

When Finn walks in, the song changes. I start beating to "Moby Dick" by Led Zeppelin. Fucking flawless.

He grabs the bass, X-man grabs the acoustic, and it's on.

The drum solo rolls around, and my ass leaves the seat. "Hang tight, little guy."

Lost in my head, feeling good, I close my eyes and feel the beat all the way to my soul.

"You ready to fuck shit up?" I ask Patrick when the song ends.

"Bang-bang!"

"All day long, buddy. Think blues riff on crack. This song is for your momma and Momma Joe."

He giggles.

"Kid, if you keep laughing at me, I'm gonna have to keep you. Now let's beat it in."

I start with a floor tom riff. Right, left, right, left, over and over again until my wrist gets loose, and my drums sound like a V8 engine revving up.

"Now we add the double bass, swing-shuffle pattern, tom accents, and I'm done, bud. Hope you got that. It's a go," I instruct little man.

I'm lost in the beat with a kid laughing and whacking me in the head to his own beat, and everyone joins in. We're now playing "Surface to Soul," and I swear he's cooking something in his diapers.

I stop playing and point to Taelyn. "Something's brewing, Momma Steel."

She laughs as she walks over, unhooks him, and lifts him up.

Little man is not happy.

"Bang-bang!"

"I know, buddy, but your dad would be pissed."

"You aren't holding my kid anymore, River." He scowls.

I see Noah, Sonya's boy, standing beside her, looking at me.

"You wanna give it a try?"

Finn leans over and whispers, "He's got some hearing issues."

"Perfect. I've got some issues myself." I look back at Noah. "Come on, little dude."

He looks at his mom, who smiles and nods. "If you wanna go ..." She laughs when he runs over to me. "Okay, then."

I wink at Xavier. "Safe again."

"This time, asshole."

"Xavier Steel, watch your mouth," Momma Joe scolds him.

"But he said—"

"I heard nothing." She turns and gives me a wink.

I look back at Xavier, who scowls.

"Noah, you know how to stick your tongue out at someone?"

He grins and nods.

"Do it to Xavier. He loves it."

After an hour of fucking around, I am sweating, and so is Noah. The kid's on me, shirtless, just swinging the sticks and beating the piss out of the drums.

"Lunch is ready," Momma Joe yells to us.

I love that chick.

*****

The place looks amazing. It's fucking made in Hollywood, so of course it does, and I am riding the hell out of this high. My wrist is feeling better than ever—must be all the "therapy." I have been "working" it a lot the past few days.

My thoughts immediately go to her.

She's strong.

I sit at the drums, making sure whoever set them up knew what the fuck they were doing. That's one thing I should love, but I don't —having someone setting up my drums since it takes a hell of a lot of time. It's always been a part of the buildup, foreplay if you will.

I look around at all the tits covered in triangles — all probably surgically enhanced—and none are as nice as hers. It's the same with the bikini bottoms: scraps of material, covering asses that my fingers would hit the bone of before I got a good, firm grip on them.

One could consider it a fantasy feast to every wannabe rock star out there. But me, it's pathetic. When I sit down to eat, I want, at the very least, a queen cut prime rib in front of me, not a half-eaten fucking chicken wing.

"You good?" Finn asks, throwing his strap around his shoulder.

"I'm better than good." I take a swig of my water and tap us in.

When we finish doing "Surface to Soul" three fucking times, pretending each time is the first for the sake of the camera, I stand up and scan the crowd.

"Looking for ass?" Memphis nudges me.

"You know I am." I wink, then walk to the bar.

"Give me a Jack and Coke on the rocks, but hold the Coke," I say to one of the tuxedo-wearing men behind the bar.

She jumps up like a fucking Jack in the Box, and I jump back, startled, holding my hand to my chest.

"Momma Joe, where the hell did you come from?"

She laughs. "I am everywhere."

"Just wanted a drink."

"*Hold the Coke.* I heard you." She pats my shoulder. "That's a good choice, but holding the Jack would be good, too."

I shake my head and look around. "Momma Joe, easy on me."

I about die when I see an all too familiar face. Fuck, I even rub my eyes because that face is one I haven't seen in eight to ten years, the only time since he fucking left us. I went to him. No fucking clue why or when; I was way too fucked up back then.

"How the fuck …?"

"Your father?" Momma Joe asks.

"Yeah, he's definitely the fuck."

She doesn't laugh.

"Who let him in?" I ask as I see him spot me.

I turn my back, hoping I am wrong.

"He called yesterday; the producers told me today. Is everything okay?"

I don't want a scene, and no one can make that fucker walk away faster than my mom and me. I can deal with it.

I pick up the Jack and slam it down. "Another please."

"River?" Momma Joe asks.

"Yeah, yeah, sure. It's fine."

"There's my boy!" His hand hits me hard on the back, and I turn around. "This is Suzy, my fiancée."

I look at Suzy. "Well, they certainly get younger and younger now, don't they?" I chuckle darkly.

Their expressions are priceless, he's pissed, she looks fucking smitten.

"River, a word?" Momma Joe asks, but I shake my head. "It wasn't a request."

I look at her. She looks at me. Then I see Xavier.

"Fuck," I mumble as I follow her.

"Don't lower yourself to his standard."

"Not to be disrespectful, but it's pretty safe to guess I really don't have standards all that high."

"River," she scolds.

"I'll be fine." I grab her face and kiss each cheek loudly. "Thanks, Momma Joe."

I feel her watching me, so when I get back to … him, I push my hand out. "Been a long time."

"Five years." He nods. "Last time I saw you, you borrowed a few hundred dollars and my car. Never saw the cash, but the police did return the car from the junkie you sold it to."

"Yeah, well, as you can see, I am doing much better now than I was back then. Thanks for checking in. I'll write you a check for the cash I borrowed."

I look at Suzy, reaching my hand out to her. She goes to shake it, and I pull it to my mouth and give it a nice kiss with a little tongue action that the old dog can't see. She sees it, feels it, too. Her nipples peak behind the white, nearly see-through gauze cover up dress she's wearing. Her face flushes, and I release her hand.

"So, when's the wedding? You looking for a band, or are you and this one gonna hit an island like you've done in the past?" I pause and scratch my head. "How many weddings since you ditched my mother and me?"

His face hardens and burns red. "This is the last." He pulls her close to him.

"Perfect. I'd like to get to know her a little better. You gonna fuck this tight, little body of hers up by pushing out a few kids? How many do you have now, Father?"

"I don't have any other children, River, and you know this," he says through clenched teeth.

"Yeah, well, it's been seven years—"

"Five," he corrects.

"Oh, shit, my bad. Yeah, about that money, maybe if Mom got child support, I wouldn't have borrowed money from you."

"She never accepted it," he tells me, and now I know I am really pissing him off. His ears are even red.

"Right, all those marriages of hers. All those men you let step in and you assumed were taking care of what you left behind."

"You seemed to always be just fine," he hisses.

"Fuck yes, I am." I turn and look at the future stepmother. "Sammy—"

"Her name is Suzy," he corrects, the pompous ass looking like he's proud of himself for remembering her name.

"Fuck, I don't know how you keep them straight." I laugh. "Come on in and get something to eat. I'll grab you a check." I don't wait for him to respond; I just take her hand. "Sammy, after you."

"It's Suzy," he snaps from behind me.

Momma Joe is watching over the buffet line like it's her job. I heard her and Xavier arguing over a caterer. You would think he would have given in to her desire to cook for two hundred people plus this insane crew.

Dear old Dad catches up and takes her hand. "Suzy, let me fix you a plate."

I step back, laughing and thinking of how good it feels to piss off the motherfucker who walked away from his woman and child.

"You okay?" Finn asks.

"Did you sprout a fucking vagina?"

He scowls at me, letting me know I'm towing the line.

"Sorry. I just have this incredible urge to whip out my cock so she can see what a real one looks like and watch it piss up and down his fucking khakis."

Finn shakes his head, and then the fucker laughs. Finn fucking Beckett laughs out loud, and I swear to God, if there is one, it's a miracle.

"Holy shit. You're laughing!"

"Yeah, that was funny. Even funnier is I've laughed before, once or twice, and you didn't know it 'cause you were too fucked up. But the best part is, a year ago, we'd have probably done it and spent the night in jail."

"Been there." I lift up my hand to fist bump him, but he looks confused. Now I laugh. "You seriously don't remember?"

He shakes his head.

"The Narcotics Anonymous meeting that judge made me go to at that church?"

He still doesn't remember.

"The one I got escorted out of because I was so fucked up I stood up and pissed in the circle when they told me it was my turn?"

He scowls. "How the fuck do I not remember that?"

"I remember it." Memphis comes up, laughing as he hands both Finn and me a drink. "Well, I remember hearing the story, I think."

"And they say drugs have no serious, long-term effects." I snicker, and they both look at me like I'm fucking stupid. "Well, that's what I tell myself, anyway. You two need to lay off the drugs."

"Oh, shit." I hear my father and look up to see he has spilled sauce down his khakis.

Finn laughs again. "There she is."

"Who?" I ask, looking around.

"Karma. She's got your back, man."

I see Thomas leading my dad to the stairs, and I look at Finn. "You got it, too?"

He nods. "Sure do, brother. Sure do."

"Good to know." I pat his back. "Give me five minutes, no more, no less. When you see the fucker looking for wife number … I don't know, five, bring him to my room."

"Dude, what are you cooking up?" Memphis asks.

"Karma needs just a little help."

I walk toward Sammy or Suzy or whatever the fuck her name is.

"Shit," I curse as I back into her, and now she's covered in sauce, too.

"Damn, how the hell did I do that?"

"Did you have too much to drink?" I ask.

"No, I haven't had a drop."

"Good to know. It was my fault. How about you and I go and find you something to change into?" I hold out my hand, and the flake takes it.

"Thank you, River." She's all sorts of fucking breathy.

As we ascend the stairs, I look back to see Finn and Memphis both shaking their heads.

I walk into my room and turn to her. "You think we should leave the door open or closed?"

She swallows hard. "Probably closed. I mean, I am going to change, right?"

I guess her to be early thirties. She's all right looking, but definitely not my type. Not that I have a type, but if I did ... She ain't it.

I kick the door closed. "You sure are."

I walk over to my suitcase and open it up. "None of these are going to look half as good as that see-through, little number you're wearing right now. I mean, I can almost see the outline of your nipples. What size are you, a D?"

"B," she whispers.

"Wow, I would have thought they were bigger." I turn around with an STD T-shirt. "I'd love to see them."

She looks at me, then around the room. "I don't know, River. Your father—"

"Will never know."

"Promise?"

"Swear to God."

"Well, it's not like we're going to have sex." She blushes as she pulls her dress over her head.

"They fake?"

"No." She shakes her head, then she pulls her bra down. "You can feel them if you'd like."

"I would like." I reach out and palm her little tits. "Nice."

"Thank you."

I use my other hand to take hers. "No fair. I gotta let you do the same." I place it on my half chub, and she gulps. "If you want a closer look, Sammy —"

"Suzy," she corrects.

"Right. Well, if you do, feel free to get down on your knees and take a peek."

"It's wrong."

"I know it, but wrong sometimes feels so fucking good."

She's instantly drops to her knees, unbuttoning my shorts. My cock falls out, and she moans. "My God."

"Yeah, I'm sure the huge cock gene came from my mother's side."

She looks up and giggles.

"Someday, he's going to piss you off, Sammy."

"Suzy."

I reach down and stroke my dick. "Right, well, when he does, you're going to wish you had that hot, little mouth of yours around this. I almost feel sorry for you."

"Almost?" her voice squeaks.

"Well, if you'd ask me nicely, Sammy" — I say the wrong name on purpose this time, and she doesn't correct me; she's too busy eyeballing the goods — "I'd force myself to live with the guilt that I allowed my stepmother to taste my cock."

"He'll never know?"

"No, Sammy, I would never tell him."

"So ...?"

"So what, Sammy?"

"So can I taste your beautiful cock, River?"

I look up as the door opens and see my father with Finn behind him.

"What the fuck is going on?!" my father roars.

"What's it look like?" I ask with a shit-eating grin on my face.

"What did you do to her?!" He runs over and lifts Suzy or Sammy up off her knees. "What did he do to you?"

I can't help laughing. I mean, seriously, the man is a fucking ass-hat, and he's fucking stupid. Like I don't know what he's doing, parading new ass in front of his rock star kid to make his saggy, old ass look better.

"I'm so sorry," she cries as he pulls her stained dress over her head.

"No, no, Suzy. I know what he's like. I know he —"

Finn grabs the back of his shirt and yanks him backward. "It's time for you to fucking go." Finn shuts the door when they are both out of my room, looking shocked, "Cover up your dick."

"You really are no friend."

"Oh, no?" He chuckles as I pull up my shorts.

"No, man, you stormed in on an almost blow job and haven't the decency to finish me off."

*****

I wake up the next morning, riding a new high, the I-fucked-my-old-man-so-hard-last-night-I-don't-even-care-what-a-shitbag-parent-he-was high. If he goes through with this marriage, every time she is on her knees, he's going to think of me, and so will she.

I roll over and grab my phone to check the time.

"What the fuck?" I exclaim when I see a message from Keanna.

I open it and see the bear-dog watching me on TV.

I sit up and type up a message.

You missing me, girl(s)?

Then I delete it.

They deserve much fucking better than me.

I toss the phone aside and get up to get ready for Finn's big day.

RJ and Frank

"Twenty-one days," I answer the new intake's question. His name is John, and he sits in my office, chewing his nails while his knee bounces up and down.

He looks down. "That's a long damn time."

"It's not, John—"

"JT," he corrects.

"Twenty-one days is three weeks, not even a month." I look down at his file. "It's less time than you'll spend in jail if you don't take the deal the judge offered."

"It's fucked up, you know."

"It's fucked up that you drove through a plate glass window because you made the decision to drive after getting inebriated."

"*Pft*, don't pretend like you know shit, bitch."

"*Pft*, don't think your choice of words is gonna offend me," I retort.

He narrows his eyes. "You think 'cause you're black you're a badass?"

"I'd be badass if I was white."

I'm arguing with an eighteen-year-old man-child who is obviously trying to push my buttons, and unlike my norm, I'm letting it get to me.

I stand up and walk around my desk. "You get to choose. Sign or not, it's up to you. I'll be back in two minutes for your decision." I unlock and open a drawer to a filing cabinet and pull out the intake information booklet for our clients. I open it up to the rules section and set it before him. "Read over these and see if you think you can handle it. But before I walk out of here, understand that disrespecting me or any of the staff is not tolerated."

When I walk out, Jonas, the director, is standing outside the door.

"You all right?" he asks, putting his hand on my shoulder.

"I'm fine."

He nods as he takes his hand off my shoulder. "Can I ask a favor?"

"Of course," I answer.

"Tonight's community meeting needs a moderator. Leslie had a family emergency."

"Of course." I nod. "Just tell me what to do."

After receiving instructions, I walk in my office to find John is gone, and so is my purse.

Dammit!

*****

I have enough time to shower, then change out of my work clothes and put on what Jonas described as street clothes.

"Natasha!" I yell as I walk in.

"In here!" she yells back.

I kick my shoes off and walk into the kitchen, laughing when I see her with an apron on.

"We should make a pact that, if you and I aren't married off or at least in a serious relationship in twenty years, we marry each other."

"Well, you'll have to propose. I had to beg you to move in." She laughs with me, setting the potholders on the counter.

"I didn't make you beg me," I retort, eyeing the wine.

When I found an apartment that would allow Tink two weeks ago, I made the mistake of taking Natasha there when I went to sign the lease.

She found a dozen reasons before we got inside the building for why it was not a good idea: fourth floor, no security, half an hour away from her, and the only park for Tink, was a ten-block walk away.

"You want a glass?" she asks.

"I'd love one, but I have to moderate a community meeting tonight."

"Oh. That's different."

"Yes, and my purse got stolen by a junkie I pissed off." I sigh. "It's been a bad day."

"Well, if we were married, I'd give you a blow job after your glass of wine."

I laugh as I walk out of the room. "You would be the best wife ever."

In the bathroom, I let the water run and the room steam up. When the mirror is fogged over, I use my finger to write the number twenty-one.

It's been twenty-one days since I heard from or saw River James. Well, aside from the week of *Entertainment Evenings* re-runs of the band playing the song that I hear over and over in my head when I'm not busy.

I get undressed and think about how nice it is to have work and Jordan and Natasha. If not for them, I would go insane.

I spent years thinking I loved Miguel; months getting over the realization that love doesn't always last, no matter how hard we wish and pray it did; and three days realizing that, sometimes, the first fall isn't actually the hardest.

The thing about it is, when I met River the first time at the office, he intrigued me. His blatant sexuality should have turned me off, but it did the exact opposite. It ignited something in me that I was sure I would only feel if I were falling for someone: desire.

After that day, I decided I needed to stop wallowing in the loss of a man who never deserved me, because now I know I can want someone else.

When I was ready, I stepped way out of my comfort zone and went out to meet some friends. That fateful night, I told myself it was to support Natasha, but deep down, I was hoping to have the same type of feeling I had when I met River.

That night when he and I left together, I had all the confidence of a girl who'd had too damn much to drink and had just stood up for herself to a man who told her on many occasions that he loved her. He never truly did, though. Love, true love, lasts through thick and thin, pain and happiness, trials and tribulations.

I step into the shower and think of what I told the kid today who stole my purse. Twenty-one days is three weeks, not even a month. He responded with "it's fucked up," and right now, in a different light, a different circumstance, he was right in a way. Twenty-one days is so fucked up.

*****

I use the key Jonas gave me to unlock the church down the block where the community meeting is held. Being physically disconnected from the rehab center yet still affiliated in a much less structured way makes many people feel more comfortable walking in from the streets.

I set the huge box of assorted pastries down next to the coffee pot and open the cabinet under it. Jonas told me where everything is, and his directions were impeccable.

"Hello," I hear and look up. "I'm sorry if I startled you. I'm Pastor Daniel. I just wanted you to know I will be in the office. If you need anything, just yell."

"Would you like a donut or some coffee?" He is tall, bald, and has a very warm peaceful presence.

"Thank you. Maybe if there are some left over." His smile is genuine and kind. "If the meeting has stragglers, I'll let them in. My office is right by the front door."

"Thank you, Pastor Daniel."

Tonight is an open meeting, meaning non-addicts can attend. I attended several after the loss of my mother with my grandma.

I was told there are normally ten to twenty people at these meetings, but on some occasions, there are none. It is eight o'clock on the dot, and I'm wondering if tonight will be one of those nights when no one shows. Regardless, Jonas made me promise to stay for the entire hour, and of course, I told him yes.

I watch three women and three men walk in the door at five after. I greet them and offer refreshments. We all sit in chairs in a circle that was set up in the church's fellowship hall. Then I wait another minute before I start the meeting.

I stand up and wipe my palms on my leggings and laugh.

"As you can tell, I am a little nervous. This is my first time moderating a community meeting. I am Keanna Sutton, and this is not the first meeting I have attended."

I pause when I see two men walking in, but I don't stop talking. I want them to feel comfortable, so as they remove their coats and hang them, leaving their hats on, I continue, "I've attended a few. You see, my mother was an addict. I can't honestly say what her drug of choice was, but whatever she shot up with on April 6th 2004 ended her life and changed mine forever."

When I see the two men stop out of my peripheral, I am afraid I may scare them off if I don't continue.

"Is this anyone's first meeting?" I ask as I casually walk over to the table and grab some information booklets.

Two women and one of the men raise their hands.

"Feel free to just say anything. I'm not a teacher or any different than any of you. I'm just the one who gets to start first."

As the two men walk over and sit, I hand out the booklets. When I smile and turn to the two latecomers, Finn Beckett is looking up at me, and River James is looking down at the tiled floor.

"Well, if everyone is going to clam up, I'll start," the oldest woman says with a chuckle.

"I'm Anita. This is my granddaughter Angel, and her child's father Zachary. I am raising the kid. She's hell on wheels, and I am too old for this nonsense. These two need a good dose of sobriety and the hand of God himself to smack them in the back of the head."

"You sure I'm the father?" Zachary chimes in.

"You know damn well you are," Angel retorts.

"Me or ten others." He stops when Anita smacks him in the back of the head. "What the hell is wrong with you, old woman?"

"The hand of God is slower than mine today. There isn't a thing wrong with me."

I hear River chuckle, and I want to yell at him, but I force myself to remain calm and professional.

"Okay, well, I'd love to suggest a paternity test to resolve the question Zachary has, but while we are here, let's talk about supporting one another in the healing process." I turn and look at Zachary. "Would you like to tell us your story?"

"I like to get high."

I wait, expecting more. When he doesn't continue, I nod.

"I see. And I hope you know that this is a place to turn when you are ready to get clean and stay sober. Are you ready for that?"

"*Pft*," is all he says.

"Angel?"

"Of course I want my kid back, but Zack makes it impossible. He doesn't want to get better for us."

"Angel," I say as I sit in the chair and tuck my leg under me, "do you want to be sober?"

"I want him to get his shit together and take care of his responsibilities to me and the kid."

"You ever think about getting clean and taking on that responsibility yourself?" I look over to see Finn looking at her.

"It's not as easy as it looks," she mutters, rolling her eyes.

"It's a choice, Angel, and it's yours to make," I tell her, knowing Finn has a short temper, and I want to avoid any more physical outbursts.

I look at the other men who came in. "Would you like to say something?"

The first man shakes his head, so I look at the man next to him who does the same thing, and then the woman stands up.

"I've been clean for forty-three days. It's been a struggle, but I am doing it because I wanna get healthy so that I can get my four children back."

"That's wonderful! Any advice for the others?"

She shrugs. "One day at a time."

"Anyone else?" I know I should look over, but I can't.

"I'm" — Finn pauses — "Frank."

I sigh inwardly at the bullshit name, but I don't call him on it.

"My mom burned down our childhood home when she was cooking meth. I was sent to foster care where my girlfriend OD'd on drugs. I've struggled from time to time with needing to get high. However, I haven't touched a drug in almost three months."

"That's great, Fi-Frank," I tell him, just like I would to anyone else. "Can you tell us your reason for staying sober?"

He nods. "I've got a wife, a stepson, and a kid on the way. I won't fuck them or myself up. Life is too damn good when you aren't chasing the storm."

He's married? I didn't know that.

"Congratulations," I tell him, then take a deep breath, knowing I have to face *him* now.

"I'm RJ. Neither of my parents abused drugs that I know of. My mom did have a shoe addiction." I can hear the smile in his voice. "After my father left, she had a man addiction. One of them had an alcohol addiction and then an addiction for abusing yours truly."

I glance over to see he is looking at me. Then he closes his eyes and turns away.

"You all keep up now, okay? Shit gets tricky." He laughs, one of River's coping mechanisms.

"When she found out after turning the other cheek to the bruises, bumps, and all the other fucking—" He pauses.

"Shit, sorry, all the other obvious signs, she sent me to visit some family and took herself to some tropical paradise with the man who abused me.

"I didn't handle it well. I was introduced to drugs that first night. I also was introduced to a chick who"—he chuckles nervously—"literally rocked my world that night. After my mother's trip, I went home. The monster wasn't there. There was never a discussion, and before I knew it, the next man was moved in. I didn't care. I got fucked up, got strong enough that I knew I could defend myself, and Jesse was what I took comfort in. Then she died.

"Ever since, I've chased the high in whatever form it came in. I'm lucky as hell to be alive and to still have friendships that I didn't completely crush in the process. Now here I am, twenty-two days sober, still riding my last high. And let me tell you all something: the best highs don't make you wake up, wondering where you are or what the hell you did."

"Congratulations," I force myself to say.

"Thank you, Keanna. I appreciate it."

DIVINE
INTERVENTION

"She fucking hates me," I whisper to Finn when she starts talking to the feisty old lady again.

He chuckles, running his hand through his beard.

"You think that's funny?"

"Yeah, I do."

I watch her. I can't take my eyes off her. I never could when she was in the same room with me.

Fucking beautiful.

"You got a plan?" Finn asks as we stand to leave.

"I plan on being buried in that pussy really soon."

"You think she'll—." He stops and laughs when I give him a look that says *fuck yes I think she'll … whatever he was going to ask.*

"I'll go and warm up the Rover for you, and then I'm gonna take off."

I nod. "Thanks, man."

I follow him out, seeing the pastor is saying goodbye to everyone.

"Where's the bathroom?" I ask, and he points down the hall. "Thanks."

In the bathroom, I look in the mirror and take the hat off. "Bad idea." I put it back on, then wash the hell out of my hands, scrub my face, and then use my finger to scrub my teeth before popping a piece of gum in. Then I decide to take a piss to pass the time, and when my dick is in my hand, I seriously consider jerking off so that I don't come too quickly when I'm riding my next high between her legs.

That's when I look up and see Jesus staring at me. Right then and there, I decide against it.

I have danced with the devil, defeated him, and overtaken his throne in Hell. But I have never done the jig with Jesus, and right now, I could use him on my side, so I opt out of blowing a load in the house of the Lord.

"I need you, man," I tell the picture hanging high above the urinals.

When I walk out, I see her shaking the pastor's hand, so I wait until she is out the door before hightailing it toward the exit.

"RJ?" the pastor calls out, stopping me.

Shit.

"Yep. Thanks for—"

"I heard you tonight." He stops, not saying anything more.

I want to tell him I'm in a hurry, that the nice, round ass that just walked out that door has me seeing stars and believing in Jesus, but even I know I can't say shit like that.

"Great. Uplifting story. Gotta jet—"

"Would you consider speaking about your struggles with some of the youth in the area?"

When I don't say anything, he goes on.

"Let your testimony be your ministry."

"All due respect, your holiness, but I'm just a drummer."

He smiles. "Steel Total Destruction."

"How the hell ...?" I stop. "I mean, how did you know?"

"I saw you on television."

I crane my neck around, trying to see if Keanna's pulled out yet.

"Give management a call. I'll see what I can do." Then I jet.

I see her standing outside her car, fighting with the door handle, and I know that, in some sick way, I just made a deal with a pastor in the house of God, and He's helping me out, because I just told his man some bullshit about talking to the youth.

"Keanna!" I yell as I get closer to her.

She jiggles the door handle faster.

"Let me get that."

"I'm fine," she snaps in an adorably annoyed tone.

"Obviously, you could use a hand." I tug on her handle, and the fucking thing comes off in my hand. "Well, now you need a new handle."

"Great," she mutters, walking around the car. I follow.

"Keanna." I grab her hand to stop her.

For a moment, my hand touches hers, and I am suddenly insecure as fuck and can't say shit.

"River," she says in a tone that makes me feel as if the world is about to fall the fuck apart again, exactly like it did all those years ago.

"When she died, I thought I had lost everything that would ever be good in my life." I tighten my grip on her hand. "I was wrong."

"I'm glad you realize that."

"I didn't until you."

"Please don't. Please don't come here, thinking I am going to fix a problem that no one can fix but you." She digs in her bag with her free hand and pulls out her keys.

"You're asking the impossible." This feeling like the bottom is dropping out from under you is not fucking cool sober. I snatch away her keys. "You have no idea how insufferable that is going to be."

"Keys please." Her voice cracks. "Please."

I open the passenger side of her car, reach in, and push the keys in, starting the car. Then I step out and shut the door behind me, blocking it because I am fucking terrified she is going to get in and leave.

"While it heats up, sit in mine with me." I reach for her hand, but she jumps back. "Keanna."

"How did you know I would be here?" she asks, and I immediately know I made her nervous.

I shake my head back and forth. "I didn't."

Her hand immediately covers her heart. "Why would you do that?"

"Do, what? Come to a meeting? I think—"

"*My* meeting. Why would you come to *my* meeting?" she snaps.

"Didn't realize it was *your* meeting."

"I don't believe you."

"And why is that? Because I'm a big fucking liar?" Now I'm getting pissed. "What the fuck would I have to gain, Keanna?"

"Oh." She shakes her head as if erasing an image, then looks down so her hair covers her face. She is hiding. "I really need to get going."

"Your car is warming up. Come and sit with me."

She doesn't respond.

"It's cold out; come and sit with me."

"I would like you to leave," she says is a soft, cautious voice. "I am so happy for you that you're trying to get sober."

"Twenty-two days, Keanna."

She looks up at me and shakes her head. "I hope you can at least be honest with yourself."

"I was never dishonest with you."

"Right." She pulls her hood up.

"You're cold, babe. Come and sit with me."

"No."

"No?"

"River, I need to get home."

"How's Tink?"

She looks up at me and rolls her eyes. "Fine."

"She miss me?"

She shrugs.

"You miss me?"

"Why would you ask that question?"

"No clue. I already know the answer. You missed me." I look back and forth from her left eye to her right. "I missed the hell out of you."

She looks away quickly, but not before I see hope. Well, at least, I feel it.

"Look, just come and sit with me. I have a lot to tell you and a lot more to ask of you."

She clears her throat. "I really have to go."

I glance over at her windshield. It's still covered in frost. "Not anytime soon."

"I can't do this with you," she says with a little more of the confidence that attracted me to her the first time we met.

"I won't let you do it with anyone else." I smirk and hold up my hand. "This is what I've been doing since I saw you last." She sighs and looks away. Immediately, I need to know. "You been with anyone else?"

She pulls her coat together, as if she is hiding.

"Don't bother. I remember exactly what every inch of you looks like, tastes like, feels—"

"Yes. Yes, I am seeing someone," she says, looking me dead in the eyes.

I immediately tense up, feeling like a fucking idiot.

"I'm gonna try my best not to flip my shit right now because I couldn't give a fuck less if you have a fuck buddy, a boyfriend, fiancé, or a fucking husband. I want that ass again," I growl.

"And I want you to leave."

"I'm not fucking kidding, Keanna. I will win. I will have you under me, filling you with my cum—"

"Shh!" she snaps, looking around.

"Jesus knows, Keanna! He fucking knows!" I tell her.

"What do you know about Jesus, River James?!"

I scratch my head. "A hell of a lot less than he knows about me, okay? But that's not the point!"

Fuck, I was not supposed to get pissed. I was supposed to be calm, sweet … Momma Joe would have my ass if she were here.

"You do know He also knows when you're full of shit." She whispers the word "shit."

"About what? That I will be in you? You and I both know that's gonna happen."

"Twenty-one days! You said twenty-two days sober, River. You're full of it. When I left you *twenty-one* days ago, you were a mess."

"Fucking right I was. Best and worst high of my life!"

"See? You lied. I know it, and you know it." She throws her hands in the air, then slaps them down on her thighs. "Jesus knows it. Yet you stand here—"

"You gave me the drug. You gave me permission! Don't you get it, Keanna? I got high on you! You fucked me up that badly. *You* did that to me."

She stands there, shaking her head. "I don't believe you. I don't—"

In one step, my hand is behind her neck and the other on the small of her back. I pull her in and kiss her hard. She tenses up, which is my cue to back up, but I have been high on this before, and I want it again.

I try to shove my tongue between her lips, but her mouth doesn't open. I don't give a fuck. It's a taste to an addiction, like coke on the gums.

When I rub my hand down her ass and pull her securely against me, she gasps, and I'm in.

She whimpers against my mouth and relaxes into me. I'm tasting Heaven in the parking lot of a church.

I hear someone clear his or her throat, and Keanna pulls back. I don't let go, though. I rub my thumb up and down her jawline as I look into her eyes.

A car starts up then, and I hear it pull away, but my eyes never leave hers, and hers never leave mine.

I know it's only a matter of time before one of two things happens: she gets pissed, which means I don't have the time to say what I need to say to her, or we fucking freeze to death before I get to feel her around my cock again.

"I spent—"

She shakes her head, but I pull her closer.

"I spent seven days in California, sober and mending fences. When they left, I spent ten more days there with my boss's mother and her man."

She scowls at me, and I can't help where my mind goes.

"No. No, kinky shit, but I like the way your mind works."

She pushes against me. "I wasn't thinking anything!"

I pull her tighter. "Well, then I like the way mine works. When my hard dick is laying against your stomach, you can't blame me. It's your fault."

She sighs exaggeratedly.

"Momma Joe is one badass woman. I drank a couple times, and before you get pissed about that, my problem was never with alcohol. But she made me talk. She made me see things I didn't wanna see, and she made me feel like I mattered. The only person who has ever made me feel like, well, like"—I close my eyes—"like the truth of my past wasn't going to kill me."

"But it was killing you," she whispers.

"No, that's not it. I was the one who put the shit inside me. I wasn't gonna let …" I stop and look up.

"You told her about … about Henry."

I feel a rumble in my chest as I shake my head.

"River, telling someone gives it less power. Talking about it makes it less—"

"*You* know." I open my eyes and look at her. "*You* know and no one else ever needs to."

Her eyes glaze over, and she takes in a deep breath. "I promise."

262

"You didn't even have to say that. You know why?"

She shakes her head.

"Because it's who you are. I knew it on our fourth date when I overheard Billy asking you something, and you pretended you didn't know."

"Our what? Fourth date?"

"Yeah. First was the doctor's office." I laugh at my skewed way of thinking. "Second, the bar where I defended your honor, because I am apparently chivalrous, or so Momma Joe tells me."

"You told her about me?" She seems shocked.

"Yeah, I told her about you. If it's not fucking obvious, you wrecked me worse than any drug I have ever put into my body."

When she leans her forehead against my chest, I take it as a good sign.

"Third date was at your apartment when I met your bear-dog and rocked your fucking world. Fourth date, I brought you flowers and saved your dog from the cop with the itchy trigger finger."

"You were coming to get your bowl," she says, looking up at me with a frown.

"Sh." I put my finger over her mouth. "This is absolutely the longest relationship I have ever had with a woman as an adult, and I've got to make it sound like a fucking fairytale."

She smiles and buries her face in my chest again. I fucking love it.

"Fifth date—"

"The one you cheated on me with the skank from the dealership?" she asks, pulling back.

"I didn't cheat on you," I huff. Hell, I didn't even think I would see her again.

"It was after our fourth date; that's cheating."

"Okay. Again, you have those three little bears and the Goldi-chick; I have River's Raunchy Bi-racial Romance."

She laughs out loud.

"Moving on." I chuckle. "Fifth date was rather uneventful. You didn't even put out, but I assume you had your reasons. Probably your period or something."

"This is now a true work of fiction."

"*Anyway*!" I glare at her. "After a morning of spooning, you talked to Billy and didn't tell him shit. That's when I knew I was either gonna have to ditch you or fuck you. And, well, our sixth date, I fucked the hell out of you. Then I got so fucking high I fell asleep. I woke to a bad dream and one hell of a blowjob. Then, well, we went through our bad spell."

"We aren't—"

"Hush up for a few more minutes, would you?"

She nods.

"You sent me a message that I responded to a million times and deleted them all. I thought you deserved better. Hell, I knew you did."

She gasps. "It didn't go through."

I smirk. "It definitely did."

"The message was a drunken accident—"

"Now who has the problem?" I look at her and raise my eyebrows.

"Hush up." She smiles.

"I was surrounded by kids, happy couples … Hell, I even stood up for Finn and helped plan a little surprise wedding for his baby's momma. So I suppose I was like, 'look at this: this dog loves me, kind of like these kids do' you all. I showed Momma Joe, and she wouldn't let it go. She taught me in seventeen days what family, loyalty, and even love was. She was more of a mother to me than mine ever was.

"She reminds me of you. Not in the way my dick needs to be inside of you, but by way of strength, confidence and" — here goes nothing and everything all at once — "love."

She is still giving me the sweet, somewhat sad smile.

"I knew from the first time I met you that you were the 'different' you hear your friends talk about or see in a cheesy, gushy, chick flick. I knew I was drawn to you. And let's be honest; I knew before even tasting or touching you that you would be one hell of a lay. But I didn't know I would be trading one addiction for another in just three days.

"I wanna get high on you, low on you, be inside and outside of you. I'm not asking, because there is no question for me to ask. I am telling you because it's the only truth that has ever outshined the darkness. You. Are. Mine."

"River—"

"I love you."

I don't know how to describe the feeling that washes over me, but the silence is killing me.

"Look, I'm supposed to talk about feelings and shit, and right now, I'm feeling like I would assume a man with a small dick would feel about being naked in a locker room. I mean, I obviously will never have that issue, but I can imagine it would suck, and me imagining how anyone else feels is a big fucking step. Epic in fact."

She looks sad — completely, undeniably sad — so I kiss her. Not hard like normal, just lip to lip because the low of not hearing the words back … sucks. And the only high I want to feel is the one that I know is there. I know she loves me. I *know* she does.

I pull back and take her face in my hands, watching her watch me.

"Say something." I feel like I'm begging. Hell, I *am* begging. "Come on, babe. I know you feel it, too." I push my forehead against hers. "Say. Something."

Sick and Dizzy

How does someone whose heart's desire is to help people, whose career choice is to show people they are worth living, end up knowing she is going to hurt someone who has worked hard to get clean, wants to be clean, and has ventured out of their comfort zone, opening themselves up to the possibilities of love and a new life?

"Oh, I see." He smiles and kisses me again.

"You do?" I ask, selfishly wanting, praying for something to change in him, to make him stay sober, yet not love me.

"You *are* seeing someone. You don't wanna say the words to me until you end it with them."

I smile without answering because he seems to have given me an out. Maybe he will wake up tomorrow and hate me.

"So the chances of me getting inside you tonight are what, fifty-fifty?"

I sigh.

"Okay, fine. Fuck!" He picks me up and spins me around, kissing me on the cheek, and then sets me down. "Can you go and break up with him, then come over?"

I shake my head.

"Okay, fine. What's one more fucking day, right?" He smiles and looks up. "What the hell are the chances of this happening? I mean, I have gone to meetings since I've been back, every night a different location. The guys said it would be better that way. No one will figure out that I'm in the band. And if they did, they wouldn't see me again. Then I come here and run into you. That's divine intervention, babe. So when you call him and tell him it's over, no matter how much he begs—the poor motherfucker— remember that, okay?"

I nod and smile.

He looks at me oddly. "You okay with this? I mean, if it's gonna be a problem, I can do it for you."

"No." I nod. "I can handle it."

His head cocks to the side. "You ever tell him you loved him?"

"No," I answer truthfully.

"Do you love him?"

"No." I close my eyes.

"Good, because I don't believe this shit that you can love two people, and I know damn well you love me," he says, bending to look me in the eyes. "Right?"

I throw my arms around him and hug him tightly because I do. I so do. More than he will ever know.

"I love you," he whispers, and I squeeze him more tightly. "If this wasn't a church, I would fuck you right here. No fucking man could stop me, and I know damn well you wouldn't, either."

"I really need to go."

He kisses me hard again. This time, I kiss him back with the fierceness of a woman who knows she is about to walk away from a love that could and would shatter her heart.

*****

When I walk in the house, Natasha greets me with a glass of wine. I thank her, setting it on the coffee table.

"Let me change, and I will be back."

"What the hell happened to you?"

"Long story. Give me a minute."

I walk in my room, knowing the floodgates are going to open, and no amount of trying to stop them is going to work.

I hate when people know my pain. I have hidden this pain. I have more than hidden it; I blocked it.

I grab the shirt I wore on his birthday, the one I hid behind the boxes on the top of my closet when I moved in since I couldn't bear to part with it. I hold it up to my nose and pretend it still smells like him, but it doesn't. It smells like fabric softener.

I pull off my shirt and kick off my pants then stand there, sniffing that damn shirt until the tears start falling.

I look down and see my dog … on my bed. She has been just as depressed as I have, so I have let it slide. I sit down and hug her tight, and she sighs.

"We're going to be just fine. You and me, Tinker Bell. I swear it. I am going to come out of this stronger than ever. So will you." I sit back and give her a scratch behind the ear. "I'll be back, or you could come out with me."

She lays her head down and sighs again.

"I understand. I'm exhausted, too."

When I walk out, Natasha is on the couch with her own glass of wine and a bottle beside her.

"What's going on? Did you find your purse-napper?"

"Shit, no. I didn't even call the police."

"What did they get?"

"Last week's Ulta binge purchases and some cash. The purse matched the shoes." I shrug.

"No ID? No keys?"

"No. I grabbed a purse that matched my shoes. I was running late, so there wasn't time to put everything in it. And keys stay around my wrist at work, thank God."

"You've been doing that a lot lately."

"I know." And the dam breaks. "I saw him tonight, Natasha. He came to the meeting. He looked amazing."

"How did he know you were there?"

"He didn't, said it was divine intervention." I cry harder.

Tink growls and barks.

"Tink, come out here, girl."

She doesn't and I sigh.

"She's fine, Keanna, but is what he said so bad?" she asks, taking my hand.

"Very, very bad. He's sober and seems happy, and he said he loves me."

She hugs me. "I'm not sure what to say. Is that bad?"

I pull back and wipe my face. "I never expected this. I thought it was a fling."

"But you should be happy. Aside from the fact that he's gorgeous and a freaking rock star, he said he loves you. Do you doubt it?"

"No, I don't." I pick up my glass and drain its contents. "If I tell him how I feel, I will eventually disappoint him. If it lasts between us and I tell him the truth about me, it will devastate him."

"What are you talking about? You're amazing."

I can't take it anymore. "I can't have children."

"How do you know that?"

"I'm a nurse. I saw a doctor — four doctors. The scarring in my tubes was caused by PID — pelvic inflammatory disease. No, I never had an STD. I was young when it happened, some sort of bacterial infection. It's one of those uncommon medical mysteries. I often wonder if it happened when I was still living with my mother and she just didn't know I was sick."

"Oh, Keanna, I am so sorry. But you can have children. You can adopt, or someone could be a surrogate; there are so many options."

"No. A man like River ..." I stop because I can't tell her his secrets. "He deserves much more than I can give him. I'm afraid for his sobriety, and I wish he had just stayed away. I mean, he didn't even actually come for me, but ..."

I stop when I hear a knock on the door.

"Are you expecting anyone?"

"No." She stands up and walks to the entryway. I hear her open the door.

She walks back in, eyes wide. "It's for you."

I stand up and hurry over, worried it's a work problem, and then I see him.

"You got a minute?"

I feel dizzy and sick to my stomach. I'm not ready for this. I'm not ready to tell him what I know will make him go away.

I shake my head, and he nods his, kicks off his boots, and walks into my bedroom without asking where it is.

"If you need me," Natasha whispers and points to the stairs, "I'll be in bed."

I take in a deep breath then exhale slowly, grab the bottle of wine, and swig it back.

When I finally walk into my room, I see him close the window.

"Was that open?"

"Let's not get into that right now." He walks quickly past me and shuts the door. Then I hear the lock. When he turns around and looks at me, his eyes are intense, and his jaw is locked.

I ask about the window again.

"Yes, it was open." Then he pulls his shirt over his head.

I close my eyes quickly. "I didn't leave it open."

"No, but you left in unlocked, which is stupid. I climbed right in."

I open my eyes and shake my head.

"Yeah, I did. Couldn't shake the feeling something was fucking wrong. Wondered if you were back together with it that dick Miguel."

"Of course not."

"Good damn thing or I'd be in jail." He sighs, " I watched you get half naked, then dress." He unbuckles his black belt, and then his pants fall to the floor.

"River," I gasp and turn to close the curtains.

"What's good for the goose is good for the gander, Keanna. You've been undressing in here for weeks, I assume, and your neighbors have been getting a show. Quite frankly, it's pissing me off." In two long strides, he is across the room and whips the curtains back open. Then he grabs my face and kisses me hard, possessively, hungrily.

When he pulls back, I touch my lips.

"Hurt?"

"I don't know."

"Good. Now tell me about this boyfriend." He stands back and grabs ahold of his erection.

I shake my head.

"So you lied to me?"

"Not because I wanted to."

He releases his cock, walks over, shuts the curtains, and then turns and reaches forward, grabbing the hem of the shirt and pulling it up.

"Arms up."

"River," I protest vocally while obeying his request physically.

"I want your tongue running slowly down this dead fucking tree on my side."

"I don't—"

"You don't need to, just do as I asked."

I don't move.

"You want it. I know you do, so don't act like it's a chore to lick my skin."

I close my eyes and step toward him.

"Good. Now, as your hot, little mouth runs along my body, I'm gonna tell you a fucking story. Then you and I are done with the discussion as soon as my cum hits the back of your throat."

"That's awfully presumptuous of you," I say because I know I should.

"Trust me."

I want him. In fact, I need him right now more than I have ever needed anyone. And yes, I trust him … completely.

As soon as my lips touch his skin, he hums, and I feel it throughout my body.

"I had this tattoo done four years ago."

I begin moving my tongue slowly down his body, loving how his skin tastes: clean, manly. His scent is the same—distinctively River.

"The tree of life." He chuckles. "My life. The black crows are all dead to me yet still sucking the life out of me—my mother, my father, Jesse—until I didn't give a fuck. It hurt too much to give a fuck."

I kiss him, then lick down the roots.

"The root's base ends where life begins—my seed. Any future lives I could fuck up won't come from me."

I stop and look up.

"I got that shit taken care of." He lifts his dick up. "Incision scar on the raphe, near my balls."

"Who would allow you to do that?" I gasp.

"A doctor who liked cash, and I had a picture of him doing lines." He laughs.

I gasp. "You trusted someone to do that?"

"I'm kind of fond of my cock, Keanna. It wasn't done in a fucking alley between lines." He strokes himself and rubs the tip of his cock across my lips. "You're fond of it, too. But before you suck me off, tell me what I already know."

This is the moment when I decide if I give him the ability to wreck and ruin me. I'm terrified, but I cannot lie to him.

"I love you. I love you. I love you. I love you."

When he smiles, tapping his dick on my lips, I lean forward and attempt to take him in my mouth, but he pulls back.

"One more thing: if you ever lie to me again, I will tie you up and jerk off all over you before walking out the door."

I can't help giggling, and he smiles.

"Love you. Now show me you do, too."

I lick my lips and take him in my mouth.

THAT AIN'T
GONNA HAPPEN

"Well, hell." I scratch my head and pull her up. "That hasn't happened in a very, very long time."

"Don't be embarrassed."

I wipe a little of me off her lip before kissing her. "I'm not embarrassed," I say against her mouth. "I'm just ready to get you there."

I push her down on the bed. She is stunning in her white, lacey bra and booty shorts against her brown skin.

"Tink, girl, this bed is too small. You're gonna have to get down," I say as I rub her belly. "The hell …?"

"What? What's wrong?"

"Tink's got nipples." I push her hair aside.

Keanna sits up. "Of course she does."

"No, they're, like, long. Look."

Keanna pets her belly, examining her closely. "Yeah."

"What's *yeah* mean?"

"It means she needs to go to the vet."

"For …?"

"Well, it could mean she is pregnant."

I can't help laughing long and hard. "I'll fucking kill those bastards."

"Maybe she's not," Keanna remarks, looking at me all doe-eyed and sexy as hell.

I reach over and grab her ankle as I stand off the bed. "Tink, I know you're all grown and shit, but you've gotta get down."

She lays on her side.

"Then you better close your eyes."

I yank Keanna to the end of the bed and pull her legs so they wrap around my waist. Then I bend down and unsnap her front clasp bra and watch as her tits spill out, unrestrained. Leaning in, I lick each of her perfect and fully erect nipples. Her back arches against my mouth as I suck hard enough to make her cry out.

I reach down and rub the lace between her legs as I suck on her left then her right nipple, biting down as I push my fingers under the lace and slowly push a finger inside. Her hands grip my shoulders.

I kiss down her soft, warm stomach until I reach her hip where I kiss back and forth across her hips while I work another finger inside her. Her hips grind against my touch as I turn my wrist, twisting my fingers, rubbing her hot, wet walls as I toy with her ass.

I rub her wetness up and down her seam, coating her ass and then rubbing my pinky against it, hoping like hell she is in for another round of me claiming every part of her tonight.

As I push two fingers inside her pussy and push my finger a little farther into her ass, I lean down, lick around her clit, and suck, bringing her to an immediate orgasm. She starts to pull away.

"Fuck that. You're gonna come so hard for me, for you, for us."

"I am … Oh, River, I am," she whispers her cry.

"Let go, babe; you're holding back. I've got you literally in my fucking hand, all of you. All mine," I growl as my dick becomes almost unbearably hard.

I lick her pussy like it's been three fucking weeks since I have, because it has, and it's been hell.

"God!" she cries out and really lets go.

I suck her clit hard and fuck her faster with my fingers until she has tears coming out of her eyes.

"Fuck," I hiss, pulling my hand away before I tear her panties down and rub my cock against her hot, slick entrance, pushing in as her orgasm still rips through her.

*****

The next morning when we come out of the bedroom, Natasha immediately turns bright red, and her eyes fixate on the floor.

"Everything okay?" Keanna asks.

She nods.

Keanna covers her mouth. "Oh, God."

"Yeah," Natasha whispers. "Heard that a few times last night."

"Jordan," Keanna gasps.

"He has a humidifier in his room. Let's hope it …" She pauses and grips the hem of her shirt, and I can't help chuckling. She looks up at us and giggles. "I'm sure it was fine. Just maybe next time you … um … have a sleepover —"

"I will be quiet."

I look at her and then Natasha. "That ain't gonna happen. We'll have them at the beach house."

*****

It took three weeks to exhaust and wear her down, but I finally got my way.

I move some of the boxes off the bed and into the closet while she is in the bathroom. When she walks out, I am lying down, looking at the ceiling.

"You okay? Having second thoughts? It's moved really fast and —"

I laugh. "It's been two weeks of pure hell. I have to share you with the other junkies in the world for nine hours a day; that's enough." I sit up. "I miss the hell out of you when you're not here."

"But you have Tink."

"Now I have you both ... until Monday when we take off. I really wish you'd quit your job. I'd hire you to do something. I mean, I'm an addict; it wouldn't be like you're not doing what you love. Plus, there's always this." I pull her hand over and put it on my dick.

"I have weekends off," she says, giving me a squeeze. "I can come and meet you."

"In the hotel, on the bus, in the greenroom." I picture her bent over the back of the couch in one of those fucking rooms.

"On the stage?"

I laugh. "What?"

"I don't know what it's gonna be like standing backstage, watching you. I might not be able to control myself."

"You better wear a skirt to every fucking concert, then. No one gets to see that ass but me. You know why?"

She smiles big. "I do."

"Tell me why."

"It's yours."

"Fucking right it is."

I hear the door wiggle and laugh, knowing it's locked.

"Two minutes, man." It's Finn.

"Let's go." She jumps off the bed as I try to grab her.

"Just moved in and already running away?" I force myself up.

She giggles as she runs to the door and unlocks it. "I'm excited to watch the video."

I grab her by the hips as she steps out, pulling her back, and whisper in her ear, "Once an addict, always an addict. If I want it, I'll just take it."

"Have I ever denied you?" She looks over her shoulder at me.

I shake my head.

"Good thing, because I'm pretty addicted to you, too."

"You like the high?" I ask.

"I love the high."

I spin her around and take the lips I once had to beg for.

When I pull back, I hold her face in my hands. "Best high of my life."

EPILOGUE

We are in upstate New York at the Carrier Dome, the third concert of our tour, and Keanna's late. I check my phone for the hundredth time and send a message.

Where the fuck are you?

No reply comes.

"Everything okay?" Billy asks.

"No, she's late, not answering her text messages, and I…" I stop when my phone plays, *So Addicted To You*, my ring tone for her..

"Where are you?"

"Did you get the picture?"

"No. But seriously …" I stop when I hear her sniff. "You sick?"

"No, Tink's a mom." She sniffs again.

"Yeah, babe, she's gonna have puppies and—"

"She's having them now. She's had four."

She's fucking crying, and I hate that sound.

"I can be there in … fuck. Four maybe five—"

"No!" She laughs and cries. "No, you have a show."

"But we're kind of having babies, babe." I rub my hand over my head. "Shit. Can you get Natasha there?"

"She is here, and so is the vet."

"Male or female?" I ask.

"The pups are—"

"No, the vet."

"Are you serious right now?" She snorts, but I know she's kind of pissed. But I'm kind of serious.

"Yep."

"Part-time vet, part-time male stripper, you ass!"

I'm pretty sure I just heard her hang up on me.

"Hello?"

She doesn't answer me.

"Shit." I dial her back, and as soon as she answers, I say, "I love you."

She sighs. "I know."

"Okay, so is it really a—"

"No," she grumbles.

"Good, 'cause a show, puppy babies, and a male stripper sound like a bad fucking mix. How is she?"

"She's good. She's doing well," she says softly. "She's calmer than I am, and I'm a nurse."

"Do you think she understands?"

"I think her body knows what it's doing, and yes, I have to think she understands or it's so—"

"Wrong." I sigh. "Fuck, I wish I was there."

"You need to go rock the stage, then come home to me."

"And rock you."

"Yeah." She is still using that soft voice.

After hanging up the phone, I look at the guys. "Tink's giving birth." I smile. I can't help it. Shit like that makes me happy now.

Finn grips my shoulder. "We need cigars."

"Right after we rock the fuck out of the"— Memphis grabs his dick—"Dome."

"We still do it for us," Finn says as we stand in our now pre-show ceremonial circle.

"In the words of the great Eddie Vedder, 'At a certain point, you realize you have a responsibility more behind yourself and your need for adrenaline.' " He winks at me.

"Jimmy Page once said, 'I always believed in the music we did, and that's why it was uncompromising.' After all we've been through, it still holds true." Finn puts his fist in.

"Kurt Cobain said, 'Drugs are a waste of time. They destroy your memory and your self-respect and everything that goes along with your self-esteem. They're no good at all.' Can't disagree." I fist in.

"The beautiful Billie Holiday once said, 'Sometimes, it's worse to win a fight than to lose.' I'm glad that I didn't fight being a part of this. I never wanted it, but I can tell you all right now that nothing and no one can bring us down. Let's go fuck shit up."

*****

Keanna

Three months later...

"I can't believe I'm doing this," I say, gripping his hand as tightly as I can.

He bends down, kisses my forehead, lets go of my hand, and raises his wrist up. "I did it first." His left wrist is tattooed *She's my addiction* in a script font that will match mine.

He lifts my wrist up, kisses it, and holds it against mine. "*I am his drug*."

I know it means a lot to him, and he means a lot to me.

I nod. "Let's do this."

"You ready?" Josephina Steel asks.

"She's ready, Momma Joe." He kisses the top of her head, then sits down beside me.

I look up at the stark white ceiling in a small room in Forever Steel, a tattoo shop that is apparently where it all began for the Steel family.

I hear the buzzing and close my eyes as I feel the tattoo gun's needle drag across my skin and feel his breath against my ear right before he leans in to kiss it and asks, "You okay?"

"Yeah, I'm fine. It's like a cat scratch."

"I promise to take care of you tonight," he whispers in a mischievous tone.

"I know you will," I whisper back.

We stay close. We are always this close when we are together. When we are alone, we are much, much closer.

*****

I wake up to my phone and look at the time. It's Sunday at seven in the morning.

Fearing it may be work, I answer without looking at the caller ID.

"Hello?"

"Hello, Keanna. This is Pastor Daniel."

It takes me a moment to understand who it is before it dawns on me.

"I'm sorry. I—"

"It's early; I understand. Anita just called with some devastating news."

I look at River lying beside me, still asleep.

"Her granddaughter, Angel, and Zachary ... Well, there is no way to say this, but they are no longer with us."

"You mean dead?" I gasp.

"Yes. I'm so sorry." He pauses.

I have no idea why he would call me. I met them one time. Just once.

"I know you and River have been helping Anita out financially for the past few months, and there is no other family ... I was wondering if you'd mind watching Rain while I take Anita to identify the bodies and discuss Angel's final arrangements."

I look again at River, who stretches and then opens his eyes. "Yes, of course. Tell me the address, and I will be right there."

"What's going on?" River asks as he sits up.

I shake my head, then get off the bed and grab a pen and used envelope from my purse to write down the address. When I hang up, I run in the bathroom, strip my silk nightie off, and turn on the shower.

"Damn," I hear him behind me and look over my shoulder. He is already naked since that's the way he sleeps.

I get under the water, and he turns me around and pushes me against the wall.

"No, River," I say and turn back around. He looks shocked. "No, not no, but ... Have you been helping Anita?"

He rubs his hand over his head. "Yeah."

"Her granddaughter and that man ..." I pause, trying to think of his name.

"Zachary."

"They died. They died and Pastor Daniel needs to take Anita to identify the bodies. I have to go and watch the baby, so that's why no."

He steps back and looks at me. Then he shakes his head back and forth.

As I quickly wash the important parts, I tell him, "I love you." Then I rinse and start to turn off the water.

"No." River stops me. "Let me wash up. I'm going with you."

Once in the Rover, he reaches over and takes my hand. I squeeze it, and he squeezes back.

"Sorry I didn't tell you."

"It's your money, and don't be sorry for helping someone, River."

"Just thought maybe it would ease the old chick's burden, and maybe, if her burden was eased, she'd raise the kid, you know. No foster care like Finn and …"

"Jesse."

"Yeah, and no fucking drunk or druggie fucking with it, you know?"

"I do know, and River, I love you even more for it."

"Aw, thanks, babe." He grins wickedly. "Show me some appreciation later."

I lean over and kiss him on the cheek. "Of course."

*****

RIVER

Two Months later...

I walk out of the bedroom and look around the beach behind the house. Billy moved out a few weeks ago. He bought a condo, so that left me, Keanna, Tink, and two puppies that look like Holstein cows. All six of them are black and white. Memphis took one, Finn took two, and X-man and Taelyn took one, as well. She promised to find them good homes, but I knew damn well they weren't going anywhere.

I stand on the deck, throwing ball after ball, hoping like hell the pups will expunge some energy, the little fucking hellions that they are.

I look over and see old Mr. Magee, who still swears his dog wasn't the father of the pups. Of course, when I threatened him within an inch of his life, he allowed Tiffany, a friend of Keanna's, to take him to the veterinarian where she works and get his big, old offensive balls chopped.

Tink and the bastard, Brando, hang out all the damn time, and I hate it. However, I'm pretty fucking sure they are in dog love, and he's not mean to the pups, so I let him live.

I hear the door open and see my girl walk out.

"You're ready already?"

"Yeah." She immediately walks over and hugs me. "Do you know how happy I am?"

"If you're half as happy as me, then you're over the moon."

"And back."

I kiss her hard and long, tasting her. Fuck, I would swallow her up if I could.

I pull back from our kiss. "I'm gonna go and get showered." But then I look at her, really look at the woman who changed my life in less than six months. "Today's a game changer, you know." I take her hands.

"You getting cold feet?" She smiles, knowing damn well I'm not.

"No, and if you do, don't even try to run. I'll catch you."

She is smiling from ear to ear, glowing in the long, ivory, maxi dress that kisses her sexy curves. She leans in, pushes up on her toes, and kisses me quick-like. "Go; we can't be late."

*****

When we walk into the courthouse, everyone is there: Xavier, Taelyn, Madison, Billy, Memphis, Tales, Finn, Sonya, Noah, Momma Joe, and her man Thomas. They are all sitting on the right side while Natasha, Tiffany, a few of Keanna's coworkers, old lady Anita, and Rain are on the other.

Keanna squeezes my hand. "What are you thinking?"

I laugh. "I never walked into a courtroom and thought, 'this is the best day of my life' before today." I kiss her quickly before we walk up to stand in front of the judge.

He stands, and I swear to fuck, if he bangs the gavel, I'm gonna wake up and be pissed if this is all just a dream.

"Today is a very unique day. I can tell you I have never been asked to be part of something like this, and I find it necessary to tell you I am honored to be part of it.

"Today, Pastor Daniel and I are going to not only make this marriage legal in the eyes of the law, but in the eyes of the Lord. And if that is not cause enough to celebrate, we are not only going to witness two people who have vowed to love, honor, and cherish each other until death do they part, but we are going to watch as they walk out the door with a child who will call them Mother and Father. In my twenty years, that has never happened, so again — "

"Da!" Rain screeches.

"Ray!" I laugh and look over to see her crawling across the floor at me as fast as she can.

"What about me?" Keanna squats down.

Memphis laughs. "Fa, so, la, tee — "

"Da!"

I reach down and scoop up the little, hazel-eyed beauty who has hair like her soon-to-be momma and an attitude like mine already.

I pull Keanna in and hold them tightly.

"How fast can we do this?" I ask the Judge. "She isn't all that patient."

*****

I'm standing in Finn's old room, watching Rain sleep, while Keanna says goodnight to old lady Anita. I swear, other than Keanna, there is nothing and no one who has ever made me feel the way I do right now.

Two months ago when we walked into that little house that had barely enough room to move around in to watch Rain, I knew right then and there I couldn't leave her living like that. Keanna and I brought her to the house that day and watched her scoot around on her little booty, knowing damn well she wouldn't be able to do that at her great-grandmother's house.

Rain ended up spending the weekend with us, making us laugh harder than we have ever laughed before. The way she scooted around, chasing those pups, was pure entertainment. Watching Keanna make sense of her little, crazy head of hair was cool as shit, too. I had a feeling of joy, a different kind of high, one I didn't want to go away, but I knew it would.

When Anita and Pastor Daniel came to pick her up, the look on Keanna's face was as heartbreaking as the pain I was feeling in my chest.

Anita looked at both of us, and the darkness that was surrounding her when she had walked in to get Rain lifted immediately.

"You want her?" she asked.

I was floored and appalled that someone was asking me if I wanted a child like she had no value, like she was nothing.

Old lady Anita must have recognized it immediately.

"Honey child, I am an old woman who has raised her children and her children's children. I love this one, but I am no fool. I know she would have a better life somewhere else. Pastor Daniel and I talked about foster care and other options, but with the way your lady friend looks at that child and the way you look at both of them, I'm gonna offer you the chance first, and I hope like hell you take it." Anita looked a hell of a lot younger than she was. The woman was seventy years old.

I offered to buy a house for them, but Anita wouldn't have it. They did take Rain home that night, but after the most underwhelming sex in the entire time we had been together, we had a discussion. Then we made a phone call, and our Rain and Anita came to stay with us until we had a plan, which was to make everything legal and do it as quickly as possible.

Anita watched Rain while Keanna was at work and I was on the road. I didn't ride the bus with the band, though. I met them on our different stops and flew out after the show. I didn't want to be away from either one of them.

Keanna's last day of work was yesterday. It wasn't an easy decision, and I left it up to her.

While she was at work, Anita was with me, teaching me shit when I was home and watching the little angel baby when I was at Forever Four.

The day I came home with a new tattoo from hip to hip—a cross with two angel wings—and Keanna saw it, she decided she would quit her job. The three of us—Anita, too, if she wanted—were going to just enjoy the hell out of the blessing we had literally been handed.

Keanna walks in the room and stands next to me. "What are you thinking?"

291

"I am the luckiest motherfucker on the planet. I have the hottest wife, a crazy sweet and amazing kid, a house, and a career that allows me to take care of them." I pull her into my arms. "Never in a million years, Keanna … Never in a million years did I think this could happen."

"Me, either," she says, holding me tightly. "But like you said, it's divine intervention." She rubs my stomach where the tattoo is.

"Divine, indeed." I lift her up in my arms. "Do you feel slighted that you didn't get a honeymoon like all little girls dream of?"

"I have everything and more than I ever dreamed of. I love you, River James."

"I love you, Keanna James. Now let me show you just how much."

****

Are you signed up for the newsletter?
If so I will be sending out info on how to claim your copy of Finn and YaYa'a big day.
It is a gift from me to you.

WHAT'S NEXT?

ROCKERS OF STEEL: Billy Jeffers
We are hoping for a March 27th release.

Billy Jeffers, never dreamed of being in a rock band but reluctantly agreed to help a friend start a band. He started, as a keyboard player with Steel Total Destruction. One night at a club in Miami, the front man was injured and unable to play lead guitar. Billy quickly learns lead and is thrust into the spotlight he never wanted.

Lead singer Memphis Blacks sassy twenty one year old sister, Madison, left college to work at Forever Four. She feels an intense attraction to Billy from the first time she laid eyes on him. On several occasions she made it apparent, but he brushed off every attempt she made.

When Madison find out a secret Billy has been keeping from everyone she confronts him. Will he use her attraction to him to seduce her into keeping her mouth shut, or will she reveal a secret that would crush the bond with Billy and Forever Four?

Hearts will be broken, friendships will be tested, and all hell is about to break lose.

Have a look...

CHAPTER 1
Billy

I never wanted to be part of a band. I was a pianist from the age of three, I excelled at it, but it was not something I wanted to do as a career. I wanted to run my own business like my father.

I don't love the stage and all the attention it brings like Memphis. Music doesn't live in me and it's not necessary to breathe like it is for Finn. I don't crave the constant party, or need a warm body in my bed like, River.

Quite frankly some of the warm bodies I have woken up to after to much partying have almost horrified me. Not because they aren't attractive, but because when they open their mouths and speak, I feel like I have lost a few hundred-brain cells just being in their presence.

I am attracted to women who are well read, educated, and who can hold an intelligent conversation. A woman who dresses nicely and focus's on presentation. I value manners, confidence, and someone who isn't overtly sexual.

I like women who are not drama, because I have it in droves with my band mates.

ACKNOWLEDGEMENTS

Two words are not nearly enough for all that so
many of you have done for me.
Three years, and thirty three books later...
The stories are still continuing to pour out of my
head and on to the pages.
I feel so blessed, and those two words are whispered
to the heavens all the time.

*****

To the owner of this book:
You are the reasons I get to do this. I wish I could give
you a bazillion answered prayers but sadly I am not
able. Instead you have my pinky promise I will
continue to give you more and become better at my
craft everyday.

To all of the wonderful bloggers:
I am so appreciative to all of you. What you do is
selfless and simply amazing. I thank you from the
bottom of my heart for sharing, caring, and loving the
stories all of us who are blessed enough to have you
in our corner helping us realize our dreams. I am
honored and you are truly cherished. Please feel free
to contact me if ever I can do something for you.

To my #foreversteel readers group:
I love you to the moon! You make me laugh, push me,
support me and make me feel appreciated. I can only
hope I do the same for you!!

To join the fun go to website and click members only

To my beta's:
A million thanks #foreversteel Fran, Elizabeth, Cassandra, Courtney, Richelle, Staci, Angie, Renee, Laurie, Lisa, Bobbie, Ivy, Kelly, Debbie, Rhiannon, Laura, Michelle, Teresa, Veronica, Jamie, Heather, Christina, Maggie, Brianna, Jeana, Debbie, Annette, Christi, Selena, Tara, Joely, Danielle, Stacy, Christine, Maria, Shaunna, Jennifer, Christy, Diane, Keeana, Diane, Jamary, Sarah, Jodi, Johnna, Dannielle, Suzi, Michelle and my very first Gloria!

To all of you who follow me on social media:
So many of you have become friends and I adore you.

To all of you who message or e-mail:
Your words mean so much to me. Thank you for taking the time it is very appreciated.

To my alpha:
You know who you are and how much I love you, bunches.

To Social Butterfly:
This is our first release together.
Thank you.

To Heather:
A million thanks for all the hoop jumping and dealing with my crazy, which with this book, has been on steroids, lol.

To Joely:
Hugs, thanks and love.

To my Jules:

Still my fucking wizard. I love you. Vegas 2016 baby.

To Keeana:
Thank you for the use of your name. Love you!

To C&D:
I still enjoy going through the edit process. Thank you so much for being here.

To Kellie:
I love you girl.... 2 months and we tear up Texas!!!

To my virtual girls:
My secrets are safe with you, and yours with me. Love you all!

To K23, (author Kari March)
I am so very appreciative of you as well. My readers first impression of my book comes from you. Thank you for always giving me perfection and going way above and beyond.

To CC and my Kate:
I love you both!

To Branden (aka cover hottie):
Thank you for being so damn hot, lol. Seriously thank you for sharing in the excitement of River James. You are a great man and I can't wait to see what the future has in store for you.

To Scott Hoover:
You are a very talented man. This cover was a challenge, and you are a class act. You went way above and beyond, thank you.

Last but not least...

To my little chick:
You are without a doubt the most beautiful thing in my life.
Love you more…

ABOUT THE AUTHOR

 *USA Today* bestselling author M.J. Field's love of writing was in full swing by age eight. Together with her cousins, she wrote a newsletter and sold it for ten cents to family members.

She self-published her first New Adult romance in January 2013. Today she has completed six self-published series, The Love Series, The Wrapped Series, The Burning Souls Series, The Men of Steel Series, Ties of Steel Series, and The Norfolk series.

MJ is a hybrid author who publishes an Indie book almost every month, and is signed with a traditional publisher, Loveswept, Penguin Random House, for her co-written series The Caldwell Brothers. Hendrix and Morrison are available now, Jagger will be released in April 2016.

There is always something in the works, and she has three, yes, three, new series coming out this summer, and fall.

MJ lives in central New York, surrounded by family and friends. Her house is full of pets, friends, and noise ninety percent of the time, and she would have it no other way.

CONNECT WITH MJ AT
www.mjfieldsbooks.com

FIND MJ ON
FACEBOOK, TWITTER, INSTAGRAM AND SPOTIFY

MORE FROM MJ FIELDS

THE LEGACY SERIES

These families stories are intertwined starting with The Love series, they move to the Wrapped Series, the Burning Souls series, and end in Love You Anyways.

Many more series will spin off from these characters already written and each will be a standalone series but for those of us who love a story to continue I recommend reading in this order.

LOVE SERIES
Blue Love
New Love
Sad Love
True Love

WRAPPED SERIES
Wrapped In Silk
Wrapped In Armor
Wrapped In Always and Forever

BURNING SOULS SERIES
Stained
Forged
Merged

*****

THE STEEL SERIES

Are you ready to meet my sexy, tattooed alpha men, their exactly hot friends and the women they love?

It's BYOB, bring your own batteries, because they ain't providing any. Get ready because you're in for one hell of a party — now go meet my guys in the Steel Series.

MEN OF STEEL
Forever Steel
Jase
Jase and Carly
Cyrus
Zandor
Xavier
Raising Steel (Momma Joe's Story)

TIES OF STEEL
Abe
Dominic
Sabato

ROCKERS OF STEEL
Memphis Black
Finn Beckett
River James
Billy Jeffers (Coming March 22, 2016)

*****

THE NORFOLK SERIES
Irons 1
Irons 2
Irons 3

*****

CALDWELL BROTHERS SERIES